BEASTLY KINGDOM

As Chiun happily turned the corner, a hulking shape came to greet him. It was Hunny Bear, his porkpie hat askew.

"Hail, O bashful bruin," Chiun said.

In answer the bear heaved his honeypot at Chiun. Out of it poured a hissing, spitting white liquid. But Chiun was already out of the way, and quickly relieved the bear of his heads. Both of them. They struck the ground at the same time. The human one went splat.

Then Chiun saw a welcome sight. Waving at him from a window was the rodent himself, his lollipop ears alert.

"Ah," said Chiun. "This creature will surely guide me, for he is always helpful and kind."

But Chiun should have smelled a rat—in this fantastic death trap only danger was real. . . .

The Destroyer

#91

COLD WARRIOR

CREATED BY

WARREN MURPHY & RICHARD SAPIR

A SIGNET BOOK

SIGNET
Published by the Penguin Group
Penguin Books USA Inc., 375 Hudson Street,
New York, New York 10014, U.S.A.
Penguin Books Ltd, 27 Wrights Lane,
London W8 5TZ, England
Penguin Books Australia Ltd, Ringwood,
Victoria, Australia
Penguin Books Canada Ltd, 10 Alcorn Avenue,
Toronto, Ontario, Canada M4V 3B2
Penguin Books (N.Z.) Ltd, 182–190 Wairau Road,
Auckland 10, New Zealand

Penguin Books Ltd, Registered Offices:
Harmondsworth, Middlesex, England

First published by Signet, an imprint of New American Library,
a division of Penguin Books USA Inc.

First Printing, January, 1993
10 9 8 7 6 5 4 3 2 1

Copyright © Warren Murphy, 1993
All rights reserved

 REGISTERED TRADEMARK—MARCA REGISTRADA

PUBLISHER'S NOTE
This is a work of fiction. Names, characters, places, and incidents either
are the product of the author's imagination or are used fictitiously, and any
resemblance to actual persons, living or dead, events, or locales is entirely
coincidental.

For Don and April and Megan and Nicholas Phelps—
acolytes of the Great Round-Eared One

And for the Glorious House of Sinanju,
P.O. Box 2505, Quincy, MA 02269

Prologue

When his mind awoke, his eyes beheld only darkness.

But his mind *was* awake. His brain, long the realm of inchoate nightmares from which there had been no awakening, no refuge, and no surcease, processed conscious thoughts.

When he tried to open his eyes, they refused him. He could feel his lids strain and tug, attempting to separate.

He made a frightened noise deep in his throat, and tasted something plastic along one edge of his thick, dry tongue. His throat felt raw.

Then he sensed presences. Something popped out of his right ear and he heard sounds again. Beeping. A steady hum. An oscilloscope. To his mind leaped the image of an oscilloscope.

"Steady, sir," a youngish voice said.

He grunted inarticulately.

Something came out of his left ear, and the sounds were all around him. There were two of them. They were hovering on either side of the bed on which he lay.

At least, he hoped it was a bed. He could not tell. It felt more like a plush-lined coffin.

Fingers took his chin and separated his jaw. The hinge muscles shot fire into his logy brain and he cried out in agony. But the thing that had obstructed his mouth, the plastic-tasting thing, was no longer there.

"Don't try to speak yet, sir. We're still in the middle of bringing you back."

His mind shot into first gear. *Back!*

He forced his mouth to make sounds. They sounded horrible, corpsey.

"How . . . long?" he croaked.

"Please, sir. Not yet. Let us finish the procedure."

"Grrrr . . ."

They began unwinding the bandages that sheathed his eyes.

The darkness shaded to gray, then lightened to a pinkish haze in which faint greenish sparks hung, dancing—his optic nerves reacting to the first stimuli in . . . dammit, how long *had* it been?

"Hmmm," an older voice was saying. "Eyelids are encrusted. Seem welded together."

"I don't see anything in the manual about a procedure covering this," the youngish voice muttered.

"May be a natural phenomenon. We'll leave them. Let the retina get used to stimulation again."

He swallowed. The effort was like ingesting a rough-textured concrete golf ball.

"How . . . long . . . damn . . . it!"

"The briefing officer is on his way, sir. We're physicians."

"Status?"

"Well, your new heart is functioning normally. The animation unit did a good job. Twenty-six beats a minute, like a Swiss clock."

"It was a heart attack, then?"

"You don't remember?"

"No."

"We've had to perform certain other . . . procedures. There was some tissue damage, with resulting loss of function."

"I feel nothing."

"Technically the nerves are still frozen. Feeling will come back. There may be some discomfort."

He said nothing to that.

Then a door clicked open, and he sensed the attending physicians had turned.

"Oh, there you are. He's conscious and responding to our voices, Captain."

"As you were." The new voice was more mature, a strong voice. One he felt he could trust. Not like those wet-behind-the-ears, over-solicitous doctors. Who the hell had hired them, anyway?

"Director, I am Captain Maus."

"Maus. What kind of a name is that?"

"German, sir."

"Go ahead. Report. How long was I . . . inanimate?"

"Let's start with the good news, sir. We currently have thriving bases in California, Florida, Japan, and France. Except for some cultural problems with the French base, expansion is continuing apace."

He absorbed that with a tight smile. The empire flourished! The captain went on.

"In the last few years the Berlin Wall has fallen, the two Germanies have reunited, the Soviet Union has broken up into a chaotic collection of autonomous states with the economic prospects of a landlocked Fiji Islands, and Eastern Europe is free."

He groaned. "That long?"

"It has been a while, Director."

He frowned. "Revenue?"

"Down in the last several quarters. The global economy has been rocky. But we're solidly in the black. There has been no downsizing—"

"Down . . . ?"

"A new business term. It means, um, to lay off staff and cut back expenditures and expansion."

"Why not just say that?"

"Businessmen don't talk that way anymore."

"Humph. With Communism dead, I don't see why they'd hide their light under a bush."

"Actually, Communism isn't exactly dead," said Captain Maus. "The Reds still control China, North Korea—although there is some wild talk of unification there—and other pockets here and there."

"Bring me a map."

"Sir?"

"I want to see this new world."

A doctor's voice: "He's not ready for this yet. The optic nerve has been in utter darkness for . . ."

The doctor's voice trailed off.

"Bring me a map," he repeated harshly.

A map was brought.

"Here it is, sir."

"Someone see to my eyes."

Again the young doctor protested. "I can't allow this. There is no telling what kind of trauma this could cause. . . ."

"Either open my eyes for me, or someone fire that idiot!"

"Yes, sir."

The young doctor's stunned voice protested in bewilderment.

"But, sir, you can't mean . . . I mean, I've been an admirer of yours since I was a boy. You can't mean what you say."

"You're on my payroll. Do your damn job."

The doctors set to work, saying, "We'll try it one eye at a time."

"Just as long you do it."

As they were pouring warm saline solution into his left eye in an attempt to loosen the encrustation there, a question popped into his mind.

"What about Cuba?"

"Sir?"

"Cuba. Is it free?"

"Regrettably, no."

"Who's in charge down there? Anyone I know?" The last was a faint hope, but he wanted something to hold on to. Something familiar.

"Castro, sir."

"*Still?*"

"He'd old and gray, and they're down to short rations and bicycles, but he's still clinging to power."

"Incredible!"

The other doctor said then, "We think the eye is ready now. We would suggest you take it very slowly."

"Shut up!" he snapped.

And, taking a deep breath, he willed his left eyelid to open a crack.

A white-hot needle of light seared his optic nerve and sent his brain crashing through thunderstorms of pain and shock, and somewhere in the distance he heard their frantic shouts and above them the meek, too-young doctor crying, "I told you so! I told you so! But none of you would listen!"

His last thought before he blacked out again was that he'd have that doctor fired. He had been right in the first place, and therefore should have stood his ground. There would be no place for such weaklings in the new order.

1

In the waning weeks of the Thirty-third Year of the Revolution, Xavier Custodio went down to the beach to defend the Revolution for the last time.

In the privacy of his wood and royal palm *bohio*, he went through his morning routine, not knowing it was to be for the last time. First he dressed in his ragged fatigues, taking them off the clothesline where they had been hung, dripping, the night before. He squirmed into the harness that held the wooden cross snugly on his back. Then he picked up his Soviet-made Kalashnikov rifle—it had begun to rust in the tropical moisture—and a single clip of ammunition.

His machete, which he took from beside the door, was not rusted. It would never rust. Unlike the castoff AK-47, the machete was Cuban. Pre-revolutionary Cuban. It would last Xavier his entire lifetime.

With the machete swinging loose in his hand, he walked into the mangrove thicket and began to hack off a sapling. With absentminded skill, he wormed the thin bole into the back brace, so that the branches formed a canopy over his head. His machete made short work of assorted royal palm fronds and other branches.

These he slipped into rips and rents in his raggedy uniform. Once these things had been held in place by string and elastics—Russian string and elastics. There had been none since the fall of the hated capitialationist, Gorbachev.

When he was so festooned with greenery as to

13

resemble an ambulatory bush, Xavier strode off toward the beach, his branches and fronds bouncing happily.

The Caribbean sun was coming up, promising a glorious day. Xavier enjoyed the warm, sultry rays as they seeped through his itchy camouflage. It was a walk he had been taking since the earliest days of the Revolution, when he had been a young man.

Now he was old and bent, and his beard had turned to snow. And while his camouflage bounced, his proud heart did not.

As he trudged down to the beach, Xavier Custodio wondered where the years had gone. And thinking of the passage of time made him wonder where the Revolution had gone.

No, he thought morosely. Where the Revolution had gone *wrong*.

Oh, it had been so exciting when he was a young *Fidelista*! He could remember the day Batista had fled in the middle of the night—after a New Year's Day celebration. Xavier had been in Habana when Fidel had marched in with his *guerrilleros*.

The *santeria* priests lined the road to offer the protection of their gods to the bearded man wearing the jaunty beret, who was hailed as a redeemer and the new Pizarro. Rebels shot up the parking meters. There would be no taxes levied on the people in the new Cuba, they proclaimed. Millions came out to greet their new leader, and when he appeared on the balcony of the presidential palace, to give his first historic speech to the masses, doves actually roosted in the stonework above him. One right on his shoulder.

A glorious day. It had been the dawn of a new Cuba. A Cuba for Cubans—not Americanos or Mafiosos, but the Cuban people.

So long ago . . .

In those days it had been an honor to rise with the sun and go down to the beach, even with the putrid crab-stink.

As he thought this, a scarlet land crab scuttled out of the brush on nervous, spidery legs. It lifted its sunburned pincers angrily, as if challenging Xavier's right to walk on his own island.

Without giving it a thought, Xavier stepped on the crab. It made a sound like a Dixie cup popping, and Xavier walked on.

Behind him another land crab scuttled out, clamped pincers onto the mortal remains of its brother, and dragged it greedily from sight. Crunching cannibal sounds came from a mangrove thicket.

Near a stand of sugarcane, Xavier stopped for breakfast, too. He selected a moderate shoot of cane, and cutting it so close to the ground that the shoot would not stop growing, deftly spun it in his hand as he hacked off the bitter tip, letting it drop to decompose and fertilize the still living parent stalk.

As he walked, Xavier sucked in the sweet brown sucrose juice without enjoyment.

There was a time when breakfast had been more nourishing, he thought sadly. And somehow sweeter.

There had been a time when Xavier had driven down to the beach in his 1953 DeSoto. Until the irreplaceable parts had begun to decay. A motor scooter had replaced that. Until gasoline had become scarce and a Chinese bicycle had replaced that—until its tires had been confiscated to make tires for the military trucks that had drunk the entire gas ration of the island.

Where did the Revolution go wrong? Xavier asked himself.

Was it when the leadership organized the Committees for the Defense of the Revolution in every neighborhood? Before the Revolution, to be a *chivato* had been a shameful thing. Now every Cuban was an informer. Every Cuban carried a secret shame.

Was it when the Russians had insisted upon converting the Cuban economy to sugarcane harvesting— even though El Lider Maximo had earlier abandoned sugarcane as an industry for peons and *imperialista* lackeys?

Was it when the flower of Cuban youth had been

sent to Africa to fight in liberation wars that had resulted only in returning coffins?

No, Xavier thought. Things had truly begun to go awry after the Bay of Pigs.

He had been on the beach then, digging ditches. Then, as now, he had been a militiaman. Then, as now, loyal to Fidel.

The B-26s came flying Cuban Revolutionary colors. They buzzed in low, and Xavier laid down his spade to wave at them with both arms. But then he noticed something the American CIA had overlooked in their preparations: They had solid metal noses. The B-26s of the Cuban Air Force—all three of them—had Plexiglas noses.

The false Cuban warplanes opened fire. Xavier rolled into his half-dug trench just ahead of the blunt teeth of death, and lived.

The Bay was soon alive with invading forces. Xavier had helped sound the alarm. As a guide for Batallion 111, he helped capture nearly two hundred mercenaries. They thought they had captured Americans. They had taken only Cubans. Exiles.

For his bravery that day, the Maximum Leader himself had decorated Xavier and assigned him the honor of guarding Playa Giron, the beach at the mouth of the Bahia de Cochinos. It was not only an honor but a gift.

For no one ever expected the U.S. or their tools to attempt another Bay of Pigs. Certainly not at the site of their greatest humiliation. Certainly not in the Bay of Pigs itself.

Yet as he thought about it, Xavier realized that everything had changed in that first flush of triumph. For it was after the Bay of Pigs that Fidel had declared himself a Marxist-Leninist.

Xavier could recall his surprise when he'd heard the news. Then, with Latin resolution, he had shrugged his leafy shoulders and muttered, "Well, now we know what we are."

Before the Bay of Pigs, Xavier had been a defender

of the Revolution. After, a defender of Socialism.
And now . . .

Socialism was dead where it was not dying. And
it was dying with tortuous slowness on the island of
Cuba.

As he walked down to the beach, the memorials to
the fallen of the Revolution began to appear at the
side of the dirt road. Weeds had grown up around
them. Over thirty years had passed. The young men
of Cuba knew not of the Bay of Pigs. It was sad.

The land crabs began to accumulate in the road.
Those that had died the day before—both eaten and
not—had been baked orange by the relentless Caribbean sun.

As he sucked on the too-sweet cane, Xavier casually
popped the crabs with his worn shoes. Coolie shoes.
Imported from China. Suitable only for the feet of
children, not men like Xavier.

How long, he wondered, before we are reduced to
eating the indigestible land crabs?

How long until the long-promised fruits of the Revolution fall at the feet of the people, in whose name
the Revolution was carried out?

As the warm turquoise water—so clear it was like
rippling azure glass—came into view, Xavier popped
with each step. The crabs died and the crabs were
carried off by the buzzards and the other crabs to be
eaten. But the crabs were always just as plentiful the
next day.

Xavier recalled a phrase he had heard: "A revolution always eats its young."

It was not that way in Cuba. Cuba was different.
Its people were different. Its leaders were different.

Down by the beach, a copy of *Granma* flapped
among the crabs. Since it was his task to keep the
beach clean as well as safe, Xavier stooped to retrieve
it.

Idly he flipped through its pages. There were fifteen
pictures of El Lider scattered throughout its eight
pages. In each of them Fidel wore his familiar designer

fatigues. In each of them his paunch hung over his cinched-tight webbed belt.

Perhaps it was his downcast mood, perhaps it was because Xavier was approaching his sixtieth birthday, but the sight of the once charismatic leader of the Revolution bursting at the seams, while Xavier actually weighed less now than he did in 1961 when he'd fought at the Bay of Pigs, brought bitter tears to his sun-wrinkled eyes.

"This Revolution did not eat its young!" he said bitterly. "El Loco Fidel ate the Revolution!"

He tore the newspaper apart, scattering fragments everywhere. What did it matter if the beach was littered with the detritus of Socialism? It was already littered with the stinking husks of the unkillable crabs. It was a beach men had died for, one whose white sands had drunk their blood—and it had all been for nothing.

Cuba had gone from being an American colony to a Soviet colony. And once the two superpowers had made their peace, they had turned their backs on the island.

Thirty years of struggle, and Xavier Custodio patrolled the same stretch of stinking beach, his leathery old man's skin rubbed raw by the branches and fronds, the promise of his youthful ideals squandered.

He let the last sob break from his sun-dried throat.

And behind him he heard a sporadic popping.

Xavier turned to see who was walking along his beach.

Behind the fronds that shielded his face, his warm brown eyes went wide.

He was looking at soldiers. They wore olive-drab, just like him. But their uniforms were clean and whole.

And on their shoulders they wore no patch or insignia. They did not need to. Xavier knew that the shameless Stars and Stripes of the United States army belonged there.

Xavier dropped to his knees, his old training taking hold. His heart pounded as he watched them. They were disembarking from rubber rafts that even now were being rent by bayonets and sunk with stone weights.

Xavier hesitated. Should he attack them? Or should he retreat and sound the alarm?

He looked to his AK-47 and its single clip—and his heart broke. The Revolution had taken his teeth. He could not fight. And his pre-Socialist machete was not equal to the hour.

Rustling and skulking like a heartless dog, he retreated into the muck of nearby Zapata Swamp and ran all the way to his humble *bohio*.

He would alert Habana. Because he was a Cuban, not because he cared anymore about the failed Revolution.

Less than thirty rods down the road, Xavier stopped running. He remembered that his telephone no longer worked. He could not call Habana. He would have to go to Zapata. And it was too far to run, for an aging *Fidelista* with the zeal sucked out of him by hunger and privation.

The President of the Republic of Cuba was wondering where the Revolution had gone wrong.

He sat in his office in the Palace of the Revolution with his advisers, the men of the mountains who had waged guerrilla warfare with him in the Sierra Maestra.

"Mi amigos," he began, exhaling clouds of aromatic tobacco smoke. "Be truthful now. Did we fail?"

"No, Fidel," said his brother, the Vice-President for Life, after a moment's consultation.

"Yet here we are, our goals unmet. Surely there have been errors? Certainly we have made some mistakes along the way?"

The advisers looked to one another. They shrugged and looked to their Maximum Leader for guidance.

"Was it in 1959, when we postponed elections, proclaiming, 'Real democracy is not possible for a hungry people'?" he asked.

"No," the Minister of Ideology insisted. "For with-

out that decree, Cuba would not have El Magnifico
Fidel to guide them to greatness."

The Maximum Leader nodded soberly. His frown
deepened. He puffed thoughtfully.

"Was it perhaps a year later, when we instituted
food rationing, thereby insuring perpetual hunger?"

"No, Comandante en Jefe," the cultural minister
protested. "For had we not instituted rationing in
1960, there would now be no food at all."

"Good. Good. That is good. I had not thought of
that."

Smiles brightened dark faces. Their leader was
pleased. The rum was flowing freely now. They were
drinking Cuba Libres.

"Was it when we announced our Harvest of the
Century?"

"No," he was assured. "For who could have foreseen that the harvest would fail? The Revolution
makes workers, not weather. The workers were with
us, the weather was not."

"Good. Good. I like it," said the Maximum Leader,
jotting these phrases down on a tiny note pad balanced on one big knee. The stubby pencil looked tiny
in his huge fist.

His brow furrowed once more. "Perhaps we blun-
dered when we sent our soldiers to Africa to fight
oppression there. Many died. Many were widowed or
left childless."

"No, Fidel," insisted the Minister of Agriculture.
"For if those soldiers were with us today, they would
have to be fed. There is little enough food as it is."

"Excellent point." The big bearded man rolled his
fine cigar from one side of his mouth to the other,
like a bear with a candy cane. "And what about the
time we allowed any Cuban to leave through the port
of Mariel?" he asked. "Thousands did. It was an
embarrassment. It made Cuba look like a place to flee
from."

"No," said his brother, in his other capacity of
Defense Minister. "For they were traitors to Socialism, and what need have we to feed them?"

"Another excellent point. I shall make a speech tomorrow. It will be about the importance of food to the Revolution."

The sound of enthusiastic applause rippled around the marble room like unseeable doves.

Pounding feet came up to the door, and someone on the other side began to knock furiously.

"El Presidente!" a voice cried. "It is the Americans! They have returned! They are attacking!"

"Where?"

"Playa Giron!"

At the mention of that legendary place of class struggle, the eyes of the presidential advisers went round, their expressions turning sick.

"We are lost!" they cried, visions of Tripoli and Baghdad flashing through their rum-besotted minds.

"No," rumbled their Maximum Leader. "This is exactly what the Revolution requires."

"*Que?*"

"An enemy to vanquish."

The Leader of the Revolution stormed into the two-story home in a Havana suburb that had served as his emergency command post since before the first Bay of Pigs.

"Report," he snapped.

A captain seated before a radio took off his earphones and said, "A militia man discovered the incursion three hours ago."

"Three hours! Why was I not notified before this?"

"He was unable to contact us by telephone. It had fallen into disrepair."

"Then he had failed Socialism. He should have maintained the instrument better. He understood its importance. Have him shot."

"But he was a hero of the first Bay of Pigs, Comrade Fidel."

"And he was a failure of the second," the Cuban president said dismissively. "Tell me of the campaign."

"I have ordered the invaders destroyed to the last man."

"*Mulo!* What good are dead invaders?"

"Dead invaders cannot establish beachheads."

"And dead invaders cannot be interrogated!" El Lider snapped. "I want prisoners, not corpses!"

"*Sí*, comrade." The captain returned to his World War II surplus radio set and began issuing rapid orders in Spanish. He listened through headphones and looked up to the hulking figure of his *comandante en jefe*.

"Grito Batallion reports that the invasion has been quelled. They have taken prisoners."

"Have them brought to me. No, I have a better idea. I will go to them. In a tank. We will bring cameras, and show me leaping off a tank at the battle site. It will be as it was in 1961. What need have the people for meat, when Fidel entertains them so lavishly?"

"*Sí.*"

There were only five surviving prisoners, he found when he entered the shack on the beach. The Maximum Leader was disappointed. Five was not much of an audience. He decided against televising their interrogation over TeleRebelde live. It would be recorded instead, and selected portions aired as it suited him.

They were, he was disappointed to learn, not Americanos but Cubans. He would rather have had Americanos. They were more valuable.

He began to speak. He paced back and forth, one hand crooked at the small of his back and the other busy stabbing the air with a Romeo y Julieta cigar.

"You are *gusanos*—worms!" he told them in Spanish. "You are betrayers!"

The men looked at one another, abashed.

Good, good, thought Fidel. He would shame them as he did the thousand-some invaders of 1961.

He had had those ones assembled in the Palencio de los Desportes—the Sports Palace. For four days he had lectured them, browbeaten them, humiliated them as the cameras rolled, recording every drop of traitorous sweat. They had wept. They had begged for forgiveness. And in the end, they had spontaneously stood up and given him a standing ovation.

Here, he would do all this again. Since there were only five survivors, it would take but the afternoon.

"You have allowed yourself to be puppets!" he continued. "Puppets of the *imperialistas*! You are men without conscience, lacking even a single ball between your spineless legs!"

They winced at his lashing words. The fear was in their eyes. Pleased, he pressed on.

"You have come to the paradise of the Caribbean to despoil it. Or so you parasites thought. Instead, you have tasted the bitter gall of your defeat on the sweet Socialist sands of our beach. You are fools and lackies of fools!"

A stiff-backed Cuban major cleared his throat. Annoyed, the Leader of the Revolution glowered at him. He paused and then nodded, giving the man leave to speak.

"Comrade Fidel. These men . . ."

"Spit it out!" he snapped.

"They do not speak Spanish," the major said. "We have already determined this."

The President's right eyebrow crawled upward. His left, hesitating, joined it.

He whirled on the five nervous prisoners.

"This is true?" he howled in English. "You do not speak the mother tongue of your fathers?"

They shook their heads furiously. At least they remain scared, Fidel thought.

"What manner of Cubans are these, who storm our shores now?" he raged.

One of the invaders spoke.

"Second-generation ones," he said simply.

El Lider Maximo blinked. His mouth went slack, making his rangy gray beard bunch up on his olive-drab chest like a cloud of steel wool dashing itself against a mountainside.

"Madre!" he grumbled. "I will waste no time with such as you!" he snapped, knowing his English was not equal to a five-hour harangue. Besides, the lan-

guage was not nearly eloquent enough for his pur-
poses. "Tell me who has sent you here!"

The men remained stonily silent. For the first time,
he noticed under their camouflage paint how young
they were. Mere boys, it seemed.

"Tell me!" he roared.

The mouths of the prisoners thinned resolutely.

"Have them tortured, and call me when they are
prepared to speak," he snapped, storming from the
beach.

It is not like the old days, he thought huffily as he
left the shack.

It took less than twenty minutes. His cultural minister employed the Russian technique known as "making a snake." It was as simple as it was effective.

They took the strongest of the prisoners, held him
down, and before the eyes of the others, split his
tongue down the middle with a sharp knife.

The blood flowed alarmingly, in crimson rivers.

The others found their tongues, and began to speak
rivers of words.

The Maximum Leader faced them triumphantly.

"I knew you lacked balls, but I did not think you
were also bereft of spines," he spat. Glaring at one,
he added, "You! Who engineered this cowardly,
incursion?"

"Uncle Sam."

El Presidente, standing straight up, almost stag-
gered at the news. He blinked. He could scarcely
believe it. Had the Americanos become so bold?
Always before, they had insulated themselves from
blame by layers of proxy commanders.

He turned to the next in line. "What do you say?
Speak your leader's name!"

"Uncle Sam."

And so it was on down the line.

"Uncle Sam."

"Uncle Sam."

Even the maimed tongueless one gurgled out two bloody words that sounded like "Uncle Sam."

This came as such a surprise that the grizzled President of Cuba let his cigar fall, hissing, into the pool of blood at his feet.

He lifted a balled fist to the height of his shoulder, and shook it furiously.

"Then it is war! At long last, it is war!"

2

His name was Remo, and he was trying to order duckling.

The room service manager of the Fontainebleau Hotel, overlooking Miami Beach, was graciously apologetic.

"I am sorry sir, but the duck is unavailable."

"Uh-oh," said Remo, his strong face warping in concern.

"Sir?"

"My roommate isn't going to like this."

"Please convey to your roommate our deepest apologies," the room service manager said in an unctuous tone, "but as I said, the duck is unavailable this evening."

"This is terrible," Remo said.

"From time to time there is a problem with our suppliers. It cannot be foreseen, and there is nothing we can do about this."

"You see, I have a sneaking suspicion my roommate picked this hotel expressly because he liked the duck," Remo said.

The room service manager's voice grew solicitous. "I shall so inform the head chef. I'm certain 'he will be gratified."

"You see, normally we don't check into a hotel a second time. We kinda like to move around, experience new things. But we were here a few months back and my roommate ordered the duck. Now here we are back at your nice hotel; and now no duck."

"I can assure you it will be on the menu by the end of the week. May I suggest our beef Stroganoff?"

"You can suggest all you want," Remo countered, "but my roommate and I are allergic to beef."

"A pity."

"We eat beef and we go into toxic shock."

"We would not want that. Would you prefer the lamb-kabobs?"

"Lamb's greasy."

"Not our lamb."

"And lamb makes us hurl."

"Hurl?"

"Puke."

"I shall have to remember the word 'hurl,' " the room service manager said dryly. "It has a certain charming . . . *force* to it."

"My roommate and I," Remo went on, "are on highly restricted diets. We eat fish and duck and rice and not much else."

"In that case, let me suggest the trout Almondine."

"Good suggesting, but my roommate has his heart set on duck."

"As I have explained, the duck is unavailable tonight, but it will be available again later in the week. Possibly by Thursday."

"Don't know if we'll be here that long," Remo said.

The room service manager's voice dropped several degrees Fahrenheit. "May I make a further suggestion? Why don't you ask your rather finicky roommate if, under the circumstances as I have outlined them, the trout Almondine might not be acceptable after all?"

"Hang on."

Remo cupped his hand over the hotel suite phone receiver and called into the next room.

"Hey, Little Father!"

"Trout have bones," came a squeaky, querulous voice.

Remo took his hand off the receiver and said, "He says trout is bony."

"We bone our trout, sir."

The squeaky voice came again. "Ask for the duck."

"I did. They say they're out."

"Has every duck in the universe expired?" wondered the squeaky voice.

"Doubt it," said Remo.

"Then I shall have the duck. In orange sauce."

Remo spoke into the receiver. "Says he's really, really set on the duck. And he'd like it in orange sauce."

The last of the oil evaporated from the room service manager's tone.

"Sir, as I have explained—"

"Listen, by chance did you hear about the bellboy?"

"I seldom pay attention to the doings of lower-echelon personnel," the room service manager said bluntly.

"The poor guy ended up in a body cast."

"I believe something was mentioned along those lines. Regrettable."

"He nicked my roommate's trunk carrying it to the elevator," Remo pointed out.

There was a pregnant pause on the line. "This roommate of yours, by chance would he be an elderly gentleman of Asian extraction?"

"Oh, I wouldn't call him 'elderly,'" said Remo, knowing that he would be overheard by the occupant of the next room, who was sensitive about his age. "And I think you shouldn't either. That's worse than nicking a trunk."

"Understood, sir." The tone changed again. This time, it was helpful. "Well, if this is the case, there may be something we can do. Perhaps I could ask the head chef to dig a little deeper into the freezer, as it were. Ah, I trust your roommate would not be offended by frozen duck?"

"Not unless it showed up on his plate that way."

"Splendid. Then duck in orange sauce it will be. I assume you would like the same?"

"Not me. I want the trout Almondine. A side of steamed white rice for both of us, and absolutely pure natural mineral water. Got that?"

"Your meals shall be delivered within the hour," the room service manager promised. "You have our eternal gratitude for your patience."

"And you get to keep your mobility," said Remo happily. He hung up. He looked into the mirror. The face that stared back at him was distinguished by two features: the deep set of his dark eyes, and the high cheekbones. It was a strong face. Too angular to be called handsome, yet too regular to be unpleasant. In certain lights, it looked skull-like. When he frowned, it looked cruel.

Remo wasn't frowning now. He was smiling. He adjusted his smile and put an innocent expression on his face. Then he walked out into the living room of the sumptuous hotel suite, hoping his expression held.

"I got you the duck," he said brightly.

The occupant of the other room sat cross-legged on a reed mat before the hotel television set. He didn't stir a hair. Not that there was much hair to be stirred. The back of his head resembled a seamless amber egg decorated by tiny ears, whose tops nudged twin puffs of cloudy white hair set directly above.

"The duck in this place is greasy," he announced.

"It is?"

"It was greasy last time."

"Want me to call back, have them do it right?" Remo said helpfully.

"It will do no good. They are incompetent. If we demand they leech out the grease, the duck will come dry."

"Better greasy duck than dry duck, huh?"

"Better properly prepared duck."

Okay, Remo thought, he didn't drag me back here for the duck. It must be something else. Remo decided to get to the point.

"Little Father, I am curious."

"So is a monkey."

"True," said Remo, trying not to be dragged into a fight. "But monkeys can't order room service for their jungle friends. And monkeys don't usually find themselves suddenly rushing off to Miami one morning. Especially since they've been there recently."

"On what channel does Cheeta Ching come on here?"

Remo picked up the local TV directory. "Channel 6."

The Master of Sinanju picked up the remote channel-selector and punched up 6. His face came into view then. It resembled the papyrus death mask of some impossibly ancient pharaoh that had been sucked dry of all moisture. A wisp of beard clung to the papery chin. His age was impossible to gauge. Even his wrinkles seemed wrinkled.

A low sound emerged from his wattled throat, curious and faintly pleased. "The black box says 6, and behold, Channel 6 appears on the glass screen."

"I think the cable box is dead."

"Perhaps we will abide here for a time."

"Suits me. I'd just like to know why."

"We are homeless, are we not?"

"Since Smith kicked us out of our home, yeah. I guess I prefer to think of us as footloose vagabonds."

"There are many homeless in this sad land."

"To hear Cheeta Ching tell it, yeah. But what does that have to do with camping out in Miami?"

"The homeless of this land, how do they come to such a sad state?"

"Let me see. They lose their jobs. They don't pay the rent."

"Exactly," said Chiun.

"Huh?"

"We are homeless, therefore we are unemployed."

"Don't tell me we've been laid off."

"I will not."

"Good."

"We have reached an impasse in our contract negotiations with Emperor Smith," explained Chiun.

"How big and how bad?"

"Enough that we are hiding from him, with all our worldly belongings, until he comes to his senses."

"So *that's* why we're back in Miami. We're hiding from Smith!"

"Exactly. He will never think to look for us here, knowing that we abided in this very place but short months ago."

"Good point. How long you expect to tough it out?"

"Not long."

"Really?"

Chiun nodded sagely. "Smith will cave in shortly."

"Why do you say that?"

"Because only this morning he ordered us to a certain place, there to await further instructions."

"He gave us an assignment?"

"Not exactly. He merely asked me to go to this place and await word."

"Holy Christ, Chiun!" said Remo, reaching for the telephone. "What if it's important?"

"Then the sooner Smith will capitulate," said the Master of Sinanju reasonably.

Remo picked up the receiver. He listened to the beeping and electronic chirping in his ear as he stabbed the 1 button repeatedly—the foolproof contact number he used when he had to reach Harold W. Smith.

Normally, after a dozen or so chirps, an electronic relay kicked in and Remo got a ringing bell.

This time, the chirping simply stopped and he was listening to dead silence.

Remo hung up and tried again. This time, he didn't get so much as a chirp.

"Something's wrong with this phone," he complained, turning.

And the severed plastic line to the wall plug clicked onto his Italian leather shoes.

Remo looked down, saw the neatly snipped end, and looked toward the Master of Sinanju, who sat on his reed mat like a wispy little Buddha, as if he had not moved. Remo hadn't seen or heard him move. Chiun was the only person on earth who could slip something past Remo. His long-nailed bird-claw hands rested open and loose on the bright lavender lap of his kimono. Those deadly nails, Remo knew, had severed the line.

"I gotta contact Smith," he said. "He'll be frantic."

"Exactly."

"He'll put his entire computer system to work tracking us down," Remo said.

"Let him."

"Look, if you won't let me call him, at least tell me where we're supposed to be."

"In a certain city."

"Does this certain city have a name?" Remo wondered.

"Yes."

"What's it called?"

"Miami."

Remo blinked.

"This Miami?"

"Do you know of any other Miami?"

"No," Remo admitted. "But that doesn't mean anything. I've been to three Daytons and five Quincys in the last five years. There might be another Miami tucked up there in Alaska. Smith happen to say Miami, Florida?"

"He said Miami. I took him to mean this very Miami."

Remo's dark eyes took on a puzzled gleam. "So we're hiding out in the place he told us to go?"

"Exactly."

"Any particular logic to that?"

"Yes."

"Care to enlighten a colleague?"

"If such a person existed, I would."

"Har de har har har. How about telling *me*?"

"Wisdom bestowed upon a monkey is wisdom squandered. But Cheeta Ching will soon be on, so I will tell you in return for silence."

"Deal."

Chiun hit the volume control, silencing the set. The local news was on.

He turned on his mat. Remo brought up his mat.

He assumed a lotus position identical to Chiun's own. Their eyes—unalike except for a similar deep confidence—reflected one another. Otherwise they were as different as two people could be. Chiun was tiny, and looked frail in his garish kimono. Remo was tall, lean, and wore a white T-shirt and brown chinos. His hair and eyes were almost the same shade as his pants.

"I am the Master of Sinanju," said Chiun in a low voice.

"True," said Remo agreeably.

"You are a Master of Sinanju."

"Also true."

"Together we are the only true living Masters of Sinanju, the greatest house of assassins in the history of this planet."

"No argument there," agreed Remo.

"We are the best. I am the very best. You are somewhat less than the best, but good nonetheless."

Remo brightened at the rare compliment. Chiun, seeing that he had overpraised his pupil, instantly amended his rash judgment.

"At least adequate," he said. "Better than most monkeys."

"Cut to the chase," grumbled Remo.

"Smith has hired us because he wished the best. Without us his silly organization, which he continually harps does not exist—"

"Officially exist," Remo corrected.

"Without us, his organization would be toothless. For over twenty winters we have served him. In harsh times and glad times. Yet now he argues over tiny matters. Insignificant details in our new contract."

"Like what insignificant details?" Remo wanted to know.

"Such as gold."

"Since when is that insignificant?"

"Since he refuses to acknowledge its importance."

Remo suddenly looked doubtful. "Come again?"

"Gold is not important in and of itself," said Chiun.

"Am I hearing right? Is this you talking?"

"What matters," Chiun went on, as if not hearing

the rude outburst, "is loyalty, understanding, and
proper respect. Gold is merely the symbol of these
things."

"Horse crap."

Chiun slapped the hardwood floor with a yellow
palm.

"Silence! I am speaking."

And because he respected the Master of Sinanju
above all others, Remo Williams fell respectfully
silent.

"You asked for logic and I give you wisdom,"
Chiun snapped. "Wisdom takes time. You will listen."

Remo listened. He did not look happy about it.

"Smith has done the house disrespect," Chiun continued. "He claims he cannot shower us with the tribute of before, meager as it was. He claims it is because
of this Procession."

"Recession," Remo corrected.

"I countered that more tribute is not at issue,"
Chiun said, ignoring the trivial outburst. "I will forgo
additional gold and take instead certain considerations, I told Smith."

"Such as?" Remo prompted.

"A new home."

"We've been trying to get him to fix that for over
a year now," Remo pointed out.

"And I have asked him for a place he once before
declined," Chiun countered.

"Yeah? What place?"

Chiun waved a dismissive hand. "It is of no
moment. We are not speaking of such trifles now. We
are speaking of respect and understanding between a
head of state and his royal assassin. There is decorum
to such a delicate arrangement. Smith has seen fit to
defile this arrangement, so I have spirited us to a place
of concealment."

"Which just happens to be the place we're supposed
to be."

At that, the Master of Sinanju's sere face softened.
He smiled thinly, his wrinkled face becoming a happy

cobweb in which his hazel eyes, like playful spiders, danced.

"When Emperor Smith realizes we are not to be found, he will be beside himself," Chiun confided. "He will mourn our absence, and be forced to reflect upon the ruinous state of his empire without us. Then he will redouble the efforts to locate us, sparing no expense, leaving no stone unturned."

"Running up one humungous phone bill."

"And when he at last succeeds," Chiun went on, "we will feign ignorance, and swear to vanquish his enemies with all the awesome skill at our command."

"Once the fine print is settled," Remo added pointedly.

"No time will be lost in travel. Only negotiations."

"Okay," Remo admitted. "It's smart. Maybe it'll work. But what if the world is about to come crashing down around our heads? What if it's a big one?"

The Master of Sinanju shrugged. "Then it will all be the stubborn Smith's fault, and so it will be recorded in the histories of the House of Sinanju."

"What if it's a really, *really* big one?" Remo pressed.

"There is nothing big enough to compel the Master of Sinanju to retreat from principle," Chiun said firmly.

"Listen," Remo began, but the Master of Sinanju lifted a frail arm for silence. He had been looking neither at the television nor the clock radio dial, but as if a chime had rung he announced, "It is now time for Cheeta."

Remo looked to the screen. As the Master of Sinanju repositioned himself so that he was facing the screen, the sound came up.

"Good evening," said a female voice like steel nails caught in a trash compactor. "This is the *BCN Evening News with Don Cooder*. Don is off tonight."

"Don is off every night," Remo growled.

"Hush!" Chiun admonished.

Remo folded his arms at the sight of the Korean network anchorwoman called Cheeta Ching.

Her face was a flat mask of some jaundiced ivory, expressionless except for a perpetual frown on her viper-slim eyebrows. Her mouth—the only part of her that seemed to move—made shapes that reminded Remo of some blood-sucking flower.

"She is more beautiful than ever," Chiun said happily.

"Looks fatter," Remo pointed out.

"Philistine! That is the bloom of motherhood you see."

Which only reminded Remo of the unpleasant series of events that had brought him and Chiun into contact with the anchorwoman who had become a heroine to career women everywhere, but who was known—and feared—as "the Korean Shark" to her network colleagues.

For years, the Master of Sinanju had nurtured a secret crush on Cheeta Ching. Recent events had brought the three of them into contact, first during the bloody special governor's election in California, and more recently in Manhattan, where they had been called in to deal with a bizarre, seemingly haunted Fifth Avenue skyscraper.

During the first contact, Cheeta had been rescued by Remo and Chiun—after which, she and the Master of Sinanju had disappeared together. Only days later, Cheeta had announced that her heroic struggle to become a fortysomething mother had resulted in an ovulatory breakthrough. Chiun had declined any comment, but was looking forward to the birth. It had been his stated goal to ensure a male child by Cheeta for the express purpose of creating the next heir to the Sinanju line.

No matter how much Remo had tried, he could not get Chiun to either confirm or deny paternity. As the due day approached, Remo grew more and more worried.

"Tonight," a puffy-faced Cheeta was saying, "tensions between the United States and Cuba are increasing, in the aftermath of what some are calling 'Bay of Pigs Two.' "

The graphic behind Cheeta's head expanded to fill

the screen. It showed a battle-torn beach, where the Maximum Leader of Cuba was storming about like some hulking, olive-drab Moses.

"Pah!" Chiun said, as the face of Cheeta Ching vanished from sight.

"Relax, Little Father. You know Cheeta's got her face time written into her contract. She'll be back in thirty seconds."

The footage rolled on as Cheeta screeched on.

"What Havana is calling 'a cowardly imperialist attack on the heroic Cuban Revolution' began in the early-evening hours when a team of unidentified mercenaries infiltrated the Bay of Pigs area, site of the cowardly botched 1961 invasion launched by the quasi-legal CIA."

"Since when is tyranny heroic?" Remo grumbled.

"Remo! Be still."

The footage showed a line of shackled prisoners being herded into a Soviet-made BMP armored vehicle.

"U.S. officials deny culpability," Cheeta screeched on. "But reliable sources abroad, as well as the historical significance of the landing site, clearly suggest U.S.A. fingerprints."

"How about giving the American side for once?" Remo complained.

Chiun glowered. Remo subsided. When Chiun merely shouted, he was blowing off steam. When he glowered, it meant a volcano was rumbling in warning. Remo decided he could do without a lava-and-pumice shower.

Cheeta's flat face returned to the screen. "In a furious, three-hour-long speech given this afternoon, Cuban President Fidel Castro promised swift and—"

Snow filled the screen with a swiftness and violence that caught them off-guard. It hissed and crackled. Cheeta Ching's mouth continued to make flexible shapes, but her words were drowned out. Then her face was gone, replaced by busy white pixels.

Chiun leaped to his feet. "What outrage is this!" he demanded.

"Easy," Remo said. "It's probably just a reception problem."

A moment later, it was clear that reception was not the problem.

A new face appeared on the screen. It was mostly beard—gray and curly. From a mouth hidden in all that unruly hair, a cigar about half the length of a Louisville Slugger jutted.

A meaty hand reached up to take the cigar from the mouth. And the mouth began speaking.

"Ceetizens of Miami!" it proclaimed in a distinctly Latin accent. "Ceetizens of the world! The Imperialists have declared war on Cuba and its magnificent Revolution. So be it! The Socialist Revolution now declares war on Imperialist interests everywhere! For every blow struck against our peaceful shores, a greater, mightier blow will be struck against the aggressor!"

"Crap," Remo said.

"Who is this man, Remo?"

"Don't you recognize him? It's Castro."

"He is ugly."

"I thought so when I was a kid, and I still think so now."

The President of Cuba resumed speaking. He gesticulated with his free hand, with his cigar, and as often as not with his bearded head. The man looked spastic. His voice rose and fell feverishly, his accent at times so thick his words ran together and were indistinguishable from one another.

Worst of all, he went on and on for what promised to be hours, warning, threatening, blustering, and making Remo, less than twenty minutes into the performance, mentally wish for the return of Cheeta Ching, owl-screech voice and all.

"Why don't you change the channel?" Remo suggested.

Chiun tossed the channel-changer in Remo's direction and stormed out of the living room. His bedroom door slammed shut.

Remo ran up and down the channels. The same

picture was on every channel. The same bombastic voice continued to pour out of the speaker.

"I wonder if this is what Smith wanted us down here for. . . ." Remo muttered.

3

USAF Captain William "Trusty" Ayres III despised Cuba.

His hatred had nothing to do with the Cuban political system, its climate, exports, or people, whom he was reliably informed were both friendly and hardworking.

William Ayres III hated Cuba because the threat it presented to Florida meant that Ayres had had to sit out the Gulf War, flying coast-wise patrols in his F-16 Fighting Falcon out of Homestead Air Force Base on the tip of Florida, a mere ninety miles from the island of Cuba.

He could have been an ace by now. Would have been, he was sure—except that some Pentagon war-simulation computer had spat out a scenario in which Havana decided to side with Iraq and fly sorties against Florida pressure points, one of which was the Turkey Point nuclear power plant, conveniently adjacent to Homestead. Cuban defectors had sworn their on-board MIG flight computers were programmed for strikes against Turkey Point.

It had never happened. Oh, sure, Fidel had made a lot of speeches. But they were just the same old hot air.

So when the scruffy face of the leader of the Cuban Revolution appeared on the Homestead AFB rec room TV during a rerun of *Hot Shots,* William Ayres III impulsively threw a can of diet Dr. Pepper at the screen.

"Banana-republic jerk!" he jeered.

His fellow pilots hooted and shouted abuse at the screen. Some of them had flown combat in the Gulf. They lorded it over Captain Ayres. Called him "Rusty" Ayres, until he wanted to drain the oil from their engines.

"What's he sayin'?" someone asked over the raucous din.

"Who cares? The guy's a big windbag."

"Yeah. Just a dinosaur looking for a cushy museum."

Eventually, they settled down. Castro was going on and on as if he were spring-wound.

They listened attentively as the Maximum Leader of Cuba proclaimed, "We are surrounded by a sea of capitalism! But we shall prevail! History will vindicate us! Our cause is true! Our slogan will always be: *Socialismo o Muerte!*' "

"What's that mean?" Ayres asked Janio Perez.

"Socialism or death," grunted Perez.

"I say death," someone else growled.

"Let's put it to a vote."

They never put it to a vote.

Instead the scramble Klaxon started yowling, and they were pelting for their waiting F-16s.

Ayres was first into the air. He received his vectors from the tower and realized he was being sent over the Gulf. Not the Gulf he had missed out on, but the Gulf of Mexico.

"This is it!" he said. "We're at war with Cuba. Damn!"

All thought of the glories of air combat drained from his brain. He was a professional now, doing the job his country had trained him for.

His radar picked up a single bogie, flying low on the deck. The Identify Friend or Foe transponder read it as unfriendly.

"Bogie sighted," he said. "IFF says Foe. Instructions."

"Splash bogie," crackled his helmet earphone. "Repeat: Splash bogie."

Captain Ayres initiated target acquisition. The heads-up display IDed it as a MIG-23 Flogger. Cuban. Defi-

nitely. No one else flew MIGs over the Caribbean.
And nobody flew down on the deck unless they were
bent on attack.

Captain Ayres got a radar tone, locked on, and with
a businesslike "Fox-1," launched his sidewinder missile. It erupted from his wingtip and flew true.

It was that simple. Lock, launch, and get the hell
out of the airspace, as the MIG jumped apart in a
nasty popcorn of flash and ash.

"Bogie splashed," Ayres said, his voice thin.

"Roger. Stay out there."

"Any others?"

"Negative on other bogies."

"Roger," said Captain William "Trusty" Ayres,
who had now tasted combat and wondered why the
taste was so metallic.

4

Dr. Harold W. Smith controlled the most powerful computer network on the face of the earth.

Not the most advanced. There were supercomputers far more advanced than Smith's. Nor the largest. Smith had only a quartet of mainframes at his disposal. Oddly enough, they were secreted behind a concrete wall in the basement of his place of work.

Nor were Harold Smith's computers the fastest. Nor the newest. Modern technology had long outstripped their microprocessors and old-style integrated circuits.

But they were powerful. In this case, knowledge was power. Thirty years of maintaining the system—which had been upgraded often in the early years, but seldom these days for security reasons—had filled its vast memory banks with highly specialized data of specific value to Smith and his work. Long years of toiling behind his shabby oak desk under the shaky fluorescent lights in his Spartan office that overlooked Long Island Sound had enabled Harold Smith to crack virtually every computer net he might have to access in the performance of his duties.

The combined computers of the FBI, CIA, Defense Intelligence Agency, NASA, the Social Security Administration, and the IRS, on down to the lowliest police department terminal in the most rural corner of the nation, were like open books, waiting to have their electronic pages turned by the unseen fingers of the anonymous Harold W. Smith.

Corporate computers, among the most rigidly controlled and protected, had surrendered their passwords to him long ago.

Government systems, despite continual upgrading and password updating, inevitably fell under the brute-force assaults of his keen analytical mind.

If it could be accessed by telephone line, Harold Smith could enter it.

None of it was, strictly speaking, legal. Smith could, in theory, be sent to prison for penetrating government files and siphoning off their secrets.

But all of it was sanctioned.

For Harold W. Smith was a unique man with a unique responsibility.

Back in the grimmest days of the Cold War, when America was beset with foreign enemies and being systematically corroded from within by domestic troubles, a soon-to-be-martyred President had summoned Smith—then a middle-aged CIA bureaucrat—to the White House to offer him a post that Smith had never heard of.

Officially the post did not exist. It was Director of CURE, a supersecret agency that didn't exist either. In any official sense.

Smith had been chosen because of the unique combination of qualities that had made him uniquely Harold Smith. His unswerving loyalty to his country. His inflexible sense of responsibility. Perhaps most of all, his lack of imagination. For what a worried President was contemplating was giving a faceless bureaucrat the power to unseat him—if he had the imagination and ruthless ambition to pursue that goal.

Smith had no such ambition. His imagination was virtually nonexistent.

And so it was that he sat behind his shabby desk thirty years later, his patrician nose almost touching the computer terminal that fed off his hidden mainframes, trying to imagine where his enforcement arm and his trainer could be.

He could not. It baffled him. He had clearly instructed Chiun to go to Miami with Remo. To await orders in the Biltmore Hotel.

They were not registered at the Biltmore. Not under any of their usual aliases.

"Are you certain you do not have anyone registered with the first name Remo?" an exasperated Smith had asked the Biltmore desk clerk.

The desk clerk, after patiently deflecting Smith's question, snapped, "We are not a telephone directory." And hung up.

Smith had hung up too. Then he had dialed into the hotel's own computer records. It was part of a chain and its system was connected to the other hotels in the chain, and thus accessible by modem.

Smith paged through the registration file.

There were no Remos. There was no guest whose name suggested an Asian flavor. Remo always retained his first name, owing to his general difficulty with technical details. And Chiun invariably chose a Korean-sounding cover name—when he bothered with a cover name at all.

This odd development had baffled Smith. He wondered if there had been a plane crash. He logged over to the wire services. There had been none. Neither were any of the flights from New York—Remo and Chiun's most recent address—to Miami hung up by delays, according to the airport traffic-control computers he checked.

Smith next accessed Remo's credit card files. Remo had thirty of them under thirty different cover names, all first-named Remo.

None of those nonexistent Remos had used his card to book a flight that morning, Smith determined.

Smith logged off the last of the credit card companies, absently adjusting his rimless glasses.

He was a gray man. Gray was the hue of his dry skin, and gray was the color of his eyes. His hair was more white than gray, but it was still grayish. He wore a gray three-piece suit enlivened only by a green Dartmouth tie.

Even his worn old wedding ring looked somehow colorless.

As he leaned back, his face pale, Harold W. Smith

found himself facing a complete dead end. He could not account for the whereabouts of his enforcement arm.

And all hell was breaking loose.

The first call had come from the President of the United States that morning. Smith had picked up the red handset of the dial-less red telephone sitting on his desk in the middle of the first strident ring.

"Smith. We have a problem."

The President was respectful. He was the seventh president Smith had been privileged to serve. They had all been respectful. Not because they feared Smith and his organization, but because they understood how it functioned.

CURE was set up to operate outside of constitutional restrictions. It was answerable to no one. Not even the Executive Branch. The President was the only person outside the organization who knew it existed. To admit there was a CURE would have been tantamount to admitting the Constitution didn't work and the great modern experiment in democracy was a broken, flailing mechanism.

The President was prohibited from ordering Smith to undertake operations. Chief Executives could only suggest missions. That way, there could be no opportunity for a ruthless officeholder to abuse CURE.

Presidential control was limited to one simple instruction: Shut down.

Smith's instructions were clear in that event. The computer files would be erased, the enforcement arm disposed of, and when those details had been attended to Smith was to ingest the poison pill he kept in the watch pocket of his gray vest. It would leave no trace—other than a gray corpse.

And he would execute this order without hesitation. Because he was Harold Smith. Every President for the last thirty years had known this, and so none had given the order to shut down.

And so this latest President was saying in a reserved

tone of respect, "I have something you might want to look into."

"Go ahead, Mr. President," said Smith with equal respect.

"Someone has just tried to invade Cuba."

"Yes?"

"They landed a small force on the Bay of Pigs. It was wiped out. The survivors have been captured. They are currently being interrogated."

"Havana will blame us," Smith said without skipping a beat.

"Havana be damned. We gotta find out who these guys are!"

"Cuban exiles. There has been stepped-up harassment of Cuba for the last year or so. After Castro executed that last group of freedom fighters, they have been bent on revenge."

"I have no intelligence on the who, Smith," said the President. "But tensions between Washington and that grubby flyspeck of an island are growing worse. The Cold War is supposed to be over! And we're still having to look over our sovereign shoulders at this guy!"

"What would you like me to do?" asked Harold Smith.

"Find out who these guys are, and muzzle them."

"Are you certain this is what you want? Cuba is ripe for revolution. The people are starving. Basic necessities are rationed where they are not nonexistent. Defectors are risking their lives to come to Florida in droves. A new leadership—almost any leadership—would be infinitely preferable to the people in power now."

"Agreed," said the President, as if speaking to an equal. "But we're trying to keep the lid on in Russia— I mean, the Commonwealth. We have a secret agreement with Moscow, Smith. Hands off Cuba. That way we don't embarrass the former Soviet military—and they stay out of Commonwealth—and therefore world—politics."

"I see," said Harold W. Smith.

"And we don't need to give Castro any more of a seige mentality than he already has. The man is poised to land on the ash heap of the twentieth century. And he's railing about the future of Socialism in the Americas. He's cornered. And there's no telling what a cornered dictator will do."

"Understood, Mr. President. I will send our people to Miami."

That had been morning.

By afternoon, things had gotten worse. Smith was monitoring message traffic. There were signs of increased activity, according to Department of Defense intercepts of coded Cuban radio traffic.

The President had called again.

"Smith, the DoD reports that Havana is telling their people the prisoners have been interrogated and they implicate Washington."

"Which is not the case, I assume."

"Absolutely. We have—want—nothing to do with this. Get your people moving. We gotta root out the real culprits and flush them into the open. This cannot be allowed to stand."

That was the point when Harold Smith had reached out to his enforcement arm without success.

Now he was frantic, trying. The red phone shrilled again. Smith hesitated. He lifted the handset on the second ring.

"Is something wrong?" asked the President, tone worried.

"Sir?"

"It took you two rings. You usually grab it on the first."

"I was preoccupied," Smith said carefully.

"The situation is going critical."

"Sir?"

"Somehow, that lunatic has overpowered TV transmissions in South Florida. We always suspected Havana had the capability, being that he's only ninety miles off our shores, but we didn't dream he'd dare provoke us that much."

"What is Castro saying?" asked Smith. He had

already brought out a portable TV set and turned it on. It had been purchased at a yard sale, and usually took its time warming up.

"I think he's giving Speech Number 33," the Chief Executive said tiredly. "They all sound alike to me. They start with 'We are the defenders of the Revolution' and end with ' "Socialism or Death" is our battlecry.' You'd think he'd make a master tape and just play it every once in a while."

"God," Smith croaked, as his set blinked into life. "What is it?"

"I'm watching him now. I hadn't realized he'd gotten so fat."

"Smith, any progress?"

Smith hesitated. "No," he said truthfully.

"Very well. Stay in touch."

"Yes, Mr. President," said Smith. He returned to his humming computer.

Harold Smith knew only one thing. That the Master of Sinanju was upset over the stalled state of their current contract negotiations. Usually they were contentious. This time, they had become interminable as well. Never before had they gone on so long. Technically, the old contract had expired. Such a situation had never been allowed to go unresolved for this long.

But Smith had been unable to break down the impasse. The Master of Sinanju had demanded the impossible.

Had Smith been blessed with imagination, he might have been able to imagine where Chiun had gone. But he could not. So he doggedly returned to his computer, his fingers on the keyboard making hollow, manic clicks.

Somewhere, in the vast databanks of the nation, he knew, there must be a lead.

The bulletin came while Smith was staring at a blank screen. The computer beeped musically, and an AP bulletin digest began scrolling before his bleary eyes.

It was brief.

An Air Force jet out of Homestead AFB had shot down a MIG Flogger over the Gulf. The fighter-bomber was presumed of Cuban origin.

"My God!" croaked Smith again.

This time the President did not call. Smith knew why. He was too busy conferring with the Joint Chiefs of Staff in an attempt to deal with the escalating situation.

This was no longer a CURE covert operation. It was lurching toward war.

While updates poured in, Smith redoubled his efforts.

The engagement had been brief. The press was speculating on the lone MIG's mission.

"Suicide mission," Smith muttered. "But what was his target?"

Smith logged off and brought up a schematic of the Florida coast. He input the MIG's intercept position, using signals intelligence siphoned off Pentagon main-frames. Then, he projected the jet's probable course.

His gray face blanched as the line plotted through the Turkey Point nuclear power station on the tip of Florida.

"My God!" said Smith. "He's long threatened that plant. This time he actually went for it."

Smith returned to his search, his eyes stark.

It might be too late for Remo and Chiun to enter the crisis, but he would have to try.

If only he had some inkling of their location . . .

5

Remo Williams was torn between duty to his country and his responsibility to the House of Sinanju.

It was not the first time. Almost since the day he had been framed for a crime he didn't commit and subjected to a chillingly convincing mock execution, only to wake up in Folcroft Sanitarium with a new face, all traces of his past erased, and then placed in the hands of the Master of Sinanju to be trained in Sinanju—the first and last word in the martial arts—Remo had experienced divided loyalties.

In the early years, the choices had been clearer. Remo was an American. A former Newark cop. A Vietnam veteran. America was his home. America his choice, hands-down. No contest.

Over the long years of training, Remo had begun to change. He had become Sinanju, which made him kin to the long line that had stood beside the thrones of history. Although the blood of the past masters did not flow through his veins, their responsibilities had fallen onto his shoulders.

In North Korea, on the West Korea Bay, lay the village of Sinanju, a cold, stark place of mud huts and ignorance. It was from this village that the art of Sinanju had emerged. In the harsh village there was no arable land, and the fishing was unreliable.

In the good years, the simple folk of Sinanju eked out a meager existence.

In the bad years, the children were drowned. First the females. Then, if the times demanded it, the irreplaceable males. It was called "sending the babies home to the sea."

Centuries of this heartbreaking cycle had forced the leaders of the village to seek another way. And so the men of Sinanju had hired themselves out as mercenaries to other provinces. This practice grew, and before long the name of the Master of Sinanju and his cunning mercenaries—the night tigers of Sinanju—had become feared throughout the kingdom of Korea.

With their increasing reknown, the Masters of Sinanju had taken to foreign lands to ply their cold trade. The courts of China, India, Japan, Persia, and Egypt came to know them. Not as mercenaries, but as assassins.

They were a dynasty unrecorded by history. An invisible power that had changed the course of empires. The art they plied was at first simply the seminal martial art. But in a time harsher than any other, a Master, Wang the Greater, had discovered a secret deeper than the hidden historical role of the House of Sinanju. He had unleashed the sun source— the power of the unlocked human mind.

This secret had been handed down from Wang to Ung to Chen to each succeeding master, until, in the latter part of the twentieth century, the last true Master of Sinanju, Chiun the Younger, bereft of an heir and without clients, had been summoned to serve the newest and greatest empire in history: The United States of America.

Chiun had trained Remo. Remo had learned well. He also unlearned bad breathing, unmasked his senses, foresworn the use of weapons, and waxed in skill. And became the secret enforcement arm of CURE. America's unknown assassin.

As he grew in Sinanju, Remo became one with Sinanju. The village of the ancestors-who-were-not-his became as important to him as America.

Now, in the hotel that was more palatial and wonder-filled than the royal halls through which the old Masters of Sinanju had moved with uncanny stealth, Remo Williams fretted about his choices.

His responsibility to the organization and to his country demanded that he call Harold W. Smith.

But he had a responsibility to the House of Sinanju, too.

Above all, it was to feed the babies of the village, lest they be sent home to the sea once again. It had not happened in over a generation. But the gold that emperors paid was the sole coin of value in Sinanju.

To shirk this responsibility would be the same as betraying the country of his birth.

Worse. The worst Harold W. Smith would do to him was to hunt Remo down and kill him—if he could. Remo was under no illusions. He was an expendable component of a supersecret "black budget" operation.

On the other hand, if he pissed off Chiun badly enough, he would suffer horribly. Chiun would see to it.

And to Remo Williams, raised in the orphanage called St. Theresa's, never married, and cut off from his past, the Master of Sinanju was the closest thing to family he had ever known.

A clear choice. In the early days, he would have called Smith. Now, his gut told him to obey his Master.

Still, Remo was torn. Maybe there was a way to finagle things so Smith could locate them.

The arrival of room service brought Remo out of his worried state. Whatever he ended up doing, it could wait until after dinner.

He let the waiter in. The man wheeled in a gleaming stainless-steel cart that was busy with silver and linen napkins.

"Looks great," Remo said, handing the man a twenty. It was Smith's money, so he felt free to squander it.

"Complimentary bottle of champagne from the room service manager," the waiter said. "Shall I open it for you?"

"No. Why don't you take it?"

"I couldn't, sir."

"Okay," said Remo, pulling the six-hundred-dollar bottle from its ice bucket and tossing it over his shoulder.

The waiter watched as the bottle, as if in slow motion, tumbled like a sweaty candlepin across the room, caromed off a wall, and mimicking a billiard ball, landed in the kitchenette sink with a resounding crash and splash.

"That was the best champagne we have!" the waiter gulped.

"Next time, consider taking it," Remo said, gesturing toward the open door.

"Next time I will."

After the front door had closed, Remo knocked on Chiun's.

"Soup's on!" he called.

The door flew open and there stood the Master of Sinanju, his eyes steely.

"Uh-oh," said Remo, noticing the color of the old Korean's kimono. It was black. Black silk. And cut high at the sleeve and hem. The better for combat.

It was the traditional night-fighting garment of the Master of Sinanju. Designed for optimum stealth. Remo had a Western-style version, which consisted of a black silk blouse and flowing beltless pants.

"Your Duck in Orange Sauce is here," he said, hiding his surprise.

"I have no time for duck," said the Master of Sinanju, sweeping past Remo like a black patch of darkness. "I must avenge this insult to my viewing pleasure."

Remo followed him anxiously. "Are you going somewhere?"

Chiun shook a tiny fist in the air. "I am going to pluck every hair from the ruffian's ugly beard."

"Not Castro?"

"That is who he will be by the rising of the morning sun," Chiun spat.

"Huh?"

"Not Castro. Not anyone."

Remo snapped his fingers. "I got an idea."

"What?" asked Chiun, hesitating by the wheeled cart, where the heavy smell of Duck in Orange Sauce fought with the more delicate aroma of trout Almondine for command of the suite.

"Let's call Smith."

"I do not call emperors," Chiun sniffed. "Emperors call me. To do otherwise would be unseemly."

"I have a hunch Smith sent us here to deal with the Castro thing," Remo added hopefully.

"Then he sent us too late. The damage has been done. I have been deprived of the sight of my beloved Cheeta."

"And so you're going to sally off and box his ears."

Chiun paused, his expression intrigued. "I had not thought of the ears. Perhaps I *will* save them in a box. Should Smith come to his senses, they will make a suitable present."

"That's not what I meant by 'box,' but never mind. What I'm saying is that you're about to perform a service for Smith."

"I am doing nothing of the sort!"

"But if you do it, and wasting Castro is what Smith wanted done," Remo pointed out, "you'll be doing it for nothing. Thereby violating Sinanju Rule Number Two. No free lunches."

"But I cannot contact him. It would be wrong."

"But you can't go after Castro, either. You'd be giving away the store. The job done, Smith wouldn't have to come to the table on the negotiation."

The Master of Sinanju listened to the words of his pupil. His eyes narrowed. And narrowed some more. The conflicting thoughts racing through his brain were mirrored on his wrinkled parchment face. He stroked his trembling beard thoughtfully, then with agitation.

"I must do this," he said harshly.

"No, you mustn't," countered Remo, sensing victory.

Now the puffs of hair over each delicate yellow ear were trembling too. The Master of Sinanju was at an impasse.

He exploded. "Why are you doing this! Why are

you telling me these things? You are up to some mischief!"

"I pulled a you. Okay? Smith sent us here for a reason, and you're playing games. Something big is brewing. We gotta deal with it directly."

Chiun stamped a sandaled foot. "I cannot call Smith!"

"Fine. Just let me do it."

"And bring shame down upon the house?"

"Well, there's gotta be a way. And the duck is getting cold."

Angrily, the Master of Sinanju went to the covered tray. He lifted the cover and sniffed dubiously, his tiny button nose wrinkling like a dried apricot.

"It smells greasy."

"Then go to Cuba and squander the negotiational high ground, if that's what you want," Remo said hotly.

The Master of Sinanju frowned.

Thinking *I've got him now,* Remo closed in for the kill.

"Tell you what," he said. "I'll go down to the lobby and call someone on my phone card."

"What good will that do?" Chiun wanted to know.

"The card number will appear on the AT&T computer net and Smith will see it," Remo explained. "He'll reach out to touch us. And bingo: problem solved."

"I will accept that." He raised a cautionary finger and added, "But be certain not to call Smith."

"Trust me," said Remo, going to the door. "And don't let my trout get cold."

Remo took the elevator to the cavernous lobby and used his phone card to call the local Dial-a-Joke.

The joke was: How do you get a one-armed man out of a tree? Remo hung up before the punchline.

By the time he got back to his room, the bedroom phone was ringing.

He scooped it up and said, "Wave to him."

Smith's voice was high and anxious. "Remo! I've been trying to reach you all day!"

"Well, we've been here," Remo said innocently, "Chiun and I, patiently waiting."

"I told Master Chiun to register at the Biltmore."

"He brought me here, Smitty."

"According to the front desk, you are registered under the names Frodo Jones and Mr. C. Lee."

Remo rolled his eyes. "I think I'm Frodo," he growled. "Chiun checked us in. You'll be happy to know he's been very security-conscious lately."

"I am pleased to hear this, but I think he's gone too far. I have no record of any of your credit cards being used to check in."

"Chiun must have picked up the tab. Amazing as it seems."

Smith's voice sank to a lower register. "Has this anything to do with the current contract dispute?" he asked.

Before Remo could answer, the Master of Sinanju's voice came loudly: "Remo, your meal is becoming cold. Please inform the illustrious Emperor Smith that you will be happy to converse once we have dined."

"No, Remo, don't hang up! We have a crisis. An unknown military force has landed at the Bay of Pigs, and in retaliation Castro has attempted to take out the nuclear power plant at Turkey Point."

"He did!"

"Yes. Fortunately, the MIG was shot down before it could inflict any damage. But we expect another attempt."

"So what do you want Chiun and me to do?" Remo asked sourly. "Patrol all of southern Florida with our slingshots poised?"

"No. I have conferred with the President. Castro is convinced this is a CIA-U.S. operation, but it is no such thing. It is critical that we locate the true provocateurs and expose them."

"Wait a minute! Hold the phone! Are you saying we're supposed to go after the guys who are attacking Castro?"

"Yes. And it is imperative."

Remo lowered his voice. "Uh, Smitty, I hate to

break this to you, but Old Bushyface has been jamming the TV channels down here."

"I am aware of that."

"Are you aware that he cut in on Cheeta Ching's evening screed?" Remo added.

"Why is that important?" Smith asked, testy-voiced.

"Oh, I don't know," Remo said airily. "Maybe because Chiun was watching and got pissed."

"I will have a tape made," Smith said quickly. "He will have missed nothing."

"And just as you called," Remo added, "he was on his way out the door to assassinate Castro."

"I was not!" Chiun called from the other room.

"Remo," Smith hissed. "Do not let Chiun provoke that lunatic. Our highest priority is to keep the lid on an explosive situation."

"I can't make any guarantees," Remo said slowly.

"Those who are without gainful employment are unpredictable," Chiun called out. "The homeless are without hope, and where there is no hope, passions run high."

"What is he saying?" Smith asked harshly.

"Tell you what, Smitty," Remo said. "Maybe you should talk to Chiun. Get this contract knot unraveled."

"There is no time," Smith said, his voice rippling with concern.

"I will perform no service without certain considerations being met," Chiun announced.

"Tell him I'll meet them," Smith said quickly.

"I thought you were too broke," Remo asked.

"Remo, I will meet them. Now tell him!"

"No need," said Remo, handing the phone to the Master of Sinanju, who had suddenly appeared in the doorway. Chiun took it and listened quietly, the receiver pressed so tightly to his ear that Remo heard nothing of Smith's end of the conversation other than an intermittent lemony buzz.

At length the Master of Sinanju said, "Remo and I will do what we can." Then he handed the phone to

Remo, saying, "You will receive the instructions. I must finish my meal."

Remo clapped the receiver to his ear. "Okay, Smitty. Nice move. Shoot."

"We are in the dark," Smith said urgently. "There is no time for stealth or finesse. You must start in the Cuban community of Little Havana. Go there immediately. Turn the place upside down if you must. Find out who sponsored this Bay of Pigs incursion and put a stop to any further activity."

"Sounds simple enough," said Remo. "Any name in particular I should start with?"

"Yes. Dr. Osvaldo Revuelta, reputed leader of Ultima Hora."

"Ultima what?"

"Ultima Hora. It is Spanish for 'Eleventh Hour.' Revuelta is a wealthy Cuban expatriate who is suspected of financing Ultima Hora, a group of Cuban mercenaries bent upon retaking the island. It is believed that Revuelta's ultimate goal is to establish himself as the first democratic President of Cuba."

"Sounds like he's on our side," Remo said.

"Not if his activities put the U.S. and Cuba on a collision course," Smith said, flat-voiced.

"What's the big deal? We can take those Caribbean losers in an afternoon. Remember Grenada? The Cuban troops ran for their lives."

"Remo, you know the situation in Russia. It is extremely delicate. There is a mood to return to the Soviet model. Our government and theirs have a tacit understanding: Hands off Havana. If we embarrass the former Red Army, they may agitate to intervene. War fuels depressed economies, as you know."

"I still don't like it," Remo said, face and voice bitter.

"Nor do I. But we live in a changing world, and we must adapt. Castro can't stay in power forever. But he can cause great harm if he seizes upon this incident as a way to rally his people behind his crumbling regime."

"Okay, Chiun and I are on the way."

"Report as necessary."

Remo hung up and sauntered back into the kitchen.

There, the Master of Sinanju was patting his tiny mouth with a linen napkin. On the plate under his bearded chin lay the bodily remains—largely spine—of a trout.

"You ate my trout!" Remo shouted.

"The duck was greasy," Chiun said.

"But you knew that!"

"I did not know *how* greasy. Besides, the trout would have been cold by the time you returned to it, and both of our dinners would have been ruined. Why should two suffer when the wisdom of one can prevent this?"

Remo picked up a bamboo chopstick and poked at the duck. The crackling brown skin broke. No steam leaked out. He could see by the gelatinous state of the orange sauce that the meal was stone-cold.

"I wasn't in the mood for duck," he complained. "And I'm sure not in the mood for cold duck in congealed orange sauce."

The Master of Sinanju stood up and shook back into place his black silk kimono sleeves, which had been folded high over his bony elbows.

"Fasting is good for a Master of Sinanju—especially one who is about to embark on an important assignment," he said sagely.

"Oh, yeah? Then why didn't *you* fast?"

"Because," cackled the Master of Sinanju, "I was faster than you. Heh heh. I was faster, therefore I had no need to fast. Heh heh heh."

6

Dr. Osvaldo Revuelta considered himself a soldier of the Americas.

He was proud. He was brave. He was a Cuban through and through. There was nothing he would not do to restore his beleaguered nation to its former glory.

When the ragtag *guerilleros* of the Sierra Maestra began their campaign, he had laid down the shining tools of his lucrative La Plata gynecological practice, absolved himself of his Hippocratic Oath, and taken up arms against them.

It was a terrible day when Fidel rode through the streets of Havana. Dr. Revuelta had gotten on the first Cubana plane to Miami. He had seen how the crowds were with Fidel.

He had thought it would be a temporary thing. But the years had rolled on, slow and terrible. And when he'd realized there would be no soon return to Havana, Dr. Revuelta decided to fight the *Fidelistas* from a distance.

His first act was to shoot at a Bulgarian tanker. He used a bazooka purchased on the black market. The bazooka rocket punched a neat hole through the bow of the Bulgar ship, which sailed stubbornly on. The government of Bulgaria had protested to the United States.

The FBI came knocking at his door, since Dr. Revuelta had taken to boasting about his act of retaliation to his compatriots in the watering holes of Little Havana.

"Yes, I did shoot the Bulgar *bastardos* with my bazooka," he admitted forthrightly. "What of it? They are the allies of our great enemy, Fidel." And he spat at the feet of the two unblinking FBI men.

"You'll have to come with us," one said with a toneless politeness.

"Jou have use for me, perhaps?" Revuelta said eagerly. "I will gladly lead the charge up San Juan Hill, eh?"

"I'm sorry, Dr. Revuelta. You are under arrest."

"*Por qué?* Why? I have done nothing illegal."

"You fired a bazooka at a ship of foreign registry while standing on U.S. soil. A clear violation of the Neutrality Act."

"Hah! Jou are wrong! I was in my cabin cruiser. She is a speedy yob, that ship. I call her *What a Country!* Is true, no?"

The FBI men did not laugh. They barely moved. And they continued to insist that Revuelta was under arrest.

Dr. Revuelta went with them. He answered their tiresome questions truthfully, and when he saw that—amazement of amazements—they were taking this matter very seriously, he pretended to break down.

"I am anguished with shame," he said mournfully. "Jou are correct. I have done a terrible thing, and now my friends are about to commit a worse act of heinousness."

The chief FBI interrogator became very interested indeed. "What act?" he had asked.

"My compatriots. Fellow exiles. They are placing bombs in ships down at the docks."

"Which ships?"

"I will take jou there." He dabbed at his dark eyes. "I am so remorseful."

A drab sedan whisked them to the docks. As they got out, Dr. Revuelta lifted his manacled hands and brought them down on the chief interrogator's crewcut head. The man had crumpled like a trenchcoat crammed with potatoes. The driver was harder to conquer. Dr. Revuelta had to punch and kick him many times, and still he did not lose consciousness.

As the man lay stunned, Dr. Revuelta rushed along the docks, trying to unlock the handcuffs with the tiny key he had rummaged from the first man's pockets.

He was looking for Spanish names on the ships. When he came to the *Santander*, he smiled broadly and started up the gangplank.

Halfway up, the handcuffs finally came loose and he flung them with all his might into the filthy water by the bow.

The sound brought all hands to the bow rail in search of stowaways. This was distraction enough for Dr. Revuelta to slip aboard and find a place to hide.

When the *Santander* docked in Pernambuco, Brazil, Dr. Revuelta walked off the boat as he did everything: boldly. No one questioned him.

In Pernambuco he continued his work, certain that he would not be criticized for his continued counterrevolutionary activities by the United States government, which was altogether too sensitive about these matters.

He learned different when the Cubana Airlines jet exploded over the Gulf of Mexico and seventy-three Cubans died. The United States denounced it as a terrorist action.

"Terrorista!" Dr. Revuelta had screamed from his palatial seaside hacienda. "It is counterrevolution! How can they call me *terrorista*?"

Dr. Revuelta happened to ask this question in a Pernambuco bistro, and soon the Brazilian security police were knocking on his door.

Fortunately, he spotted them from his bedroom window. Dr. Revuelta slipped out the back and hurried down to the docks. This time he stowed away on the freighter *Garaucan*. It took him back to Miami where, now white-haired and thin, he picked up where he had left off.

This was in 1984, and Miami had changed. Little

Havana was no longer strung along Southwest 8th Street, but spread out over virtually all of Miami. This was after the Mariel boat lift. The *Marielitos* had swollen the Cuban population until Miami was virtually Cuban.

And in that rich environment, Dr. Osvaldo Revuelta began to recruit for Ultima Hora—the anti-Fidel *guerilleros* who would be his instrument of terror.

They trained in the swamps. They set out for Cuba in boats. Sometimes they landed and blew up power lines and telephone poles. Other times they simply released propaganda messages in bottles.

Sometimes they did not return.

Dr. Revuelta never went with them. He was a soldier of the Americas, but more, he was a leader of soldiers of the Americas. Leaders who did not come back from battle did not live to lead.

Emboldened by the new spirit of Miami, where the minorities had become the majority and Spanish was the lingua franca—despite the nervous referendum that had established English as the official language of Dade County—Dr. Revuelta began to boast once more.

It was another mistake. He loudly claimed credit for the Cubana bombing, believing that sympathies had shifted, and overlooked but one minor detail: that the passengers of the flight had had relatives and the relatives—or some of these—had come to Miami to escape oppression. He was reported to the FBI. This time by fellow Cubans.

On this occasion, the government tried Dr. Osvaldo Revuelta in the courts and sentenced him to jail. The Justice Department had wanted to deport him as an undesirable alien, but no country would take Dr. Revuelta.

Except Cuba. Havana let it be known that Dr. Revuelta was very much desired in Havana.

This time, Dr. Revuelta did not attempt escape. He knew Cuban justice. Besides, the judge had given him but five years. As it turned out, he served only two. Political pressures forced his early release.

But it had been a humiliating early release. The U.S. government had demanded he sign a letter renouncing terrorism.

"What foolishness is this?" he demanded of his Cuban lawyer. "A man who was determined enough to blow up a civilian airliner would not hesitate to renege on a written pledge such as this."

"Perhaps they wish only to cover their asses," the lawyer had suggested.

"*Que?*"

"Their *colitos*."

"Ah, yes," said Dr. Revuelta, promptly signing the renunciation in his cell. He laid down his pen and rubbed his hands together gleefully. "Okay, make them let me go. I have much to catch up on."

"There is more," the lawyer informed him.

Dr. Revuelta's face fell.

"What more?" he inquired suspiciously.

"You will be placed under house arrest, and made to wear an electronic monitor."

"I cannot leave my home?"

"Only between the hours of eleven A.M. and two P.M., to do necessary things."

Dr. Revuelta's sun-browned brow gathered into deep wrinkles. "Ah, a loophole," he said, thinking he understood now. "They are giving me a loophole, these canny *norteamericanos*."

"You must keep a daily log of visitors, and submit to polygraph tests and random searches," the lawyer went on doggedly. "Your phone will be tapped."

"Let them tap," Dr. Revuelta said haughtily. "During my three hours, I will accomplish all that I wish to do."

"They are very serious about this, Revuelta."

"If they were serious, they would not release me," Dr. Revuelta countered. "This is a farce and I will play along. Now, hurry. I have two years of catching up to do."

*   *   *

Immediately upon returning to his palatial Biscayne Bay home, Dr. Osvaldo Revuelta fired his Nicaraguan caretaker staff and replaced them with *guerrilleros* of his Ultima Hora.

"This is *loco*, Revuelta," complained his lawyer. "You are not to consort with terrorists."

Dr. Revuelta drew himself up indignantly. "Are jou mad? These are not terrorists. These are freedom fighters. Besides, I will tell the snoopers that they are Nicaraguans. These Anglo FBI, they know only that a man looks Hispanic or he does not. They will never know the difference."

"What about their guns?"

"The weapons of my *soldados* will never enter this house. They will patrol outside only, to protect me from the agents provocateurs of Fidel."

"I think," said the lawyer of Dr. Osvaldo Revuelta, "that you will be returning to jail very soon now."

But Dr. Revuelta did not return to jail. Oh, he was closely watched, polygraphed every few months, and subject to searches that turned up nothing worse than his growing collection of pornographic magazines. But during his three-hour period each day, he drilled his Ultima Hora for their forays into Cuba.

Every time men did not return, it was easy enough to recruit more. Ultima Hora grew, gained adherents and patrons of great resources.

While supposedly languishing through two years of house arrest, Osvaldo Revuelta was in fact running a paramilitary organization large enough to establish a major beachhead on the island of his birth. And he was convinced that his success was due entirely to U.S. financial assistance, regardless of what the Justice Department might say in public.

So it came as a total surprise when the two mysterious U.S. agents came to visit Osvaldo Revuelta late one night, as he was studying topographical maps of Cuba.

They were not announced. They were simply there. In his den.

"Que?" he said, turning. *"Que pasa?"*

"Got a minute, pal?" said the tall one. He was an Anglo. Lean. With thick wrists, and a casual insolence that reminded Revuelta of the DGI—the Cuba security police.

Dr. Revuelta would have shot the man right then and there, but he had no weapons on the premises.

"Quien?" he asked.

"He asked 'Who?' " said the other one, the short one. This second person was as fantastic in appearance as the other was ordinary. He was Asian, and wore a black silken garment that made Revuelta think of the Viet Cong. That was a bad sign. But the fact that the little Asian had to translate for the Anglo meant that he at least was not DGI. And he appeared very, very old.

"You speak English?" asked the Anglo, in a voice definitely gringo.

"Sí. I mean, yes. Of course. Who are jou, that jou enter my humble home unannounced?"

The man flashed a card in a plastic holder. "Remo Ricardo, CIA."

"And jour friend, he is not CIA?" asked Dr. Revuelta, gesturing to the tiny old Asian.

"He's the backup interrogator," offered the Anglo.

"This mean jou are the foremost interrogator, no?"

"Something like that," said the tall Anglo, walking forward with absolutely no sound. He walked on the outsides of his feet. Clearly he was trained. *Well* trained. In something.

"Have jou signed in?" Dr. Revuelta asked nervously.

"Signed in?"

"Yes, it is the requirement of jour government. Jou must sign in."

The man looked blank.

"Here," Dr. Revuelta said, moving toward his desk, "allow me to summon a servant to bring the sign-in book."

A hand reached out before Dr. Revuelta could

touch the bell button set on the side of his desk. The hand had moved with a direct, casual grace, but suddenly the bell button had become a blob of metal clinging forlornly to the desk rim.

There was no sound of a bell. There should have been. The man had struck it so ferociously that the button should have triggered the current.

Revuelta looked closer. The button stuck out like a gangrenous nipple from a flat metallic breastlet. It would never ring the downstairs bell again.

"Since this is a requirement of jour government, and jou represent the U.S.," Dr. Revuelta said sincerely, "I will assume the sign-in requirement has been waived. How may I assist jou fine yentlemen?"

"Somebody tried to invade Cuba this morning," said the Anglo.

"So?"

The other man, the Asian, had slipped up and around to stand near him. Revuelta began to sweat. He did not like this. This was not how U.S. agents ordinarily acted. Of course this was the CIA, not the FBI. So who could say?

"So everybody knows you run a training program for anti-Castro guerrillas," the Anglo said simply.

"I do not know this."

"Don't screw with us," said the Anglo. "Some of us missed supper because of you."

"Since when is it a crime to be anti-Castro?" Revuelta asked in an injured tone.

"Since Fidel started flying MIGs over Florida nuclear plants and jamming TV transmissions," said the Anglo.

"These are terrible things, but I think if jou have complaints jou should take them to Havana."

"Count on it," said the Anglo.

Revuelta smiled broadly then. "So we are on the same side?"

"Depends."

"I have always suspected the CIA of steering certain—how jou say?—*assets* my way."

"What assets?"

"Ah, but I am a good *soldado*. I do not reveal these things. If names are known to jou, there is no need to repeat them. If not, jou have no—what is the phrase?—no need to know."

"Remo, what is this idiot babbling about?" asked the Asian suddenly, his wizened face puckering.

"May I inquire jour name, señor?" Dr. Revuelta asked.

"You may not."

"Jou are not Vietnamese?"

"I am never Vietnamese! I am Korean!"

"Ah. South Korean, yes?"

"North."

At that, Dr. Osvaldo Revuelta took an involuntary step backward. The North Koreans were among the last of Castro's close allies. What was transpiring here, that an Anglo CIA operative and a North Korean agent would come together to see him?

"I do not understand," he said carefully, backing away.

The others moved with him.

"You launch the Bay of Pigs operation?" demanded the Anglo.

"No."

"Liar!" snapped the North Korean. And suddenly the little old man was between Osvaldo Revuelta and the window he'd been planning to break, in a desperate effort to summon help in the form of his Cuban guards who patrolled outside, somehow unaware of this invasion.

"Speak the truth," the Korean demanded, and took hold of Osvaldo Revuelta's wrist.

There was strength in the little man's wrist. Great strength. It was like being seized by a tiny steam shovel powered by a dynamo of great size. Birdlike yellow fingers constricted, and things began popping out all over Osvaldo's body. Veins. Tendons. Sweat.

"The *pain*!" screamed Osvaldo Revuelta.

"The faster you come clean," the Anglo said coolly, "the sooner it goes away."

"I send no one!"

"We don't believe you."

"I only loan *soldados*!"

"What's a *soldado*?"

"A soldier," the tiny Korean said before Osvaldo could. But he said it anyway. Anything to lessen the fierce agony.

"Soldiers! I loaned my Ultima Hora soldiers to a man. A brave man."

"His name?" demanded the Korean, inflicting crushing force. Revuelta lowered himself to his knees, unaware that he was doing so. In his scarlet agony, he thought the tiny man was growing in strength and stature before his very eyes.

"He is Leopoldo Zorilla!" Revuelta shrieked.

"Who's Leopoldo Zorilla?" asked the Anglo, in a voice that seemed far, far from Osvaldo Revuelta's inflamed nervous system.

"How could jou not know?" he gasped.

"We're new in town. Haven't hit the night spots yet. Who's Leopoldo Zorilla?"

"A Cuban defector! He was former defense minister! He have been in Miami many months now! To him, I loan my best!"

"For what purpose?" asked the old Korean.

"I do not ask these questions! I am given money, and told to be prepared to return to Havana in triumph!"

The Anglo turned to the other and asked, "What do you think, Little Father?"

"He is telling the truth," the old one said disappointedly. The pain began to lessen, and the tears stopped flowing from Dr. Revuelta's eyes. He was able to see semi-clearly again.

"Why am I on my knees?" he asked wonderingly, noticing the nearness of the rug.

"Because we're here for information."

Dr. Revuelta looked up. "I do not understand. What difference would that make?"

"If we weren't, you'd be in the ground."

"Yo comprendo."

"Where do we find Zorilla?"

The pain was still there. It was tolerable. Dr. Revuelta took a chance. He spoke two words very fast.

"Little Havana."

"Where in Little Havana?"

"I do not know. He moves around." This was the truth, and it seemed to work.

The tall Anglo noticed the clock on the wall and casually said, "It's about bedtime, isn't it?"

"*Que?*"

And so swift was the night that overcame his senses that Dr. Osvaldo Revuelta did not notice he had lost conciousness, until he opened his eyes many hours later to find himself drooling into the fine rug that had once graced his Havana office.

Upon regaining his senses, he called the contact number of Leopoldo Zorilla. The phone rang and rang and rang, and a feeling of dread came over him.

There was another number he had been given. He had not been told to whom this number belonged. Only that it should be resorted to in only the direst circumstances.

He dialed and waited. . . .

7

Remo Williams used a pay phone to contact Harold W. Smith.

"Smitty? Remo. We got something."

"What is it?"

"His name is Leopoldo Zorilla. Name ring a Cuban bell?"

"Vaguely," said Smith, and the hollow clicking of fingers on a keyboard came through the phone wire. "Yes, Remo. Leopoldo Zorilla is a Cuban defector, according to Immigration and Naturalization Service computer records. He was picked up in a raft floating in the Windward Passage."

"Where is he now?"

"Unclear. He was briefly detained by INS and then released."

"If he was that big, why wasn't he debriefed?"

"I do not know. I imagine because there has been such a flood of defectors that Washington saw no intelligence value in interrogating him."

"Well, according to Revuelta, he loaned some of his Ultima soldiers to Zorilla."

"For what purpose?" Smith asked.

"Claims he doesn't know. But he was told to stand by to go back to Havana in style."

"Interesting. You have your lead. Pursue it. Find Zorilla and learn all you can."

"What's the latest?"

"Castro is still speaking."

"This could go on for days," Remo remarked.

"Let us hope not."

"You and me both. If Chiun doesn't get his daily Cheeta fix, I wouldn't give odds on Castro's survivability"

Remo hung up and turned to the Master of Sinanju, who was patiently waiting some distance away, saying, "Smith says to chase down Zorilla."

"Then let us begin."

They returned to their rented car and drove off.

Remo hadn't been to Miami in a number of years. It had changed. The palmettos still shook in the offshore breezes, the heat still soaked cloth to the skin, but the people were different. There were more Latin faces than Remo remembered.

Off in the night, he heard a sporadic *pop-pop-pop-pop* of a sound. Machine pistols. His mouth went grim.

Remo had been raised in a time when street gangs were considered unsalvageable if they carried zip guns. Now it seemed that the cheapest hood was better armed than the average Korean War-era soldier.

"This town looks and sounds like it washed ashore from the Third World," he said bitterly.

"I do not remember it this way," Chiun remarked, his narrow eyes reading the faces in the night.

"Another present from Fidel. About ten years ago, he launched a little thing called the Mariel boat-lift. Dumped the contents of his prisons and mental institutions on Miami. As well as honest refugees. I guess both flavors stuck around. I hardly see any white faces."

"This is acceptable," sniffed Chiun, arranging his kimono skirts absently.

"Listen to you, Mr. Multicultural."

"Pah! Do not speak that word."

Remo smiled. He had scored a direct hit. A few months ago, the Master of Sinanju had joined the campaign of a dark-horse candidate for governor of California. The man—an Hispanic—had offered Chiun the post of treasurer. Chiun had tentatively accepted. Only after Chiun had nearly burned his bridges with Harold Smith did he learn that the candidate was actually a fugitive banana-republic dictator, with a face made media-friendly by plastic surgery.

They had been forced to terminate the guy, and Chiun found himself in dutch with Harold Smith. He was still digging out.

The bewildering maze of Miami byways took Remo to what was supposed to be Little Havana. He slowed down and unrolled his window.

"Hey, pal. This Little Havana?"

The man turned, shrugged, and continued walking.

"I just need a yes or no. Is it?"

The man kept walking.

"People are real friendly down here," he grumbled, driving on.

Remo took the next right and cruised by a row of bars whose neon names were flowery and Spanish.

This time he pulled over and asked a knot of people, "I'm looking for Little Havana."

Swarthy faces turned. Eyes grew tight. No one spoke.

"Anybody speak English here?"

Apparently no one did.

"Little Havana," Remo repeated in a loud voice, pointing around him. "This?"

"No," a voice returned. "Little Haiti."

"Where Little Havana?" Remo asked, thinking he was making progress.

He got a chorus of *"Quien sabes."* He didn't know what it meant, but he had seen enough *Cisco Kid* reruns to get the message.

"This is ridiculous," he grumbled, sending the car screeching along.

He found a well-lit gas station called Jose's and pulled in.

"Fill her up," he said, by way of breaking the ice.

"Que?" asked the attendant, a brown-faced teenager with a mustache like a used paint brush.

"I said fill her up. *Comprende?"*

"No, señor."

"No, you don't speak English, or no, you won't fill her up?" Remo wanted to know.

"No, señor."

There were others working on an exposed engine and Remo called over to them. "Anybody here speak English?"

The men looked blank.

"Habla ingles?" Remo asked.

"No *ingles!*" one called back, returning to his engine.

"What *is* this?" Remo demanded of no one in particular. "How can you run a gas station if no one speaks English?"

The teenager shrugged. He didn't offer to fill Remo's tank, so Remo pulled out, tires caterwauling.

"I'm here in Miami less than a day, and already I'm tired of it," Remo said bitterly.

"It would be easier if you had learned the language," Chiun sniffed.

"Language! This is America! The language of America is English!"

"The language of *North* America is English," Chiun corrected. "The language of South America is *Spanish.*"

"So? We're in North America."

"No, we are in *South* Florida."

"Which, the last time I was in this town, was still part of the U.S.A."

"None of this would be happening if you had learned Spanish."

"Why should I learn Spanish?" Remo said hotly.

"In case we ever have to work for Spain," Chiun said reasonably.

"When was the last time that happened? Really."

"The sun will not shine on this mongrel land forever. I will not be at your side forever. You must learn other tongues, so that the tradition can continue and you will not have to stoop to working for inferior nations, as have I in my declining years."

"My ass," said Remo. He tapped the brake. The car stopped short.

Remo and Chiun went forward and back, as if they were anchored to their seats by spring cables. It was a tribute to the total control they exercised over their bodies.

"Wait a minute!" Remo said. "*You* speak Spanish."

"Therefore, so should *you.*"

"That's not what I mean. Why am I wasting my time trying to communicate when you can interpret for me?"

Chiun raised a wise finger. "Because you will never learn if I keep doing this for you."

"Bulldookey," said Remo, sending the car shooting ahead. "There's gotta be at least one white guy in Miami. Somewhere."

They found one after another ten minutes of circling what seemed to be a very large Spanish area.

The white man was definitely white. He was also definitely scared. He was outrunning the pack pursuing him, even though he was carrying a middle-aged paunch and his pursuers all wore Reebok Pumps and the tight flesh of teenagers.

Remo cut in front of the pursuers and got out.

"*Habla español?*" he demanded.

"*Tu madre!*" someone snarled, drawing a switchblade. It *snicked* into the extended position and the wielder brought it down to the level of his belt, driving in for Remo's stomach.

Remo smiled. He grabbed the attacker's wrist and made a sudden complicated motion with his other hand. His wrist drove the knife into the stomach of the one attacking him.

The attacker felt the dull pain that he knew was associated with being stabbed. It was not the first time. His bare brown arms were scarred and scatched from previous encounters with assorted blades and straight razors.

But this time was different. This time, he was holding the hilt of the blade that had been pushed into his vitals. Pushed deep, he saw with widening eyes.

"Dios mio!" he moaned. *"Compadres!* Come to my aid!"

His compadres backed off and withdrew assorted ordnance. Safeties clicked off. It was about to get serious.

Seeing this, Remo released the man's wrist.

The erstwhile attacker did not release the knife stuck in his own stomach. He was streetwise, and knew that to extract the blade would be to bleed profusely. So he held on to the knife for dear life—even when he found himself suddenly airborne in the direction of his amigos.

A few upward-pointing gun muzzles went *pop-pop-pop!* before they fell from surprised hands and Remo stepped into their midst.

He didn't waste time. He used the heel of his shoe to crush the weapons flat, driving his handmade sole home so fast and so hard the metal barrels went flat. His shoe leather didn't pick up so much as a nick.

Technique.

Remo tapped the toe of his right shoe against jaws, and the squirming pile of Hispanics became a slumbering pile of Hispanics. When the last one had gone quiet, the man who had stabbed himself lost his grip. The switchblade fell loose from his stomach—showing that it was in the folded position after all.

When the man woke up he would think it was a miracle, and that God had spared him for reasons unclear.

It would never occur to him, nor would he have believed it if it had, that his mysterious attacker had simultaneously folded the blade shut while driving the blunt hilt into his stomach. The pain had been identical to being stabbed.

Whistling, Remo returned to the car.

The Master of Sinanju was comforting the panting middle-aged man.

"What happened, pal?" Remo asked, as he slid behind the wheel.

"I . . . I had a flat. I got out to fix it. Those hoods tried to jump me."

"Next time, try not to get a flat in Little Havana."

"Little Havana? What are you talking about? This is Little Managua."

"Little Managua? I never heard of Little Managua."

"It's new," the man said.

"Okay. It's new. So where's Little Havana?"

"Give me a ride to a safe part of town and I'll tell you."

"Sounds fair enough," said Remo. "Hop in."

The man got in back. Remo drove off, asking, "Any place in particular you want to go?"

"The airport. I've had enough of this town."

"I know that feeling."

They drove to the airport, and as Remo dropped the man off at the terminal he asked, "So where's Little Havana?"

"It used to be all around Southwest 8th Street."

"So where is it now?"

"Now," the man said, as he turned into the terminal, "it's practically all of Miami."

"He was very helpful," Chiun said smugly after the man had gone.

"Don't rub it in," growled Remo, putting the airport behind them.

They took the Palmetto Expressway back to town and turned off on the Tamiami Trail. Soon, they were cruising along Southwest 8th Street. It looked amazingly like Little Managua. Remo couldn't tell the difference.

He tried asking passersby the question that he had been asking half the night.

"Is this Little Havana?"

People shrugged and said *"Qué?"* or sometimes *"Quien?"* And Remo fumed.

"You could lend a hand, you know," Remo said pointedly to the passive Master of Sinanju.

"Of course. *Qué* means 'what' and *quien* means 'who.' "

"Har de har har har," muttered Remo.

His dark eyes alighted on a neon bar sign: PEPE'S.

"When in doubt, ask a barman," he said jauntily.

Remo parked, got out, and went into the bar. Chiun followed silently.

It was a brightly lit saloon. Jukebox salsa music filled the air. Remo sauntered up to the bar, ignoring the hard stares at his white skin.

"I'm looking for Little Havana," he said.

"Por que?"

"He means 'why,' not 'what,' " Chiun whispered.

"Because," Remo answered, "I'm looking for Leopoldo Zorilla."

"I have not heard of this man," said the bartender, elaborately polishing his countertop. Too elaborately, Remo thought.

"I hear he lives around here," Remo said, laying down a twenty.

Disdainfully, the bartender swiped it away with his rag. "Señor, you perhaps hear wrong."

Remo looked around. Dark, liquid eyes glowered at him. He felt like Chuck Connors in a *Rifleman* rerun.

"Why do I get the feeling that we're being snowed?" he undertoned to the Master of Sinanju.

"Because we are," said Chiun.

"It would be good advice if you were to leave, señor," the bartender said pointedly.

"That *is* good advice," Remo returned lightly. "Guess I'll just keep asking around until I find my man," he added in a loud voice.

As they walked from the smoky bar, Remo and Chiun felt eyes on their backs. No one followed them out.

"Where do we ask next?" asked Chiun, looking around suspiciously.

"Nowhere," Remo said. "We just walk around." He started walking. Chiun followed.

"What will that accomplish?"

"Right now, that bartender is probably calling Zorilla or someone connected with Zorilla. We won't have to find him. His people will find us."

*   *   *

It took less than fifteen minutes.

They were about to cross a busy intersection when a large white Cadillac pulled in front of them. A black Buick slid in behind them.

"Jackpot," Remo whispered.

Doors popped open and bulky-shouldered men emerged, wielding short-barreled Uzis and other easily concealable automatic weapons.

"Jou seek Zorilla?" one demanded. He wore a plain gold hoop in one ear, making him resemble a well-tanned buccaneer.

"Word gets around," Remo said casually.

"Why jou seek Zorilla?"

"Only Zorilla gets to ask me that question."

Hard eyes looked them over carefully. Remo folded his arms. In his T-shirt and tight chinos, it was obvious that he carried no weapon larger than a concealed blade or flat .22 pistol.

The Master of Sinanju had been walking with his hands tucked out of sight in the joined sleeves of his ebony kimono. He was invited to bring his hands into plain view.

Chiun replied with a single pungent Spanish word that stung the faces of the men aiming at him.

Harsh Spanish spilled out. Chiun lashed back with short, declarative sentences.

Uneasily, the men looked to one another. Finally, in English, one said, "Jou will come with us."

"Suits us," Remo said easily.

They were herded into the back of the Cadillac. A man took the wheel and another, the front passenger seat. The latter turned in his seat and pointed his Uzi so that Remo and Chiun were covered.

"No fonny business," he warned. "Or *pop-pop-pop-pop*."

Remo smiled back at him. "Sounds pretty brave, coming from a guy who took the death seat."

The Cadillac peeled off. The black Buick followed. Remo settled down for the ride.

"What did you tell them, Little Father?" Remo asked the Master of Sinanju as the ride lengthened.

"I called them motherless sons of worthless fathers."

"I've heard worse."

"But they have not," Chiun said smugly.

8

When Leopoldo Zorilla received the warning telephone call, he was drilling his soldiers in a remote corner of the Big Cypress Swamp. They were excellent soldiers—young, strong and fiercely willed. Destined to be liberators. They would form the nucleus of the New Cuban Army, and he was proud of them.

Yet they also reminded Zorilla that, sadly, he was no longer the young man he once was.

Not that Leopoldo Zorilla was old. He was, in truth, barely forty. But forty years of living on Castro-held Cuba had taken their toll on his erect body. There was not enough flesh on his bones, from improper diet, and his eyes were sunken. Even his mustache appeared sunken—the result of too much sugar and not enough meat and vegetables. The teeth he had retained were black with metal.

He let the soldiers exhaust their weapons against the targets—staked dummies, each dressed in olive-drab that bulged at the belt line and each with a Castro beard adorning its blank, chubby face.

"Fire above the beard!" he commanded. "Between the beard and the hat. That is your target. The flabby flesh between."

The men reloaded their Belgian-made FAL rifles and fired again. Instantly, the blank white areas collected sprinklings of holes that, had any of the dummies been the true Maximum Leader, would have splashed his brains back out of his head and into the eternal night.

An orderly came huffing up.

"A telephone call, Comandante."

Leopoldo Zorilla turned smartly, ever the military man. He had been a deputy air commander in the Cuban Air Force, and now he was a full commander in the army-in-training that would replace the Cuban Revolutionary Army.

"Who is it?" he demanded.

"It is Pepe. He says that two men seek you in Miami."

"What men?"

"I do not know, Comandante."

"Carry on," he told the orderly, and stormed into the barracks building, a converted tobacco-drying shack in the sprawling tangle of swamp called Big Cypress.

The cellular phone lay off the hook in his makeshift office.

"Pepe," he said gruffly. "What is this about two men?"

"They just left, Comandante. They ask for jou by name, but I tell them nothin'."

"Who were they?"

"An Anglo. The other was Asian. They were not dressed like FBI or any other government person I could name."

Zorilla frowned. "Hmmm. Who might they be?"

"They said they would comb Miami for jou, Comandante."

"There is no need for them to go to that trouble," said Comandante Leopoldo Zorilla. "Have them brought here."

"Is that wise?"

"We are too close to B-Day to allow the authorities to interfere with us."

"They did not look like authorities," Pepe pointed out.

"All the better. Have them brought here. Now."

"*Sí*, Comandante."

After Leopoldo Zorilla hung up, he unbuttoned the back pocket of his camouflage pants. He took out a sealed pack of chewing gum. It was decorated with

the cartoon head of a mouse. The mouse reminded
Zorilla of home. Even though it was an American
mouse, TeleRebelde regularly showed his famous cartoons to all of Cuba. First by means of old pre-
Revolution films, and later, as the technology
changed, by downlinking transmissions from U.S. TV
satellites. Fidel had boasted of his ability to pirate
U.S. TV without subjecting Cubans to annoying com-
mercials, but never mentioned that the people were
forced to watch Soviet TV sets that often exploded
without warning.

He could remember how unhappy the copyright
owners of the cartoon mouse had been. They explored
every avenue of legal recourse open to them. But
American lawyers were not welcome in the Cuban
Revolutionary courts and they were reduced to sending impatient letters demanding payment, and warning
of the accumulating charges that would be presented
to the Cuban government if it ever rejoined the free
world.

Zorilla smiled at the memory. Now that the time
approached, the copyright owners would finally col-
lect. With interest.

For now, he placed the pack of *chicle* in his blouse
pocket where it would be handy. It promised to be a
long night, and filled with uncertainties. With unknown
snoopers coming, he might well need it.

Leopoldo checked his watch. It was near eleven.
Time for his injection.

He cursed the business of the needle and what it
contained, but there was no help for it. Years of living
in Cuba had brought his once invincible body to this
sad state of affairs.

He opened a drawer and charged the needle from
a stoppered bottle. He used a rubber band to block
his arm veins. They bulged up blue and thick, and he
discharged the contents of the needle into the most
wormlike of them. He swabbed the pinprick wound
with a bit of cotton dipped in alcohol.

It stung. With the stinging, he lavishly cursed the

Leader of the Revolution, who had made him so dependent on the needle.

The prisoners arrived after midnight.

Comandante Leopoldo Zorilla went out to greet them. He clasped his hands behind his back and addressed the pair.

"You have sought me, and I stand before you now," he said simply.

Then he got a close look at them. The Anglo appeared quite ordinary, except for the exceptional thickness of his wrists. He had a lean, hard look about him. His nationality was difficult to ascertain. The Mediterranean was stamped on his moderately handsome features and lurked in his dark eyes. But his skin was pale.

There was, as he had been told, an Asian. He had not been told the Asian's age. He looked . . . *advanced*. Surely, Zorilla thought, these were not agents of any government who disagreed with what had been planned.

"Who are you two men?" he demanded, as they stood before him.

Weapons were trained on them. The pair seemed oblivious to their dark-mawed threat.

The Anglo looked around. He saw the dummies on the posts, with their blank white faces spilling cotton stuffing like bleached brain matter.

"Looks like we've found our Cuban invasion force," he remarked to his Asian companion.

"For once," the other murmured, "you have hatched a plan that has worked." Then, looking at the uniform Zorilla wore, he asked, "What are you supposed to be?"

Zorilla drew himself erect. "I am a soldier of the Americas!"

The Anglo asked the Asian a foolish question. "What's that supposed to mean?"

The Asian said, "He is a Spaniard. They are very proud. In the days of the Spanish kings, the soldiers boasted that they were soldiers of Spain. This one has fallen from that lofty perch, like a haughty eagle that has grown too fat for the branch, so now he is a mere soldier of this mongrel continent."

"You insult me?" Zorilla demanded.

"The uniform does that," the Asian sniffed.

"Who sent you to seek me?" Zorilla asked tightly.

"Uncle Sam," replied the Anglo with cool insolence.

Leopoldo Zorilla blinked. "Truly?" he asked.

"Definitely," the Anglo said.

"Por que?"

"That means, 'Why?' " interjected the Asian.

"Because he's not happy with the way things are going down Havana way, that's why," said the Anglo.

Comandante Leopoldo Zorilla then lost command of himself.

"It was unforeseen, what happened!" he said quickly. "Our scouts landed with the dawn, when the sentries are less alert. Nevertheless, they were captured. It was regrettable. We did not know that Fidel would respond so harshly. But that is the nature of the man. Please tell Uncle Sam for me that Ultima Hora remains firmly on the agreed-upon timetable."

The Anglo took this with less grace than Comandante Zorilla expected.

He and the Asian exchanged blank looks, and then the Anglo said, "You telling me that Uncle Sam put you up to this?"

"You know this. For he sent you."

"Yeah, but the Uncle Sam who sent me didn't know anything about any Cuban operation," the Anglo insisted.

"He did not?"

"In fact, he specifically asked me to find out who was behind the operation."

"Uncle Sam asked this of you?" asked Zorilla.

"Maybe it was a different Uncle Sam," the Anglo offered.

"What other Uncle Sam is there?" Zorilla shot back.

"Good point," said the Anglo, frowning. "I know of just the one."

Comandante Zorilla grew concerned.

"What is your name?" he demanded.

"Call me Remo."

"Ah, Remo. A good Spanish name."

"It is?" the one called Remo said, surprised.

"It means 'oar,' " the Asian whispered.

"It does?" Remo said, astonished.

The Asian nodded sagely. "In Italian, as well."

"Who would name his son 'Oar'?" Remo wanted to know.

"A parent who would then leave his son on a doorstep," Chiun countered.

"You leave my parents out of this!"

"Why not? They left you out of their lives."

Comandante Leopoldo Zorilla looked to his men, who held their FAL rifles on the bickering pair. They shrugged, as if to say, "We do not understand these strange ones, either."

Zorilla shrugged in reply. He listened as the argument grew loud. Loud and harsh on the Anglo's side, and loud and squeaky on the Asian's. Zorilla studied them carefully. These men had said they had been sent by Uncle Sam, but they were not dressed in the business suits of the agents of Uncle Sam. They were cool, nearly oblivious to the threat of the weapons arrayed around them. Perhaps they were stupid, Zorilla thought.

Then, as the argument lapsed into a tongue Zorilla neither recognized nor understood, he began to wonder if it was possible they were not who they claimed to be.

"You will cease this noise!" he thundered.

The argument went on.

"*Hombres!* Quiet them!"

The rifle barrels were poked between the men, as if to separate them. The pair argued on, unconcerned.

Then the rifles were used to prod the two arguing ones.

Hands so fast they left no blurs in the night air rendered the weapons useless.

This was how Comandante Leopoldo Zorilla saw it:

The rifle muzzles were poked forward.

They never touched the bodies they were intended to prod. Instead his soldiers jumped back, as if startled by the unexpected sound that came from their muzzles.

It was not an explosive sound. Not even the click of chambers being charged.

The sound was more of a *runk*! Like a steel goose honking in the night.

The sound was what made his soldiers recoil, weapons coming up in their hands. The right-angle bend in their barrels was what made their eyes go round in their heads.

Leopoldo Zorilla changed his mind again. These men, for all their odd appearance and odder behavior, were highly trained professionals. He had never seen the likes of them before.

Wordlessly, he signaled his *soldados* to break up the argument.

The men, who were left clutching maimed weapons, startled expressions making their faces clownlike, retreated as the replacements came in.

Runk!

These too, stepped back, as if they had poked their barrels into the whirling blades of the most powerful fan ever constructed. But there was no fan. The pair seemed not to touch the weapons at any time. They merely used their hands to gesticulate angrily at one another. At no time did they appear to reach out and actually touch the rifle barrels.

But this was the only explanation, that they were using their hands to create this wonder.

It is either that, Zorilla concluded, or they are protected by personal force-fields.

The thought, wild as it was, intrigued Leopoldo Zorilla. He lifted his open and weaponless fingers and inched them toward the Anglo named Remo, as if he were an electrician approaching a possibly live wire.

He received a shock that was no different.

It was not electrical in nature, but his fingers stung

very suddenly. Zorilla withdrew them and looked at his fingertips.

The nails were already turning black, the way they had once when he had tried to fix a broken window in his Santiago de Cuba *comandancia*.

The upper casement had slammed down, catching the tips of his fingers. Within days the nails had blackened, eventually to fall off, leaving a black, gritty substance resembling crushed coal that was probably dried, trapped blood.

The pain this time was not nearly as intense, but the fingernails were already blackening and Zorilla felt them go numb.

"Are you injured, Comandante?" a corporal asked worriedly.

"Silence these two!" Zorilla ordered, a slow-traveling pain moving from the area of numbness up his arm and to his central nervous system. It was like a delayed pain. It shot through his muscles suddenly, and his teeth clamped down so hard he distinctly heard a bicuspid break.

This time, his *soldados* went to work in earnest. They brought the butts of their rifles around and prepared to club the still arguing pair apart.

This, apparently, was enough to make the pair notice that they were under attack.

This time, Zorilla could see their hands at work. Their feet as well. Kneecaps cracked like seashells. Fingers were bent backward, against the natural flex of the knuckle. Men were flying. Rifles cartwheeled from nerveless hands.

In seconds, the cream of his New Cuban Army was standing about as he: clutching injured members, or squirming in the dirt, weaponless and conquered.

The Anglo said, "Our information is that Uncle Sam has nothing to do with this little boot camp here."

"Your information is wrong," Zorilla muttered through pain-tightened teeth. A bloody chunk of tooth enamel dribbled from his mouth.

"What do you think, Chiun?" the Anglo asked the Asian.

"You have asked the question wrongly," said the Asian named Chiun.

And the Asian proceeded to ask the question in a unique manner.

He said not a word. He used the long, spidery nails of his right hand, which gleamed like curled ivory. He took Zorilla by the point of his chin and, neither exerting obvious pressure nor inflicting additional pain—not that any was needed—used that chin as a handle to bring Comandante Leopoldo Zorilla to his knees in the dirt like an effeminate *maricón*.

"You command this ragtag army?" he demanded.

"I do," Zorilla admitted through his teeth.

"And who commands you?"

"Uncle Sam."

"Liar!"

"I swear it is the truth! I serve Uncle Sam!"

"Satisfied?" the one called Remo asked.

"Pah!" said the one called Chiun. "We have been sent on a wild weasel quest."

"Wild goose chase, and right about now I think discretion would be the better part of valor."

"Meaning?"

"We'd better check with Smith."

"Who is Smith?" asked Comandante Leopoldo Zorilla, at the exact moment before the lights went out and he knew no more.

9

Harold Smith was very close to falling asleep.

National security depended upon Harold Smith's remaining awake, alert, and in contact with the developing situation. Yet he found himself nodding off.

It was night over Long Island Sound. The moon was high and full, and its silver effulgence washed the dark pimpled water like a luminous bleach.

The light poured through the one-way picture window behind his Folcroft desk. It was made of one-way glass so that no one could look in on the office, over Smith's shoulder, and read the computer screen that often displayed the deepest secrets of America.

The overhead lights were fluorescent, and shook the air.

Except for the medical staff and security guards, Folcroft slept. Only Smith, in the administrative wing, was working.

He was at his desk. The CURE terminal was up and running. On a corner of the pathologically neat desk sat a tiny black-and-white television set. It was turned to a network channel.

The bearded face of El Lider animated the screen. Smith had the sound turned up. Still, even with the sound of that raging voice, he could barely keep his eyes open.

"Does that man ever stop?" he complained, catching himself nod off for the fifteenth time.

The situation in Washington remained tense. After the MIG interception over the Gulf of Mexico, there had been nothing from the President. Smith continued to watch the seemingly endless Castro speech. The networks, having been overwhelmed in South Florida by the more powerful signal from Havana, had made matters worse by repeating the signal to affiliates all over the nation, with a running translation at the bottom. It was certain to heighten tensions, but nothing could be done about it.

No doubt, Harold Smith reflected as he put eye drops into his bleary gray eyes in an attempt to keep them open, the President was working the phones in an effort to convince the networks to downplay the interruption of regular programming.

In the meantime, it was all Smith could do to stay awake. For all his bluster, Castro and his tirade were having a soporific effect on him. But he dared not shut off the set while there was a possibility the networks would break in with an important bulletin.

So, while the Maximum Leader of Cuba ranted on about the Cuban people being willing to eat their shoes and pick their teeth with the nails rather than turn away from Socialism, Harold Smith continued to monitor his computer, waiting for word from Remo and Chiun.

It came when the blue contact telephone began ringing.

"Yes, Remo," Smith said, replacing his rimless glasses.

"We got a problem, Smitty."

A surge of adrenaline perked Harold Smith up in his cracked leather executive's chair.

"What is it?" Smith asked, his voice lemon-bitter.

"We found Zorilla. All tricked out in his soldier suit, ramrodding a paramilitary outfit in the Big Cypress Swamp."

"Good. You have interrogated him?"

"Yep."

"And?"

"That's the problem, Smitty. You'd better check back with the President."

"Why?"

"According to Zorilla, Uncle Sam's behind the whole thing."

"He said that?"

"He did. With Chiun squeezing every syllable from him. So he has to be telling the truth."

"I understand," said Smith, his gray-hued face going ashen.

Remo asked, "So what do we do? Back off until you clear this up?"

"One moment, Remo," said Smith. Cradling the blue receiver between jaw and shoulder, he attacked his keyboard. As he worked, he continued speaking.

"If there is a covert U.S. Cuban invasion in the works, it has to be a CIA operation," he muttered.

"Sounds about right to me."

"I am entering their central computer net right now."

"Don't startle any sleeping spooks," Remo said dryly.

"They have no idea I am in their system. I have super-user status."

"Goody for you," Remo said in an impatient voice.

Smith entered the deepest recesses of the CIA system. He executed a global search of keywords. "CUBA" brought up only intelligence intercepts and contingency plans.

"ULTIMA HORA" produced nothing more than raw intelligence.

"CASTRO" summoned up such an endless file of assassination senarios that Smith was forced to log off out of sheer impatience.

He broke contact and turned in his squeaking chair.

"Remo," he said, thin-lipped. "This is not a CIA operation. There is no active scenario fitting the description on file."

"Who said it has to be on computer?" Remo asked reasonably.

"*Everything* is on computer these days."

"Then it's somebody else. Isn't the President heavily involved in the Cuban exile community? Through his son?"

"Remo," Smith pointed out, "the President suggested this assignment."

"Maybe to cover his butt," suggested Remo.

"Remo," Smith countered, "the President would not put you and Chiun on the trail of these people if he had a stake in their eventual success. I have explained the situation to you. Cuba is hands-off. We do not wish to ruffle the Russian bear's fur."

"Are they still a bear?" Remo wondered. "I thought they were just cubs now."

"Never mind," Smith said. "Give me five minutes." And he hung up.

Smith cleared his throat and lifted the red receiver. The dedicated direct line opened automatically, causing a matching red telephone in the Lincoln Bedroom to begin ringing.

As he waited, Smith turned down the sound of Fidel Castro haranguing a world that no longer had a place for him.

The President's voice was hushed when it came on the line.

"Smith. Progress?" he hissed.

"Slight progress. We have located the comandante of the operation. He is a Cuban defector."

"Good."

"He insists that Washington is behind his efforts."

"That is insane! Unless . . . unless there's a rogue CIA effort under way."

"Not possible, Mr. President," Smith said crisply. "I have just gone through the CIA computer net. It is devoid of any such operation. Furthermore, the agency itself shows no activity or message traffic that would be consistent with the management of an ongoing operation of this magnitude."

"You have access to CIA files?" the President said, blank wonder in his tone.

"Part of the mission, Mr. President."

The President's voice grew disturbed. "Did you have it when I was in charge over there?"

"You may conclude that if you wish," Smith said flatly. "But the matter at hand is what should concern us now."

"Of course. Obviously this Cuban defector is lying through his teeth."

"Impossible. He has been subjected to an interrogation technique that is one-hundred-percent irresistible."

"But he implicated Washington," the President of the United States pointed out.

"Specifically, Uncle Sam."

"That could be anyone from a renegade senator to—"

"—to a person with high connections claiming to be operating with presidential sanction," Smith finished.

"Good point. But who?"

"Mr. President, I must ask you this question in the name of national security. You have a son who is active in the Cuban community in Miami. Can you vouch for his recent activities?"

Indignation rose in the President's tone. "I certainly can."

"If you are certain, that is enough for me," Smith said.

"Good," the President said tightly.

"Still," Smith went on, "it might be advisable to get him out of Florida if he happens to be there now."

"Why?"

"Because I am about to order my enforcement arm to terminate everyone connected with this operation."

"I didn't hear that."

"Contact your son, Mr. President. I am about to pull the plug on Ultima Hora forever."

Smith hung up and checked on the progress of the Castro speech. He was in the "History Will Absolve Me" phase. That meant the speech was coming to a climax. No more than an hour remained.

The blue contact phone rang and Smith brought the handset to his grim gray face.

"Remo," he said. "I want you and Chiun to render Ultima Hora completely and totally immobile."

"That mean what I think it means?" Remo asked.

"It does."

"And Zorilla?"

"Make sure he wakes up among the fallen."

"Yeah?"

"Then follow him to whoever he reports to."

"And lead us to his control, right?"

Smith sighed. "Let us hope. Otherwise, knowing the U.S. news media, Fidel Castro will become the next Bart Simpson."

"Huh?"

"His speech is into its fifth hour, with every network and CNN carrying it live with subtitles."

"For crying out loud, why?"

"I believe it is sweeps month," Smith said sourly. "Report when you have penetrated the next echelon."

Smith hung up. He turned up the sound. As he watched the bearded man rant on, his mind went back over the years.

The President of Cuba had been a thorn in the side of the United States for as long as Harold Smith had been sitting at this anonymous desk. Longer. Smith had once been a CIA bureaucrat, and Castro had been a CIA obsession even in those early days. Smith had been privvy to the Bay of Pigs plan, and his advice that the operation was ill conceived and would prove counterproductive if not carried out correctly was pointedly ignored.

The ultimate failure of the operation had made Smith a man with an uncertain future at the CIA. Then had come the summons to the White House and the offer to head the agency that did not exist.

Within a year, the young President had been assassinated. To this day, there were those who pointed the finger of blame for that heinous act at Havana.

But Smith wasn't thinking of that. He was thinking of the global turmoil this one driven individual had caused. The Cuban Missile Crisis had simply been the earliest and most dangerous incident.

Smith knew, because recent revelations had brought it to light, that Havana had attempted to egg the Soviet Union's Khrushchev into nuking the U.S. to protect a tiny island that had never contributed anything more important to the world than sugar and tobacco, one that had been built on the slave trade and was the last in the Western hemisphere to renounce it.

The memory made Harold Smith shudder. The U.S. and U.S.S.R. nuking themselves, and human civilization, into hot smoking ash—over a useless green speck in the Caribbean. All because of one man's rabid anti-Americanism.

Smith thought of the events of his life since 1961, of the people who had been born, the scientific and cultural achievements of mankind. None of them Cuban. And none of them would have happened had Havana gotten its way.

While the first man was walking on the moon, Havana was overturning elected governments in Latin America and Africa. While human hearts were first being successfully transplanted, Castro was ordering Cuban cows to mate with zebu in defiance of elementary genetic logic, in an insane gambit designed to produce an animal that produced both meat and milk.

On the television screen, Fidel Castro shook his fist and dripped spittle onto his iron-gray beard. One man. One madman. From Attila the Hun to Adolf Hitler, it was usually one power-crazed lunatic who piled up the most bodies.

Perhaps he had made a mistake in not ordering the man terminated years ago, after CURE had gotten its enforcement arm.

Now it was too late. By presidential decree, CURE could not undertake that task. It shouldn't even have been necessary. The Cold War was over.

Yet there he was: the last Cold Warrior, trying to push the world to the brink once more. . . .

10

Remo left the out-of-the-way gas station pay phone off the loop road, with a slow look of uncertainty settling over his lean features.

The Master of Sinanju saw this as his pupil approached their rented car.

"You are troubled," he said.

Remo eased behind the wheel. "Smith just ordered Ultima Hora hit."

"What is so troubling about this? They are enemies of the Emperor. They live to die."

"No," said Remo, starting the car. "They are Cuban patriots. All they want is to take back their homeland. Nothing wrong with that." He sent the car running down the long tunnel of a Spanish moss-overhung road. "We're supposed to be on the same side."

"They are pawns," Chiun said coldly. "As are you."

"Maybe. But I thought this kind of crap went out with the Cold War."

"If you wish, I will dispatch them."

"You will?"

Chiun raised a wise finger. "But you must tell Smith you accounted for some of the vanquished."

"Why?"

"Because while I wish the credit, I am negotiating a contract for your services as well. You must demonstrate your worth."

"I haven't done so badly this far," Remo growled, swerving to avoid a road-crossing armadillo.

"For a white. A parentless white."

"Get off that kick. And while you're dismounting, how about clueing me in on the bone that's caught in Smith's throat?"

"What is this you ask?"

"The sticking point in the contract. It's gotta be pretty big."

"If you must know, I am seeking a new residence. One worthy of our station in this ugly land."

"Yeah?"

"One with battlements and great stonework and other accoutrements befitting our worth."

Remo's bright expression darkened. "Sounds like Dracula's castle. Where is this place?"

"It is a surprise."

"Uh-huh."

They drove along in tight silence. At length, the Master of Sinanju broke it.

"What do you think of this province?" he asked.

"Florida?"

"Whatever it is called," Chiun said with a vague wave.

"Well, it's hot and steamy where it's not dank and swampy, heat rash is a big problem, the cockroaches are almost indestructible but not as bad as the snakes and gators, and there are the hurricanes."

Chiun looked over. "You prefer a northern clime?"

"Just so long as we're talking south of the North Pole," Remo said.

"My native Korea is not hot like this place. But one could get used to the heat. If one had a suitable cool place in which to dwell."

"Castles aren't cool. They're dank."

"The castle I would dwell in will be cool," Chiun sniffed.

They followed their headlights back into the swamp. When the road petered out, they got out and started across the swampy terrain. The air was moist yet unseasonably cool. Katydids chirred amid the bullfrog croakings. Red eyes low in the water told of lurking gators.

The Master of Sinanju's black silk kimono became

a flitting thing in the darkness, like an ebony bat on wing. Remo, also in black, moved easily between the cypress trees, avoiding when he could the watery sloughs and, at all costs, the black, sucking muck. Even in the water, their feet made no sound warning of their approach.

A bull alligator, like a floating log, turned up in their path.

The Master of Sinanju simply stepped onto his ridged reptilian back and, pausing only to drive a heel into his skull, moved on.

Remo leaped onto the gator's back and off again before it could sink in death.

The moon ghosted out of a thin boil of fast-moving cloud cover, and just as swiftly fell behind a patch of haze to shine, mistily and eerily quiet, through a dome of Spanish moss-draped cypress.

Remo and Chiun paused when the moonlight found them. They waited. In the silence, an egret took wing.

When the moon had faded behind fatter clouds, and the deep of the night returned, they resumed their silent progress.

The base camp of Ultima Hora was a dry highland surrounded by mangrove-festooned sentries, standing ankle-deep in stagnant water.

The Master of Sinanju drifted up to one of these men and broke his neck with a short chop to the base of his skull.

Remo caught the body and held the head underwater until the last air bubbles had ceased tailing upward.

They moved on, unchallenged.

The first time they were escorted to the camp, the guards had been clustered together, waiting to escort them in.

This time they were spread out in a circle surrounding the base camp. A common defensive posture, and one Sinanju had long since learned to defeat.

"Walk the circle," Chiun intoned.

With a silent nod passing between them, Remo went north, and Chiun south.

Each time they encountered a guard, they took him down. Not a shot was gotten off. Then they met at the opposite point of the circle. It took all of three minutes.

"The circle is closed," Chiun intoned.

Remo bowed.

They moved into the base camp.

There was no rattle of gunfire. The Castro dummies lay slumped on their stakes, faces torn, mossy beards askew.

Remo and Chiun moved in utter silence, their every sense alert.

All human signs of life seemed to be clustered in the tobacco-drying shed.

"I will go ahead," Chiun said. "You will guard."

Remo hesitated. His face stone, he said, "No."

Chiun turned.

"This must be done," he said coldly.

"It will be," Remo agreed. "By both of us."

The Master of Sinanju nodded quietly. Together they advanced.

Then, without warning, came the rip and pop of automatic weapons fire.

Splintery holes pocked the rude sides of the shack. The incessant chirr of katydids fell still.

The two Masters of Sinanju dropped flat on the dry ground.

Rounds whistled through the Spanish moss, making *clip clip clip* sounds punctuated by the creak and snap of fractured cypress branches.

"Sounds like we have a firefight on our hands," Remo growled.

Without warning, a door banged open. Remo and Chiun froze, two black shadows against the dark mossy earth.

Out of the powder smoke came a man, his body awash in the metallic scent familiar to assassin and soldier alike.

Blood.

The man paused on the open veranda, yanking an empty clip from his FAL rifle and slapping home a fresh one. He set the butt plate against his hip, moving the barrel this way and that with casual confidence.

They watched his face. It resembled sculpted brown rock inset with two black eyes that held no more expression than the buttons on an old coat. Shadows made his identity impossible to ascertain.

Nothing happened.

"Is he such a fool, that he thinks we will show ourselves?" Chiun undertoned.

"I don't think he's waiting for us," Remo said.

The wrinkled face of the Master of Sinanju grew more wrinkled still. His hazel eyes narrowed, like those of a thoughtful cat.

The salt scent of blood hung in the moist, humid air like a portent.

Chiun nodded. Remo knew then that he understood.

They waited.

The man in the camouflage uniform stepped off the shack step reluctantly and strode out into the night. A stray shaft of moonlight caught his face and they could see him clearly.

Comandante Leopoldo Zorilla. His eyes were hard, but a sad moistness hung far back in their liquid depths.

He strode out into the swamp and, like two fugitive rags, Remo and Chiun followed.

Zorilla moved with the stealth of a trained soldier.

But to the two Masters of Sinanju, he might have been an elephant dancing on its hind legs. His boots made rude splashes and crinkled undergrowth. Insects and frogs darted from his path, to come to resting places that were not abandoned even as Remo and Chiun moved stealthily by them.

Zorilla came upon the first fallen sentry. He muttered something under his breath. Then he moved on, searching.

When every body had been found, his manner grew strained. He walked more slowly now, with less care, but with long strides that turned his body a complete revolution every few feet so that the FAL muzzle, like a radar antenna, could sweep the night all around him.

They followed him to a point behind the dry hump of land, a stretch of seemingly open water. Yet Zorilla strode into it seemingly without fear of the cottonmouth moccasins that glided along, leaving V-shaped wakes.

His soldier's boots barely sank into the water.

They followed, staying low.

At the mangrove clump where Zorilla had stepped into the water, they paused.

Remo slipped a hand into the stagnant water. It was warm, pungent with life. Barely an inch beneath the surface, he felt the sliminess of submerged wood.

"Walkway," he said softly.

The Master of Sinanju nodded. Without a word of communication, they slipped beneath the water and moved through it with the soundlessness of swimming manatees.

Eyes adjusting to the lack of light, they used their ears to follow their quarry. His boots made the walkway creak, and the sound carried perfectly.

A cottonmouth, gliding along the surface, suddenly dropped toward Remo like a coil of discarded rope, its jaws distending.

Remo reached up and grasped its head, forcing the jaws together and the brittle skull apart. He released the limp reptile, shedding a cloud of blackish blood, and swam on.

When the ground began to slope upward they hung back, releasing air bubbles one at a time, three per minute, so as not to betray their position.

The creaking ceased, so they let their natural buoyancy carry them surfaceward.

Two heads broke the calm swamp surface as one. Two pairs of eyes scanned the night.

They saw a lone figure vanish between tangles of cypress, and not long after heard the sound of a car engine disturb the night. Headlight glare flared and then swept around, casting elongated shadows that made the world seem to be turning on a plate before their eyes.

"Let's go," Remo said.

They left the water erect, not seeming to hurry but moving with urgent speed nonetheless.

They found the road and spied the retreating headlights.

They were other vehicles parked there. Cars. Trucks. They picked one of the former. Remo popped the ignition with a skill picked up in the Newark streets of long ago, and soon they were following the car at a careful distance, lights doused.

They drove with a wide silence between them.

Remo broke it after a while.

"My money says Zorilla wiped out Ultima Hora."

"You may keep your money," Chiun said.

"He must have woken up and called someone."

"Obviously he woke up."

"That someone heard we were sniffing around, and ordered the operation terminated," Remo went on.

"A wise someone."

"This still smells of the CIA to me."

"I only smell blood and the lack of proper credit," said Chiun.

"Those guys back there were patriots," Remo said bitingly. "I don't care what anyone says."

His dark eyes, fixed on the moss-draped road ahead, were like pools of death.

"We may be on the same side, but I want the guy who gave that order."

"Beware of what you hope for."

"Why?"

"Because you may receive it," said Chiun, his yellowed visage tight with the wise webs of his years.

11

Comandante Leopoldo Zorilla drove north through the Florida chill without expression. His face was stoic. He was a man. A Cuban man. As such, he was *machismo* personified.

Machismo left no room for regrets, never mind tears.

Still, the tears came. He could not help them. He was a soldier true. And a soldier followed orders.

But to slaughter his own men? The hope of Cuba's future?

He let the tears flow. For Guillermo the brave. For Fulgencio the sly. Young men who knew Cuba only from TV travelogues and tales told by fathers and uncles. Young men who would liberate Cuba and return it to the welcoming arms of the world.

Caught unprepared, they had died shamefully. They never dreamed their own commander would turn on them and slaughter them so cruelly.

It had happened after they had aroused him from his state of unconsciousness.

"*Que?* What happened?" he asked.

"It was the two. The Anglo and the other," had said José. He of the quick smile and killer eyes. "They did this. We could not stop them, *comandante mio.*"

"Why not?"

Ruefully, they displayed their injured hands.

"We can no longer hold our rifles, comandante," Roberto said miserably.

Zorilla was helped to his feet. He examined their

fingers. Some were broken. The trigger fingers. It was as if these intruders who claimed to have been sent by Uncle Sam had set out to maim them.

"Give me a rifle," said Comandante Zorilla.

They scrounged up a single FAL whose barrel had not been bent.

He took them out to the target range and tested each of them. They could not squeeze triggers, except with their thumbs. Not that they did not try. They nearly shot one another trying, for they were very determined, this new generation of Cuban youth. At that moment, Zorilla felt a sad wave of pride in them.

When the last had failed even to strike a target, they stood about like castrated bulls, droopy of shoulder and morose of eye. Men. But not warriors. Some furtively brushed tears of shame from their eyes.

"What will we do?" asked one.

Zorilla had to clear his throat twice before he could answer. "I must contact Uncle Sam."

They all agreed this was for the best. Comandante Zorilla left them to deal, hot-eyed, with the pain in their Cuban hearts while he made the telephone call.

In the privacy of the tobacco shack he dialed the number that existed, unextractable, in his trained memory and no place else.

"Zorilla reporting," he said stiffly.

"Go ahead," a gringo voice said. There were orange blossoms in that voice. It was mellow, and laced with the mild southern accents of Florida.

"Ultima Hora must stand down."

"Repeat report."

"Ultima Hora has been rendered ineffective by two agents."

"Agents of whom?"

"They say Uncle Sam send them."

"Describe these agents."

Zorilla rattled off the descriptions with spare clarity.

"One moment," said the mellow phone voice.

The line hummed. Bullfrogs croaked in the swamp, and the tireless katydids made reedy music.

The clicking signaled the return of his immediate contact.

"Uncle Sam sent no agents. Repeat, the two you describe are unknown unfriendlies."

"The timetable must be abandoned until my men can heal."

"Negative. Timetable cannot be shelved. The MIG incident is driving events now."

"But what do I do?"

"Ultima Hora was first wave."

"I know. I am heartsick."

"Redundancy has been built into the plan. A new first wave must be set in place, and trained by you."

"But what will I tell my men? They live for this."

"We have to assume training camp compromised irrevocably. Return to headquarters for debriefing and new orders."

"But my men . . ."

"Must be decruited."

Comandante Leopoldo Zorilla's eyes went stark.

The code word had been agreed upon. Zorilla had agreed to the "decruitment" option. But never had he believed he would be forced to implement it.

"But—"

"You are a soldier. Execute instructions and report for further duty. Word comes directly from Uncle Sam."

"*Sí, sí,*" muttered Comandante Zorilla into the suddenly dead telephone. Through the rush of blood to his ringing ears he never heard the receiver click.

Woodenly, he hung up, adjusted his insignia-less uniform, and picked up the sole working rifle within the sentry perimeter.

He called in his men, stood them at attention, and with the suddenly too-heavy rifle held loose in the crook of his arm like a duck hunter's, began a speech.

It was a long speech. About duty, about honor, about Zorilla's deep feelings for his men. There was sadness in his voice as he spoke, sadness in the faces of his soldiers. They knew they were to be taken off active duty. A few flinched. They steeled themselves for the actual words when their comandante, circling them on dull feet, lifted his rifle and let the shameful bullets erupt one at a time.

They fell in the time it took for a string of firecrackers to become torn red paper.

It was necessary. It was also shameful. Because he could not bear to see the looks in their wounded eyes, Comandante Leopoldo Zorilla had shot them all in the back.

Then he had gone out into the night to silence the sentries. Finding them already dead, he had fled.

And now he drove through the frosty Florida night, the firefly-like love bugs bouncing off his windshield, making noises like castoff peanut shells caught in a windstorm.

The sound reminded him of the sand against the windows of his *comandancia* office back in Santiago de Cuba.

There, Comandante Zorilla had been Deputy Comandante Zorilla of the Cuban Air Force. He had been a boy the day Fidel had taken the capital.

It had been a jubilant day, and when Fidel had put the nation under arms, Zorilla, a teenager, had been glad to shoulder them. On each May Day he had taken up an actual rifle and shot at rocks along Jibacoa Beach, pretending they were the helmets of crawling *Yanqui* Marines.

It was an exciting time to be Cuban.

He enlisted in the Air Force when he came of age. Flew patrols and escorts for Soviet ships. Then-Captain Zorilla had been so valuable a pilot that they would not send him to Angola to support Socialism there.

It had been the bitterest of disappointments. Until his comrades began to filter back, telling tales of African ingratitude and the wasted lives spent defending a nation that did not care about itself, never mind Cuban sacrifice.

Capitan Zorilla had dismissed these grumblings, for he believed.

He believed even as Cuba peaked in the mid-1970s,

all the while suffering horrendous losses in its fight for ungrateful peoples all over Africa.

He believed through the Soviet intervention in Afghanistan, because Fidel had told him this was no superpower adventure, but a necessary defense of Socialism. Even as the Hind gunships massacred simple goatherds, Fidel had vowed this.

He believed when younger Cubans were sent to Grenada and were hurled back like toothpicks, heartless and cowardly, by U.S. Rangers.

He continued to believe as, one by one, the Warsaw Bloc fell, not to aggression or war, but to internal discontent and ineptitude.

Slowly, Leopoldo Zorilla had been forced to surrender his ideals. He visited Havana every year. Every year Havana remained static, the streets choked with inferior Soviet cars and proud pre-revolutionary American cars. The buildings decayed and declined. And no new buildings were built. It was as if Havana—and all of Cuba—were frozen in the late 1950s, not progressing, only deteriorating.

The rations grew steadily worse. Meats became scarce. The Berlin Wall fell. Germany was reunited. The world was at last emerging from a long political Dark Age.

Yet the regime only grew more strident, more uncompromising.

When three Miami-based exiles were captured attempting to make contact with Cuban dissidents, a Popular Provincial Court sentenced them to death. But it commuted to thirty years the sentences of the two who had been born in Miami to exiles. The third, a defector, had been summarily executed by firing squad. Even in the worst days of the Cold War, this had not been done.

The Council of State had given as the reason the doomed man had deserved his fate that he had "enjoyed the fruits of the Revolution, then betrayed it."

In the meantime, under Option Zero—the Presidential decree that required all members of the armed

forces to forage the countryside for their own food—
Comandante Zorilla had taken to eating banana rats,
which he caught in traps because the state's meat—
mostly Bulgarian chicken—was so bad. So much for
the "fruits of the Revolution." Still, he had reasoned,
it was better than eating alligator, as some did.

The night the Soviet Union came apart, Comandante Zorilla was walking the beach of his childhood,
dazed and restless. He walked all night. Buzzards flew
overhead, as if over a cooling corpse. There had been
buzzards overhead in the days before the Revolution,
he knew, but now they seemed a portent of the
exhausted carcass that his isolated homeland had
become.

Zorilla was sucking on a length of sugarcane, the
rich brown sucrose juice fueling his nervous state.

He did not remember collapsing. Not even to this
very day.

The doctor was leaning over him when he came
around.

"You are all right," said the kindly old doctor—one
of the last of the good ones because he, like all that
was left in Cuba that was good, was pre-Revolution.

"No more sugarcane for you," the doctor said.

"Why not?"

"You have diabetes," said the doctor, handing
Comandante Zorilla a plastic packet containing a vial
of insulin and two disposable needles.

"Do not throw away your needles," the doctor
directed. "Clean them in alcohol."

"There is no alcohol to be had," Zorilla had
protested.

The doctor shrugged forlornly. "Do not concern
yourself, because soon there will be no more insulin,
as well."

"Will I die?"

The kindly old doctor smiled. "Son, we will all die.
Some sooner than others."

That night, Comandante Zorilla lay on his bunk,
listening to a transistor radio whose sole battery he

had hoarded for years. He was listening to Radio Marti.

"It was announced tonight by MININT that meat rations have been cut to one a month. President Fidel Castro Ruz has decreed that Cubans will subsist on sugarcane rather than sell them to the Russian Commonwealth at ruinous prices. According to the U.S. Department of Agriculture projections, the sugarcane harvest for the previous year was poor, and expectations for a good one this year are minimal."

That night, Comandante Zorilla packed all that mattered to him: some U.S. dollars he had acquired, and his dwindling insulin supply.

As a military man, he was privy to much intelligence. He knew, for instance, the schedule of U.S. Caribbean cruise ships, although everyone knew these to some degree. For ordinary Cubans took to makeshift rafts and pushed out into shark-infested waters, knowing that if the winds were right they would be sighted by the passing ships, which always picked them up.

And if they were not, they would die.

Comandante Leopoldo Zorilla knew he was going to die anyway. So he stole a Soviet rubber raft from supply and inflated it on the beach. The inflating canister sputtered out with the raft only half-filled. Zorilla was forced to use a bicycle pump to finish the job. The handle cracked at the penultimate pump.

"Nothing in Cuba works anymore," he complained, and shoved off into the night.

It was a moonless night in April. The air was moist and free. And Leopoldo Zorilla—no longer comandante, except of his own soul—lay there dreaming of what it would be like when he reached Miami and defected.

His mind held many military secrets. Enough to expose all of Cuba's weak spots. Choke points. Ill-guarded landing spots. He was but one man, but he could lay Castro's Cuba naked and exposed to liberators.

It would be sweet, this revenge he contemplated.

When the Caribbean sun heaved out of the too-blue

waters, Leopoldo Zorilla was astonished to see that he
was not alone on the open sea here in the Windward
Passage.

All about him, other rafts floated. He looked around
wonderingly. It was like a Sargasso Sea of rafts.
Mostly, inflated inner tubes floored with mangrove
branches. Or rubber tires too bald to serve any other
useful purpose.

The *balselaros,* as they were called, greeted the sun
with reverential silence, for all knew that when the
sun set, they would either be free or they would be
lost forever.

The cruise ship *Beasley Adventure* hove into view
at high noon, when the rays burned hottest.

It was magnificently white and multistoried, like a
palace afloat.

Those who could, stood up and waved at the ship
with their straw hats. Zorilla waved with his sunburned hands.

The great ship hove to, and landing stages were
lowered.

They were taken aboard as if it were an ordinary
thing.

Leopoldo Zorilla presented himself to the white-
uniformed captain.

"I am former Comandate Leopoldo Zorilla of the
Cuban Air Force," he said, his voice choking, for this
was contrary to his upbringing.

"Fine, fine," said the captain rather carelessly.
"Welcome to our ship. We dock in an hour. Immigration will be there to process you."

"But I am a defector. I have many military secrets
in my head."

"Tell it to the INS."

"But I am a military man, like you."

The *Yanqui* captain almost laughed in his face.

"I'm just a plain old commercial captain. Now if
you'll excuse me . . ."

Zorilla had been left stunned. What an ignorant
dandy this man is, he had thought. Did he not realize
how important a defector Zorilla was?

He did not. Zorilla found himself herded into a hold with the others, like two-legged cattle. The food was good though, and he ate greedily.

At the dock, Immigration authorities came to take charge of them. They did not look pleased with this harvest of defectors.

When one of them came to him with forms to be filled out, Leopoldo Zorilla snapped to attention and saluted, saying, "I am former Deputy Comandante Leopoldo Zorilla of the Cuban Air Force, requesting asylum."

"Fine. Here's your entry form."

"I know many military secrets of value."

"Fill it out in triplicate, please."

"I have knowledge that would bring down the Havana government, if properly applied."

"Turn it in to the man in white."

"But—"

The bored immigration man moved on. Then, as if understanding for the first time, he stepped back. He looked Zorilla in the eye for the first time, and Zorilla thought, He is slow-witted. He understands now.

"Almost forgot. Here's your pencil."

Stunned into wordlessness, Zorilla accepted the yellow stub of a pencil. His tongue thick in his gaping mouth, he filled out the form. In triplicate.

With the others, he was taken to the Immigration Service's Krome Avenue Detention Center to be processed. There he was given blue coveralls and more forms to fill out.

For two months Leopoldo Zorilla told his story to any who would listen, and waited for a higher U.S. official to come and take charge of him. He had heard whispers of Cuban pilots who received handsome stipends in return for defecting. He had spit on the memory of those traitors in days gone by. Now, all he cared about was getting his very own stipend.

But there were no stipends for Leopoldo Zorilla. Nor did any high-ranking U.S. official show up to take charge of his case.

Instead, after the obligatory two-month cooling-off

period had passed, he and those with whom he had shared a Spartan barracks existence were summoned to a room and given green cards.

"What is this 'green card'?" he asked.

"Residency permit. You can get work."

"I do not wish to work. I wish to reveal the secrets of Cuba military machine," Zorilla protested.

"Not interested."

"But I have been told of the vast sums my junior officers have received for flying their MIGs into this country."

"You got a MIG on you?" the processor asked.

"No . . ." Zorilla admitted.

He pointed. "Get your clothes and wait in one of those vans."

Dejectedly, Zorilla did as he was told. These men were dolts! As bad as the functionaries in Havana, who would refuse to change a light-bulb if it were not their assigned task to do so.

Leopoldo Zorilla hitched a ride to Washington and attempted to interest the CIA, the FBI, and the Pentagon in what he knew.

He was rebuffed at each institution. With the exception of the Pentagon, which offered him a janitorial job at $5.40 an hour.

Depressed and defeated, Zorilla had returned to Florida and an unknowable future.

It was not so bad. The Cuban community had virtually taken over Miami. The mayor was Cuban. A senator was Hispanic. It was, Zorilla thought, like Havana would have been if that bearded monster had not thrown a monkey wrench into the clock of time itself.

He got a job in a restaurant, and although the work was menial and hurt his pride, Zorilla was told that he was in the land of opportunity and good fortune was sure to come his way.

It did. One day a man named Drake walked into the restaurant and offered him more than just a job.

"I understand you know some things about current Cuban defenses," he said in a smooth, low voice.

"This is true. Why do you ask?"

"The Director would like to speak with you."

And it had been just as his fellow Cuban-Americans had promised. Leopoldo Zorilla laid down his busboy's plastic tray and became a leader of men once more. A soldier of the Americas.

That had been a year ago. A good time. A new beginning.

But now, it had all been dashed to pieces.

As the last bitter tear slid down a track on his face to leave a dried, tight, saline line, Comandante Leopoldo Zorilla vowed to make the person responsible pay: The despised Fidel Castro.

The mission would go on.

He pressed his heavy booted foot to the accelerator and, like a robot, held the snaketrack road.

Behind, the shame of his life lay in slow-drying pools of blood.

Ahead, lay his manly destiny.

As he rushed through the Florida night, Leopoldo Zorilla vowed to himself that he would build a monument to the fallen of this terrible night, of the purest granite he could find.

He could do no less. For he knew personally the mothers of many of the glorious dead.

Captain Ernest Maus slipped his magnetic passcard into the slot and entered the quietly humming control room after the door had slid upward.

The humming came from the banks of computers and control consoles. It made the room sound cool. In fact, the temperature hovered around ninety-five degrees. He began to sweat profusely as he walked past the guards in their immaculate white jumpsuits.

He stopped where an old man sat hunched over a computer terminal. The old man was using a mouse to draw a fox in glowing red lines. His hair, visible over the chair back, was the color of snow.

"Director?"

"What is it, Maus?" the Director asked in a chilly voice.

"Dr. Revuelta called the emergency contact number, and left a cryptic message on the machine. Do you authorize contacting him directly?"

The Director used the mouse to make the fox stand up. He gave the fox a Marilyn Monroe face, large breasts, and a wealth of bushy pubic hair.

"Director?"

"Why is it so cold in here?" the Director asked peevishly. clicking the mouse. The fox-girl began to revolve, swaying its generous hips like a hula dancer.

"The heat is on high," Maus reported.

"Damn doctors. Said there'd be no aftereffects. If that's so, why am I freezing all the damn time?"

"I'll have the heat increased, Director."

"And go to Threatcon Squeaky. No telling what the cat might drag in."

"And Revuelta?"

"Find out what his problem is. That idiot is probably just jumping at shadows."

The Director made the fox girl's naked rump a size larger. Then two. He chuckled appreciatively.

"I love this thing," he said as Captain Maus left the room, his uniform blouse sticking to his skin.

12

Remo Williams drove through the cool Florida night in tight silence.

Beside him, the Master of Sinanju said nothing.

The road ahead ran in straight lines that became cutbacks at unexpected moments. Remo was completely focused on it and his car. He was at one with the car, feeling the tires hug the road through vibrations coming up through the steering column.

The modern automobile was as far removed from the purity that was Sinanju as was Donkey Kong. Still, the reflexes Remo had acquired made him a superb driver.

He had been running without lights for hours, his vision fixed on the distant taillights of Zorilla's car.

They were on Interstate 75, heading north, toward Tampa. Cool, salty breezes were blowing in off the Gulf of Mexico.

Remo turned on the radio and punched up the stations until he got a newscast.

". . . in Florida, military bases and law enforcement agencies are reportedly on a high state of alert in the wake of the Cuban interference of broadcast channels. The Pentagon is being uncharacteristically tight-lipped, but sources here confirm contingency plans are being reviewed for a possible retaliatory action against microwave TV-transmitters on the Cuban mainland."

"Good," Remo muttered.

"No, it is not good."

"Why not?" Remo asked Chiun.

"Because the oppressor cannot oppress unless he has external enemies."

The newscaster continued, "According to a Cuban television broadcast monitored in Mexico, Fidel Castro told his people today, 'We will fight them without quarter, with the force of the masses and the law, in the political field and in the ideological field with every means. If the *Yanquis* come, it will be another Vietnam, only worse.' "

"Guess he never heard of Desert Storm," Remo said.

"If there is one person who wishes for invasion, it is the oppressor," Chiun said.

"Say that again," Remo said, turning off the radio.

"It is very simple, Remo. I know what is happening on that island of sugar. The tyrant cannot feed his people. They clamor for food and grow restive. It is the beginning of the end. Only a miracle can save him now." Chiun turned, his voice pointed. "Or an enemy to be invoked, the better to draw the people around him to protect the man, under the pretense of protecting his throne."

"Makes sense. But Castro isn't doing this."

"What has he to lose?"

"I still think it's the CIA. They've had a bug up their ass over this guy since day one."

"They should pass gas then, and be done with it," Chiun said blandly.

"Chiun?"

"Yes?"

"When we get to the head guy, I get Zorilla, too."

"Why?"

"He slaughtered his own men. He deserves to die."

"If all your wishes come true, my son," Chiun said in a low voice, "we will have a very busy night before us."

As they neared Tampa, the taillight angled east. Remo followed onto Interstate 4, as if riding a wheeled lodestone being pulled by another lodestone. The driver never suspected he was being followed.

The countryside changed character. They began to see cattle farms, surprisingly enough. Lakes were common sights.

The signs began to say: LAKELAND. WINTER HAVEN. KISSIMMEE. FURIOSO.

The Master of Sinanju, seeing the last of these, perked up in his seat and said, his voice squeaky with pleasure, "Look, Remo, we are going to Furioso."

"Big hairy deal," Remo growled.

The Master of Sinanju frowned. "It is a big hairy deal to some," he said.

"Not to me."

"We have no time to stop?"

"Chiun, we are not going to you-know-where while we're on a freaking mission."

"Now I know," Chiun said forlornly.

"Know what?"

"That I am unappreciated by ingrates on all sides."

Remo sighed. "Maybe on the way back."

" 'Maybe' is not 'definitely.' "

Silence fell over the darkened car interior.

Somewhere in the night, fires raged. They were passing through fields of orange groves now. The air was filled with a strange mixture of orange blossoms and burning kerosene, and dense with dragons of rolling black smoke.

"What are these fires?" Chiun asked in a doubtful voice.

"Looks like the orange growers got hit by a frost."

"Frost does not burn."

"No," Remo said patiently. "But the growers have millions of dollars tied up in their orchards. They can't afford to lose them to frost. So they burn smudge pots and use electric heaters to save the crop."

"This works? Smoking the fruit?"

"Usually. If the frost doesn't go on too long."

The Master of Sinanju grunted. "Did I ever tell you of the Master who was so foolish that he performed a service for a solitary orange?"

"No. And I think you're making it up."

"I do not make up legends. It was in the time of

Cathay. Oranges were unknown to Sinanju, and an emperor of . . ."

Remo tuned out Chiun, and the singsong tone in which he was relating a possibly true story of the early days of the House of Sinanju. He was in no mood for it. All he wanted was for the trail to end and the bodies to start piling up.

Miles short of the outskirts of Furioso, Florida, the fugitive taillights dimmed, flared, and winked out.

"Damn," Remo said.

Chiun pointed into the night. "I see him. Follow."

Remo pulled off the road—he had no idea what road, or where he was exactly—and onto a sandy access road that was nothing more than a knot of switchbacks rank with kudzu weed.

Either side was lined with old billboards. Mostly ads for local theme parks. The kudzu was working its way up those, too.

"This isn't a posted road," Remo said.

"It is a road," Chiun countered. "That is enough."

For nearly a mile they negotiated the road. Ahead, the night horizon was a jagged line of strange shapes.

Chiun examined this critically. "What vista is this?"

"Search me," Remo said.

Chiun pouted his lower lip, his hazel eyes thoughtful.

The road came to a dead halt at the end of a pond bordered with wilting pink camilla blossoms.

Remo eased to a stop in time to keep the front tires from slipping into the water.

"What the hell?" he muttered. "Where'd he go?"

They got out, shades of black in a deeper blackness.

"See anything, Little Father?"

"No," Chuin said thinly.

Remo looked for tracks. There were none. In fact, his own car had made no impression in the sand. Remo knelt. The sand, he found, was actually glued in place. Glued over asphalt.

"Well," Remo said, standing up. "we know Zorilla wasn't driving a submarine car." He looked up. "I don't see anything in the sky, either."

"Come," said Chiun, moving back the way they had come.

Remo followed.

"What are we looking for?" he asked, curious.

"We are looking for nothing. We are smelling the air."

Remo focused on his nostrils and drew in a sip of air. The air passing over his sensitive olfactory receptors was reasonably clean, for all its proximity to the sprawling city of Furioso.

"I don't smell anything," Remo complained.

"But you will."

Remo did. He picked up the tailpipe emission from Zorilla's car a quarter-mile back. It went off to the left.

Remo spotted the crushed-down kudzu on one side of the artificial road.

"Must have missed it in the darkness," he said.

They moved into the kudzu. The carbon monoxide vapor, odorless to most noses, was heavy in theirs, so they switched to breathing through their mouths. It made their thoughts heavy.

Against a low hillock, they found it. A concrete bunker, nearly buried in the dirt and obscured by kudzu. The door was a big slab of steel, painted brown and green to blend in with the surroundings.

There were no signs. No guards, no anything.

"Looks military," Remo said quietly.

Chiun nodded. "We have found the lair of the plotters."

"All we have to do is get in."

"All we have to do is get in," came the voice over the overhead loudspeaker.

"Director, we have a security breach."

The Director looked up from his console, where he had been wireframing three touching circles. He was in the act of commanding this remarkable newfangled computer to "draw" a pair of eyes in the large bottom circle when the word came.

He turned in his swivel chair to the overhead monitor, cursing the eye patch that restricted his vision and adding another for the stupid doctor who could have saved the eye—if only he had had the gumption to stick to his guns.

He saw two men moving through the stark high-contrast image transmitted from the infrared scanner.

"Who the hell are they?" he demanded in a gravelly voice.

"Unknown, Director."

"The little guy looks like he strayed out of a bad Saturday morning cartoon."

The Director picked up the telephone handset at his elbow, inadvertently hitting the dial buttons embedded in it.

"Damn these things! What was wrong with the rotary dial?"

He hit the switch hook and tapped the pound key. "Yes?"

"Get me that weasel Drake," he snapped.

"At once, sir."

A cautious voice came on the line.

"You wanted me, Director?"

"There are two of them, and they're sniffing at the back door like a couple of hound dogs at a fireplug."

"I'm patching into the visual feed now."

"Good for you," the Director said acidly. The man was a toady.

"Director, they fit the description of the pair Zorilla encountered earlier this evening."

"That idiot must have let them follow him. Where is he?"

"On his way to my office for debriefing and reassignment."

"Decruit him."

"Yes, Director. What about the intruders?"

"I'm going to have them let in."

"Director?"

"Well, we can't very well let them go running back to the CIA or the Cuban DGI, now can we?"

"No, Director. We can't."

"You deal with Zorilla. He's your speed. I'll handle these two."

The Director hung up abruptly. He turned to a blank-faced uniformed figure, standing guard at the door.

"You, flunky. Open the door for our curious guests."

"Yes, Director."

"And have them interrogated and processed out with the rest of the trash."

"Yes, Director."

The Director went back to his computer screen. He tapped a key and the eyes drew themselves. He added a smiling mouth and a button nose.

"Not bad," he murmured contentedly. "Not bad, if I do say so myself."

He added his famous signature with the tap of another key.

"We are being observed," intoned the Master of Sinanju.

"Infrared?" Remo asked.

"I feel warm rays."

"Infrared," Remo said.

They were crouched in the rank kudzu, studying the massive portal.

Remo's dark eyes raked the structure. The ground under his feet thrummed and throbbed, as if from mighty machinery.

"Think they can hear us, too?"

"It does not matter," said Chiun.

"I don't see any way in except through that huge bulkhead, but there's gotta be a vent shaft or something."

Just then whining servo-motors cut the air, and with a metallic uncoiling the great door began to rise.

"Looks like we've been invited in," Remo said doubtfully.

The Master of Sinanju stood up. His hands going to his wrists and both disappearing under closing sleeves, he said, "Then let us be gracious and accept this kindness."

Face calm, he started forward. Remo followed, not looking happy at all.

13

Comandante Leopoldo Zorilla walked the cavernous walkways, which were scrubbed clean with military spotlessness.

Two soldiers in insignia-less uniforms came along driving a rubber-tired utility vehicle, like a golf cart on steroids. It was an unmilitary turquoise.

The driver said, "Hop on, sir. Drake will see you immediately."

"Gracias," said Comandante Zorilla, getting in back. He sat facing away from the driver. The rubber-tired utility vehicle turned smartly and zipped back the way it had come.

The tunnels were a bewildering maze of alabaster conduits and ivory corridors. Overhead pipes and aluminum ductwork of all descriptions clustered against the high ceilings. It is a wondrous place, Zorilla thought to himself, marvelous for all the things that are controlled down here.

Along one long stretch the air reverberated with a rushing like a vast vacuum, and the ceiling appeared to be one huge pipe.

"What is this roaring pipe?" Zorilla wondered.

"Waste-disposal," the driver said. "Takes all the trash and debris from topside and dumps it into trash-compactors for removal."

"Ah, brilliant," said Zorilla admiringly.

The utility vehicle came to a dead end and stopped, with but an inch between its rubber bumpers and a steel sliding door.

Zorilla was taken to the door and the driver inserted a magnetic card into a chrome-mouthed slot. The door rolled back, revealing a common elevator interior.

"The lift will take you where you need to go," said the driver.

"Gracias," said Zorilla again, stepping aboard. The door rolled shut. The lift rose.

The ride was short. The doors slipped open, and he was looking into a conference room rich in woods and indirectly lit.

When he had stepped off, a cherry-wood panel rolled back into place, concealing all traces of the lift.

"Please be seated, Comandante," said a voice. It was coming from a lonely-looking speakerphone atop the long conference table.

Zorilla took the seat at the end.

"Comandante, I have been in touch with the Director. He sends his sincere regrets. The loss of Ultima Hora was an avoidable tragedy. They are the worst kind."

"Gracias, Señor Drake," said Zorilla in a thick voice.

"The organization commends your bravery under fire and your willingness to execute distasteful duties."

"I am a soldier of the Americas," Zorilla said simply.

"We know you are. And we know that you would never willingly betray the operation, as Dr. Revuelta has."

"Revuelta?"

"He was in touch by phone. The two who followed you here approached him. Revuelta gave you up under torture."

"Followed me here? What do you mean, followed me here?"

"Dr. Revuelta has offered his sincere apologies."

"I accept," Zorilla said quickly. "But by what do you mean, 'followed me here'? No one followed me here."

"The two unknown unfriendlies did," Drake's voice said flatly. The tonality of the speakerphone was perfect. There was no distortion. It was as if the man were in the room, but invisible.

"I do not believe it," Zorilla said bitingly.

A frosted wall panel glowed into life. On the oversized screen appeared corridors similar to the ones Comandante Zorilla had just traveled. The lean Anglo and the ancient Korean were visible, examining a line of trucks.

"Impossible," he hissed.

"But as you can see, true."

"What would you have me do?"

"The Director asks that you accept decruitment."

Zorilla recoiled, as if from the lash of a whip.

"But I am prepared to go on," he protested. "I have trained to lead the landing party."

"The operation has redundancy built into it at all levels."

"But I am a key component."

"None of us is key. Except the Director. We have to assume the unknown unfriendlies have superiors they have already reported to. Your name is known. But the trail ends here. No one leaves. Therefore there are no further leads."

"But—"

"Comandante, the future of the operation, not to mention the fate of your native land, hangs in the balance. I ask that you reflect on the situation, and your operational responsibilities. You have your orders."

"*Sí,*" said Comandante Leopoldo Zorilla, unbuttoning the blouse pocket of his insignia-less uniform and extracting a pack of chewing gum.

His eyes on the screen as the camera tracked the two strange men, he mechanically slid off the paper wrapper and peeled the foil from the gum. Ever the military man, he took the refuse and with the remaining pack replaced them in his blouse pocket, which he rebuttoned.

Then, he put the stick into his mouth and began to chew.

He was still watching the screen when his eyes rolled back in his head and he keeled over.

After a few minutes, the cherry-wood panel slid open and two uniformed soldiers stepped out. They checked the body for signs of life and, finding none, went to a blank wall.

A magnetic keycard caused a chutelike drawer to drop down.

A faint howling came from far below.

Comandante Leopoldo Zorilla's still warm body went feet-first into this. The drawer closed on his thick black hair, and the soldiers disappeared into the elevator.

After a moment the image of the two figures on the screen winked out and the room was still, except for the quiet hum of the air conditioner.

14

The great door dropped, and a locking latch as big as a nautical anchor rolled up out of the poured concrete floor and secured the guillotine of steel.

"This," Remo said uneasily, "reminds me of one of those underground nuclear command centers."

The Master of Sinanju looked about the space before them. It was a parking area. There were cars, vans, a few forklifts, and a pair of golf cart-like utility vehicles.

Some of the vehicles sported insignia. Curious, Remo went to one and examined it.

It consisted of a white circle encompassing three black disks. A large bottom circle topped by side-by-side smaller duplicates. All three disks overlapped.

"Looks familiar," Remo muttered. "But I can't place it."

"I, too, have seen this arcane symbol."

"Where?"

The Master of Sinanju stroked his smoky tendril of a beard. His eyes narrowed. "I do not know. Perhaps it is the symbol of some cabalistic secret society."

"Could be," said Remo, looking around. He tested the back of one of the vans. It came open.

"Hey, Chiun! Check this out!"

The Master of Sinanju came around to the back.

The entire van was stacked with cloth-covered poles, like cordwood. Remo pulled one from the top of the stack.

A corner of a red cloth unraveled. Remo gave the

pole a crack and unfurled a red flag, on which the three-black-circles-in-a-white-circle symbol swam.

"It's some kind of national flag," Remo said.

Chiun made a face. "I know of no such nation."

"Maybe it's supposed to be the flag of the new Cuba," Remo mused. "The three circles must stand for something. Either that, or the Neo-Nazis are into circles these days."

"Hark," Chiun said suddenly.

"Hark?"

"I hear something."

"Oh." Remo tossed the flag away and went to one of the rubber-tired open carts, saying, "Come on."

Remo found a key in the ignition. The head was shaped in the three-circle style. He turned it and an electric motor caught.

Remo sent the car around in a circle as the Master of Sinanju leapt aboard.

"Why walk when we can ride?" Remo said.

"Hear hear," said Chiun.

There was only one exit from the tunnel, so Remo sent the cart humming into that.

They passed into a long service corridor filled with the monotonous thrum of air conditioning and other mechanical sounds.

"Big place," Remo said.

"Remo. What is an animator?"

"A guy who draws cartoons," Remo said, noticing a closed door with a sign that said: ANIMATORS' MESS.

"We know that can't be right," he grunted. "Must be a goofy code name. Military types love to play word games."

Just then a lavender cart scooted out of a side passage and turned in their direction. It was driven by a soldier in a white jumpsuit and helmet. Another soldier sat blank-faced behind him. They looked like identical twins going to some sort of military First Communion.

Remo steered over to the left and said, "Signal a right, will you, Little Father?"

"Gladly," said Chiun, as Remo pressed the accelerator to the rubber floorboards.

The two carts barreled toward one another in a quiet game of chicken.

The other car swerved first. It went right, because there was no way to go left without slamming into the wall.

As they passed, the Master of Sinanju jutted out a bony arm and decapitated the soldier next to the driver.

The driver lost control when the person seated beside him became an organic red fountain that gushed hot liquid into his face.

The cart went nose-first into a wall and turned over, pinning the driver.

Remo took the left-hand tunnel, saying, "Nice job."

"Director, we have a problem," said Captain Maus.

"Solve it," said the Director, making the face on the computer screen revolve on an imaginary axis. His signature revolved with it, became alternately readable, a thin stitching of electronics and reversed. He frowned.

"How do you get this thing to freeze the signature?"

"Director, the unknowns have just decapitated a soldier."

The Director turned and looked up. The screen showed the overturned utility vehicle and the quivering mess that had been the guard.

The Director sniffed, "I've seen worse," and returned to his play. If this operation was to succeed, these snot-noses would have to learn to solve the little problems for themselves.

As the tunnel walls whipped by, Remo Williams was saying, "I figure this for a military installation, probably funded by ultra-right-wing Cubans out to topple Fidel. There's probably an orange grove or something over our heads. It's the perfect cover."

"I do not understand this 'wing' thing," Chiun complained.

"Our ultra left wing is the same as Cuba's ultra right wing."

"Thank you for enlightening me. Not."

Remo shrugged.

"All we need is to find the big cheese, wring some truth out of him, and contact Smith," he said. "Smith will tell us if we take down this place or leave it to the Marines."

They passed side tunnels every few yards. Brief glimpses showed white-uniformed soldiers pushing white-handled push brooms.

"Whoever runs this place must have a mania for cleanliness," Remo said.

"There is nothing wrong with that," Chiun sniffed.

"You'd think, since they know we're here, they'd have the place on alert. But I don't see any signs of panic."

"The answer to that conundrum is obvious."

"Yeah? Explain it to an ex-Marine then."

"The overlord of this vault does not yet know he has allowed Sinanju into his lair."

The way was suddenly blocked by two rows of white-uniformed soldiers.

"But he's about to find out," Remo muttered, bringing the utility vehicle to a slow stop.

"Halt, please," ordered a soldier.

Remo lifted empty hands off the steering wheel. "Too late. We already did. Next order?"

"Dismount, please."

"We under arrest, or just prisoners?"

Rifle safeties latched off.

"You will please dismount instantly."

"Ride's over, Little Father," said Remo, stepping off the truck.

The Master of Sinanju stepped away from the vehicle as well.

They were surrounded at riflepoint.

"Last guys who did that to us ended up with their

trigger fingers in splints," Remo offered in the way of friendly information.

"Place your hands atop your heads, please."

"Since you're all so polite I guess we can't say no, can we Little Father?"

"We will allow them to keep their fingers," Chiun said thinly. "For now."

They placed their hands atop their heads. Remo took a moment to scrutinize the faces surrounding them. The men all had a fresh, well-scrubbed look, like Boy Scouts coming into early manhood. The weapons at their shoulders were American-made Colt AR-15s. Purchasable at many sporting-goods stores. There was no hint of ethnicity in any of the faces. In fact, they looked corn-fed, most of them.

Remo frowned. More and more this was looking like a U.S. military operation. But who the hell was running it, and why?

Remo decided there was only one way to find out.

"Take us to your leader," he said, straight-faced.

The circle broke, and half the soldiers formed up behind them. The others formed an honor guard of sorts.

"March, please," the leader requested.

They marched.

"Why are they so polite?" Chiun wanted to know.

Remo shrugged as best he could. "Search me."

"No talking in the ranks, please."

"We are not of your ranks," Chiun sniffed.

"No talking, please. Thank you."

Remo and Chiun exchanged glances.

They were walked through a labyrinth of spotless tunnels. White-coveralled soldiers swabbed the pastel walls with ammonia-scented rags. Others dusted the exposed ductwork with white-enameled foxtail brooms.

Remo started whistling "Whistle While You Work" to break the silence, and the captain's head suddenly jerked around. For the first time, an expression crossed his set features.

"What's the problem, pal?" Remo asked. "You don't like my taste in music?"

The man said a tight-lipped nothing, but he picked up his pace. Consequently they all picked up their pace.

"These guys are too perfect to be U.S. military," Remo said, after some thought.

This time, the captain hissed for silence.

"Struck a nerve," Remo said.

The captain whirled, his corn-fed face white and tight. It almost matched his coverall uniform.

"I have instructions to shoot one of you to ensure the cooperation of the other."

Remo smiled tightly, "You forgot to say 'please.' "

"Separate them!" the captain snapped.

The Master of Sinanju shook his black silk sleeves off his pipe-stem forearms. He folded them resolutely, saying, "I will not be moved."

Remo folded his arms as well. "That goes double for me. I'm tired of all this pussyfooting."

"Shoot the old man."

Remo got between the captain and the Master of Sinanju and said in a low tone. "You forgot to say 'May I?' "

"Fi-*yeeii*!"

The captain's order had been interrupted by a sensation like a tightening vise in the specific area of his testicles. He looked down to see that the skinny man had grabbed his crotch with one hand. The old one now took him by the throat.

While he was still screaming, the captain went ballistic.

Had he not been wearing his helmet, his head would have been split open against the overhead conduit pipe. It was as large as a sewer main, and as heavy.

The helmet protected the top of his skull from being caved in. It punctured the pipe and hung there, forming a solid cup that collected the compressed remnants of his pulped head.

The other soldiers looked up at the dangling white boots, to the skinny guy with the thick wrists, and remembered the captain's unfinished final order.

They trained their weapons on the old Asian. Fingers squeezed triggers.

Remo moved among the soldiers. He came in low, bent at the waist, and slammed the AR-15 muzzles ceilingward, like a handball player deflecting a rebounding ball.

Bullets erupted straight up, riddling the pipe and making the limp body of their captain jerk and jitter and string blood from points along his torso.

The overhead pipe suddenly cracked apart with a roar and a section crashed down, spewing assorted paper trash, soft-drink cans, used camera-film boxes, and colorful napkins. All propelled by a hurricane of air.

Remo and Chiun retreated as the soldiers were swiftly inundated.

"What the hell is going on?" Remo shouted over the din.

"I do not know."

"What the heck is that thing?" Remo said, retreating from the spreading sea of refuse.

From the relative safety of several yards down the corridor, Remo and Chiun watched as the soldiers, weapons forgotten, tried to wade from the snowstorm of debris. They were not fast enough. The stuff covered them faster than they could wade. They slogged waist-deep, then shoulder-deep, and then, like men drowning in some frothy white water, their helmeted heads were soon covered.

Somewhere someone must have thrown a switch, because with a silence that made their ears ring, the whooshing roar ceased and all was quiet.

A final paper cup tumbled out of the fractured ceramic pipe, and all was still.

Remo and Chiun walked around the mound of trash, their faces bemused.

"They must have a whole division under arms, from the look of all these food containers," Remo pointed out.

The Master of Sinanju noticed a corner of the mound shift. The gleam of a white helmet appeared.

With the heel of his hand, he gave it a tap. The emerging helmet rang like an old bell, and fell silent.

Then the Klaxons started.

Remo looked up and down the gleaming corridor worriedly. "Uh-oh. Now we did it."

"Perhaps this might be the correct time to escape, my son," Chiun pointed out, his bearded chin indicating the severed pipe.

"Just a sec."

Remo went to a wall-mounted video surveillance camera and with an extended forefinger shattered the lens, blinding it.

"No sense leaving a trail," he said over the Klaxon howl.

Remo got under the ruptured pipe and took hold of its cracked maw. He pulled himself up. The Master of Sinanju, being somewhat shorter, leaped high, fading into the maw like a spider slipping into a web hole.

Crouched low, they moved along the pipe. It was dark and surprisingly clean, in spite of being a conduit for trash and food refuse. The inner walls were teflon-slick.

The way was dark, but their visual purple compensated for the lack of illumination.

At a bend in the tunnel they came to a clump of trash.

Remo cleared it with distaste on his hard features.

They continued on.

They found the body of Comandante Leopoldo Zorilla wedged in a catch basin, where the pipe angled up into a sheer vertical well.

"Guess he was too heavy to make the turn," Remo said, checking the body's carotid artery and finding no pulse.

The body of Zorilla had landed in a kind of tangled ball of outflung limbs. They dragged him free and laid him out. There were no obvious marks or wounds. The man's eyes were wide, and already turning to dull glass. Remo noticed that his mouth was open and there was something in it.

He pried the jaws apart and saw the pink wad crushed against his wisdom teeth.

"Gum," he said, dismissing it without a second thought.

Remo went through the man's pockets and found a pack of gum in the blouse pocket. He barely glanced at it before tossing it aside. There was an INS green card, and a plastic syringe filled with liquid. The needle was stoppered. That was all.

"Must have been a drug addict," Remo said, dropping the needle.

"Or a gum fiend," sniffed the Master of Sinanju, retrieving it. He tossed the instrument aside after examining it curiously.

Remo straightened. "Well, they wasted him without wasting any time. Serves him right, too. Murdering his own men like that."

The Master of Sinanju moved to the point under the vertical length of pipe. His wise old face frowned tightly.

"It is time to see what lies above," he said firmly.

"Want me to go first?" Remo offered.

"No," said Chiun, making a fist like a block of old bone and punching a dent at the level of his head. He reached up and made another off to one side.

Then, leaping high so that one sandaled toe caught the lowermost dent and the other the next one up, the Master of Sinanju quickly created a ladder of indentations, climbing as he went.

Remo followed. He was halfway up when he heard a metallic screech.

Past his head came a ball of twisted steel.

"What was that?" he called up.

"An inconvenient propeller."

"Must be part of a pneumatic system," Remo said, continuing on. Unlike Chiun, Remo lacked the long fingernails of the traditional Sinanju master. He had to knock deeper holes here and there.

Near the top, Chiun's voice came, high and squeaky.

"Remo! Remo!"

"Yeah?"

"I know where we are!"

"Where?"

"Home! We are home!"

"Huh?"

"Director, I have bad news."

"What is it now?" demanded the petulant, chilly voice.

"The two unfriendlies are topside."

The Director looked at his famous smiling watch. "We're two hours from opening. That should be enough time to erase them from the drawing board."

"Instructions?"

"Send the Wolf Pack after them."

"At once, Director."

"And have a mop-up team on standby to take care of the damned blood. I want topside to sparkle. And turn up the heat. I'm freezing in here."

"Yes, Director."

"Wolf Pack, you are go for the hunt."

Warily, Remo emerged from the disposal pipe, not knowing what to expect.

A section of the pipe, an elbow, had been knocked aside by the Master of Sinanju. Remo found himself staring into another horizontal stretch.

He walked around it and saw that he was in a semi-dark concrete bunker, and that the final length of pipe was jutting from a giant piece of machinery studded with air-compressors.

"I was right." he said. "This is a giant pneumatic tube. That means it's like a vacuum in reverse."

Then he noticed the Master of Sinanju standing at a window, staring out with a pleased expression on his face. Chiun was standing at his full height now, his chin uptilted slightly, like an emperor surveying his domain.

"This doesn't look like any home I've ever seen," Remo said, approaching the window.

The Master of Sinanju stepped aside. "Open your benighted eyes to their fullest then," he said proudly.

Remo peered out the window. The expression on his face was an odd mixture of curiosity and bafflement.

He saw in the near distance the tessellated ramparts and spindly towers of a castle.

The curiosity drained from his face as the bafflement took over. His mouth dropped open. His deep-set eyes seemed to crawl out of their enshadowed orbits. He blinked. And blinked again.

No matter what he did, the castle was still there.

"What the hell?"

"Is is not magnificent?" Chiun asked, beaming.

"Huh?" Remo gulped.

"That is where we will live," added Chiun. He clapped happy hands together. "It is what I have always wanted."

"No doubt there," Remo growled, "but what is it?"

Chiun's tiny mouth went round. "You do not recognize this place?" he squeaked. "You, a child of this generous nation?"

"It looks familiar, sure," Remo admitted. "But I can't place it. I was expecting an orange grove."

"Come. Perhaps this wondrous place which Harold the Munificent has granted to the House of Sinanju contains such things."

The Master of Sinanju floated to a closed door.

Remo followed. "Smith gave you this?" he asked, small-voiced.

"It was my final demand, and he agreed to meet it."

Remo Williams was so befuddled by the disorienting experience of escaping an underground military installation, only to find above it a place Chiun called home, that he couldn't think of any comeback. He let his brain shift into neutral and went with the flow.

Chiun opened the door, and the building flooded with too-bright sunlight. They passed through and out into an immaculately landscaped fairyland that Remo instantly recognized.

"Oh my God!" he said.

Chiun drew in a long breath. "Smell, Remo. Orange blossoms." He beamed. "Here, all wishes come true."

"This is Beasley World!" Remo said, aghast.

"Yes," said Chiun happily.

"Beasley World. *The* Beasley World."

"Yes!"

"Somebody built a secret military installation under Beasley World!" Remo said, his voice incredulous.

"A minor annoyance which we will soon remedy," Chiun said.

Remo looked around.

The summit of Star Mountain reared up in the early-morning sun, the shadows of fast-moving clouds dappling it.

They were standing near an artificial pool. It appeared to be empty. At the far end of a long white-cobbled walk, past colorful children's rides, loomed Sorcerer's Castle, emblem of "the Enchanted Village," as Beasley World—the greatest theme park in the universe—was sometimes called.

"This is a dream," Remo muttered.

"A wonderful dream," Chiun said.

"A bad dream," Remo said. "A nightmare."

Chiun frowned. "What is wrong?"

"We can't live here. It's wide open!"

"The sun will be good for you, Remo. You look pale." The Master of Sinanju began to walk, his merry hazel eyes darting this way and that, his perfect white teeth dazzling in his tiny mouth.

Remo followed. "No, I mean this is a public place. Millions of people come through the gate every year."

Chiun shrugged unconcernedly. "I have left them Beasleyland. They may go there instead."

Remo's incredulous eyes took in an Alice-in-Wonderland panorama that was familiar to children throughout the entire world.

"I can't believe Smith gave this place to you."

"Why not? I deserve it—even if you do not."

"That's not what I mean, and you know it. It isn't Smith's to give. One of the biggest corporations in the world owns all this. And from what I hear their lawyers are real piranha."

"Let them plotz," Chiun said disdainfully.

Remo looked back. The building they had just left was some kind of disguised waste-disposal collection center. The walls were covered with open-mouthed cartoon faces. The mouths were round holes, and beside one of them was a pair of covered plastic barrels. The covers were adorned with puppet heads.

"That pipe we came through was part of the trash-disposal system for this place," Remo decided aloud.

"It is very efficient," Chiun agreed. "I hereby make you Lord High Sanitation Engineer of Assassin's World."

"*Assassin's* World?"

"The old name needs updating."

"You weren't listening to what I said," Remo said tightly.

"What else is new?" Chiun returned carelessly.

"That means the military guys are in cahoots with the Beasley Company."

Chiun turned, his mouth going prim. "Remo! Such blasphemy! Was this man Beasley not one of your childhood heroes?"

"Sure. What does that have to do with anything?"

"Uncle Sam Beasley would never go against the wishes of Emperor Smith."

"He never heard of Smith. Besides, he's dead."

"Nonsense."

"He died back in the sixties. Everybody knows that."

"Humph," sniffed Chiun, resuming his promenade. "If this is so, then who draws the wonderful cartoons bearing his illustrious name?"

"A bunch of artists, that's who. Uncle Sam never drew the cartoons himself."

"Slanderer! Defamer of greatness!"

Remo stopped, blinked, and said in a very small voice, "Uncle Sam . . ."

"Come, Remo. We must find Monongahela Mouse. I will accept the keys to the Enchanted Village from him personally. No lesser functionary will do."

"Chiun!" Remo croaked.

The Master of Sinanju stopped, turned, his eyes narrowing.

"What is wrong with you, Remo? This is the culmination of my years of hardship in your ugly country. This is a moment about which the future children of Sinanju yet unborn will sing. For no Master of Sinanju was ever bequeathed a kingdom as wondrous as this one."

"Chiun, listen! I just said the name 'Uncle Sam.' Uncle Sam *Beasley*—the founder of Beasleyland and Beasley World."

"You did," Chiun allowed.

"The creator of Monongahela Mouse, Screwball Squirrel, and Dingbat Duck."

"His reknown has reached even Sinanju," Chiun said. "Although he is a mere white artist, his greatness is unsurpassed."

Remo said, "Everybody from the captured Cubans to Zorilla swore Uncle Sam was behind the operation. Remember?"

Chiun's eyes squeezed to walnut slits.

"Not the Washington Uncle Sam, but *Uncle Sam Beasley*! This is a Beasley Corporation operation!"

"I will believe this only from the lips of Uncle Sam himself," Chiun said firmly. "Come, the famous rodent can wait. We must speak with Uncle Sam himself."

In a swirl of black silken skirts, the Master of Sinanju flounced off toward the towers that Remo had first seen what seemed like another lifetime ago, as a wide-eyed child watching a cheap black-and-white picture tube back at Saint Theresa's Orphanage.

There was a lump rising in his throat.

Ronald Phipps had grown up on Sam Beasley.

Every Sunday night, he had watched *The Marvelous Realm of Sam Beasley* in his fire-engine-red Dr. Denton's. He had collected *Sam Beasley Comics and Cartoons.* Colored in *Mongo Mouse* and *Screwball Squirrel* coloring books, with Sam Beasley-brand crayons. If it bore the flourishing signature of Uncle Sam Beasley, Ronald Phipps had collected it.

The first time he had visited Beasley World was akin to a religious experience. He was nine. By the age of eleven he had been to Beasleyland and Beasley World what seemed a million times. He liked Beasley World better. It was bigger and—more to the point—

he could go more often. Ron Phipps lived just outside of Furioso, Florida, Vacation Center of the Galaxy, site of Sam Beasley World.

When he reached high school age and other boys were discovering cars and beer and girls, Ron Phipps spent his weekends at Sam Beasley World.

After high school, he horrified his parents by announcing that he wasn't going to Yale after all. He had applied to a much more exclusive institution.

"I'm going to be a greeter at Sam Beasley World," he announced proudly.

His father glared. His mother broke down. His younger sister asked, "Does that mean you can get me in for free?"

Ultimately, his disappointed parents had not stood in his way. They thought it was just a phase. It would pass. And Yale would still be there next year.

They were wrong. The day he first donned the furry costume and oversized lop-eared head of Wacky Wolf, Ron knew he had found his true calling. But being a greeter, he discovered, was not quite as much fun as being a greetee.

There were rules, and violators could be summarily fired. One could never appear in public out of costume. Or with one's character head removed. One mustn't speak. One must be unfailingly polite and kind.

Once a greeter dressed as Screwball Squirrel had come upon a little girl who had fallen into the Phantom Lagoon. As her parents watched helplessly, the little girl splashed and cried piteously for rescue.

The Screwball Squirrel greeter had doffed his bucktoothed head and plunged in. He pulled the girl to safety and after applying mouth-to-mouth, brought her around.

The crowd had applauded the man.

The CEO had hauled him onto the carpet within the hour.

As Phipps later heard it, the CEO opened up the confrontation with a curt, "You're fired!"

"But sir, I saved a little girl from drowning."

"And removed your squirrel head. That wasn't necessary."

"I had to resuscitate!"

"You could have done it through the mask, or let the parents do their own CPR. You stepped out of character, and worse, you deprived the organization of a wonderful public relations bonanza."

"Sir?"

"A ton of tourists took photos of you giving mouth-to-mouth. Had you kept your head on your shoulders, we could have had that photo run in everything from *People* to *Isvestia,* furthering the glorious Beasley legend."

"But—"

"We're selling fantasy here, and you popped the bubble! Can you imagine that little girl's trauma when you took your Screwball Squirrel head off?"

"She was unconscious!"

"Turn in your tail and pick up your last check."

When Ron Phipps heard the story from the tearful greeter that very same day, he wondered aloud, "What would Uncle Sam have said if he could have seen it?"

"The same thing the CEO did," the greeter overseer said. " 'You're fired.' Keep that in mind, Phipps."

Ronald Phipps did. He never, never wanted *not* to be a part of Sam Beasley World. So when the demands on him increased, he made sure he was equal to them. If the organization said to dump that old lady out of a Beasley-owned wheelchair, he did so. If a fellow worker grumbled about working in "Mouseschwitz," he turned him in. None of it was what Ronald Phipps had thought Beasley World stood for, but orders were orders.

But this . . .

"You all know how to use these things," the security overseer was saying, in the underground dressing rooms where all the cartoon costumes were stored.

Phipps accepted the short-barreled machine pistol, with its oversized trigger guard so he could slip his padded wolf's-paw fingers inside. The weapon felt enormously heavy.

The overseer went on.

"We always knew that terrorists would one day try to penetrate Sam Beasley World, symbol of all that is America. You've trained for this day. You're prepared for this day. Now that day is here."

Ron Phipps looked around, and saw a disturbing sight. Screwball Squirrel was brandishing an Ingram. Mother Goose had a pump-action shotgun. Everyone had known about the potential Cuban threat, but it was incredible that Beasley World actually had been targeted. The overseer said Cuban terrorists had already penetrated the park.

"Rule number one is 'Aim at your target and hit what you aim at.' " reminded the overseer.

"Rule number two is 'Try not to damage the attractions,' " he added. "There are only two terrorists. This should be a walk in the Haunted Grove, so to speak."

There came nervous laughter from a dozen happy heads, as they marched single-file to the freight elevator that would take them topside to their rendezvous with destiny.

Remo followed the Master of Sinanju through Sam Beasley World, a dull, stricken look on his face.

"This isn't happening," he said under his breath.

Then Chiun's squeaky voice called out, "Look, Remo! Wacky Wolf! Let us ask the befuddled canine the way."

Remo looked up. The Master of Sinanju had veered off toward Horrible House, a Louisiana Gothic mansion whose shuttered windows held ghoulish faces.

"Hold up, Chiun. I don't think we should take anything for granted here."

"Yoo-hoo, Wolfie!" called Chiun.

And to Remo's horror, the giant form of Wacky Wolf dropped to one knee and brought up the muzzle of an Ingram submachine gun.

The weapon blatted nasty sound and a tongue of fire.

The Master of Sinanju leaped high in the air, over the scream of bullets that tore past Remo's dipping shoulder and perforated a child-size Ferris wheel. The creaking seats rocked and swayed, some dangling, damaged.

The Master of Sinanju landed atop the Wolf's funny hat. The head jammed down with a dull, mortal crack, and the rest of the creature folded to the immaculate cobblestones.

Chiun stepped off the corpse, frowning.

"Obviously some of the inhabitants have not been informed that Sinanju now rules their happy domain," he sniffed.

Remo stopped to lift off the absurd wolf's head. The face revealed was unexceptional. Remo replaced it, sick. The guy looked barely twenty.

"These guys are supposed to be *greeters*," he said, aghast. "What are they doing toting automatic weapons?"

"Uncle Sam can explain this to us," Chiun said firmly.

"Listen!" Remo said sharply.

And all around them, the cool air carried furtive sounds. Pounding heartbeats. The sip and whistle of people breathing carefully through their mouths. Padding feet. Floppy, padding feet.

"Don't look now," Remo said, "but the bears are coming out of hibernation."

In the long shadows of the rising sun they spied peering, semi-human faces. Flat, too-round eyes seemed to regard them. Unreasonably large paws reached around gingerbread corners. Or clutched assorted weaponry.

"What say we split up?" Remo suggested. "Maybe get to whoever's giving the orders faster?"

"Let no harm come to Mongo Mouse, Remo," Chiun admonished.

"What if he's the ringleader?"

"Take him prisoner. One as famous as he will surely fetch a bountiful ransom."

"Gotcha," said Remo, thinking that he *couldn't* hurt Mongo Mouse, no matter what. Once he had been the round-eared rodent's biggest fan.

They went in opposite directions.

17

"Director, they're splitting up."

"Damn!"

"And Wacky Wolf is down."

"Process his mangy carcass according to park guidelines. And burn his timecard. He did not show up for work today."

"Yes, sir."

The Director turned in his chair. The overhead screens were cutting from monitor to monitor, scanning for the intruders.

The Director heaved himself out of his chair and clumped over to Captain Maus's station.

"Relinquish your chair," he snapped. "I'm directing this damned production from now on."

"Yes, Director."

The Director clumped over and eased himself into the warm chair, taking care with his sterling-silver left leg. His hands went to the control-button array. He began calling up cameras.

It was a frustrating search. The greeters stood out like marshmallows in a coal bin. The two intruders might as well have been invisible.

Once, the Director caught a glimpse of a fugitive rag of black slipping behind a polyurethane candy cane. When he called up a different angle, there was no sign of the owner of the ebony garment.

But Screwball Squirrel lay on his back, impaled by his own umbrella.

"Damn! The Squirrel is down, too."

"I assure you we have the two unknowns outnumbered," Maus said from his station.

The Director worked his cameras impatiently. There was Dingbat Duck, his pride and joy, crouching at the edge of the Phantom Lagoon, his beady crossed eyes alert.

"The hell!" he snarled suddenly.

"What is it, sir?"

"Will you look at that idiot quacker! You can see the seam at his neck. Pull him out of it. I want my people looking like their inspirations, damn it!"

"At once, sir."

Captain Maus went to a console and spoke into a microphone mounted on a flexible steel stalk.

"Overseer. Withdraw the duck. He's out of character. Repeat: The duck is out of character."

The Director moved on, knowing his orders would be carried out to the letter. It was like the Jesuits used to say: "Give me a boy at seven, and I will show you the man."

It was his second favorite saying.

The first was: "The Mouse means revenue. Shield the Mouse, and you protect the revenue."

A roving camera mounted near the Tom Thumb Pavilion happened to pick up the top of someone's head. The hair was brown and human.

"Got one!" he exulted.

As if the owner of the hair had somehow heard him remotely, the brown-haired head stopped, turned, and looked up. And the deadest eyes the Director had ever seen were looking directly at him.

"He's by the Tom Thumb Pavilion," he snapped to Maus.

"Acknowledged." Maus began issuing orders into the mike.

And on the screen, the owner of the dead eyes lifted two splayed fingers and poked them in the Director's direction.

The screen spiderwebbed and went dark.

"Damn!" spat the Director, punching up another camera.

"Sir. The overseer reports the duck is down."

"Not Dingy?"

"Afraid so, sir. That seam? When the overseer went to check, the quacker was in a crouching position and refused to respond to vocal commands. He pulled the Duck's head off to reprimand him."

"And?"

"Nothing but a stump where the neck ended."

"That's it! We're changing tactics. Sweatbox them!"

"Yes, sir!"

"We're at Threatcon Gumpy. Go to Threatcon Spooky. I want the entire park on a military footing. All pavilions and attractions convert to combat readiness. Now!"

"Executing."

"See if you can get the fruity-looking guy with the brown hair into the Tom Thumb Pavilion."

"I'll instruct the greeters to flush him in that direction."

"Flush, my pink ass! *Lure* them in. I want them dead and disposed of. We open to the public in two hours and we have a duck head unaccounted for. What if some snot-nosed brat picks it up? The lawsuits will go on into the next century."

"At once, Director."

It was too easy.

Remo slipped between the places where the skulking greeters lurked. He didn't want to kill any, but he was forced to ace the squirrel and the duck. It left a bitter taste in his mouth.

Near the Tom Thumb Pavilion, he paused. A faint whir brought his head up alertly.

Remo turned. Through a tiny window, he sensed an electrical hum. Another concealed camera. The park was riddled with them.

He used two stiffened fingers to blind this one and then moved on.

Then the patterns changed.

Up until now, Remo had been aware of every

nearby stalker. Their hot breaths and clumsy walks gave their positions away.

Now, they retreated. Flat, wide eyes withdrew from windows.

Something was going on. Moving low, Remo floated down to Phantom Lagoon, where piles of papier-mâché rocks hugged the artificial shore.

He slipped onto the landward side and went up the rocks.

Remo lay flat on the sun-warmed summit, looking around. The position kept him out of sight, and also distributed his body weight so that the rocks wouldn't buckle beneath him.

Beasley World looked peaceful in the morning sun. Here and there a 'toon edged around a corner, his machine pistol poked forward incongruously. There was no sign of Chiun. Which actually was a good sign.

Behind him, he heard a warning gurgle.

Remo looked over his shoulder. Just in time.

Breaking the stillness of Phantom Lagoon was a baroque purple submarine, its narwhal-nosed bow pointed in his direction.

"Uh-oh," Remo muttered, remembering the movie the attraction was modeled after.

The water bubbled and boiled—and something shot out of the sub's unicorn nose. It arrowed toward Remo's flimsy perch.

Remo bounced to his feet and kept going. He executed a slow, languorous midair backflip that took him backward, over the churning torpedo.

Remo dropped behind the armored safety of the sub's conning tower as the torpedo struck the fake rocks.

The explosion was muffled. Papier-mâché flew in fiery rags, mixed with pebble shrapnel.

When the echoes had ceased reverberating, Remo stood up to look. There was a smoking pit where the "rocks" had been.

Then Remo began peeling plates off the sub's colorful hull. It was like peeling a banana with an onion skin. Every layer revealed another. Muttering, "The hell with it," he drove his fist into a point along the waterline, making a hole.

Water rushed in, and Remo rode the sub to the shallow bottom. An escape hatch blew in a boil of bubbles, and a frogman swam out. Not a man in a wet suit, but one in a rubber frog skin. Eyes goggling, he kicked his webbed feet toward the surface.

Remo caught him by the back of his green neck and held him just under the surface, until his flippers stopped kicking and the last air bubble struggled from his gasping mouth.

Then Remo let his natural buoyancy bring him back to the surface.

Remo popped up and found himself face-to-snout with a gray polyester aardvark, standing on the shore.

He didn't recognize the aardvark. There had been a lot of Beasley cartoons produced since Remo was a boy, and over the years he'd lost track.

Consequently he didn't know what to call the aardvark.

So he said, "Don't make a mistake, pal."

The aardvark didn't seem to take the advice to heart. He lowered the muzzle of his short-barreled machine pistol in the direction of Remo's dripping head.

He didn't get to use it.

Remo shot out of the water like a porpoise. He went up and, with his ankles still submerged, suddenly changed direction, veering toward his assailant. He left a modest wake and landed upright on shore, where he took possession of the pistol by yanking it from its owner's furry grasp.

The aardvark's paw came away with the weapon, trigger finger caught in the ringlike trigger guard.

"Betcha can't do this, even in cartoons," Remo said, squeezing the weapon in his steel-hard fingers. They found weak points in the metal. The weapon began shedding parts amid metallic squeals of complaint.

The aardvark cried "Tarim!" in a funny voice and turned tail. Literally.

Remo started after him.

He was easy to follow, for he waddled as he ran. Remo decided to follow him back to his hole—or wherever it was aardvarks lived. *Someone* had to be in charge of this insanity.

The gray 'toon bobbled and slipped among the plastic palms, looking back often as he worked his way to the Tom Thumb Pavilion. His eyes, unreal as they were, looked positively frightened.

At the pavilion entrance he turned one last time, lingered, and, when he saw Remo coming in his direction, ducked in.

"Looks like a trap," Remo muttered. "Okay," he said, shrugging. "So it's a trap."

The Master of Sinanju paused to ask directions.

"Excuse me," he inquired, of the figure standing before an old-fashioned outdoor clock resembling a numerically calibrated all-day sucker. "I seek the illustrious Mongo Mouse."

The figure, its clear eyes very bright in its homely, bearded face, ignored the Master of Sinanju.

The Master of Sinanju tugged at its sleeve.

"I said, I seek the illustrious—"

Suddenly the figure jerked to life. Only then did the Master of Sinanju recognize it as one of the previous rulers of this odd nation. He wore the royal crown of that era, known as the "stovepipe hat."

Then the figure of Abraham Lincoln spat out a croaky, *"Fuck you,"* and went stiff once more.

Insulted, the Master of Sinanju narrowed his hazel eyes.

His acute hearing picked up no sounds of human biology. So he stamped the simulacrum's feet into shattered piles and stepped away as it fell on its gaunt face and shattered.

He walked on.

Here was wonder at every step, Chiun thought. Here was an abode worthy of the Master of Sinanju. With a critical eye, he made a mental inventory of the ugly structures that would have to be razed. Future World would be the first to go. But the monorail might be retained. For his personal use only. Remo could drive.

Off to one side stood the Haunted Grove, where the trees had faces. Curious, he moved toward it.

A hulking shape loomed out of the plastic copse.

It was Hunny Bear, his porkpie hat askew.

"Hail, O bashful bruin," cried the Master of Sinanju in greeting.

The bear had a crockery honey jar under one arm, and he lifted it over his head with both hands. He heaved it at the Master of Sinanju.

The spot where the old Korean had been standing was cobbled in plastic. The jar broke, and splashed a hissing, spitting white liquid onto that exact spot. The white paint browned and bubbled like a witch's cauldron. But there was no one there anymore.

The bear stared at the phenomenon, long jaw agape. He was still staring when the angry form of the Master of Sinanju came out from behind a growling tree and relieved him of his heads.

Both of them.

The goofy bear head sailed up and then returned, a falling spacecraft separating into two reentry vehicles: Bear and not bear.

Both heads struck the ground at the same time. The human one went *splat*.

The Master of Sinanju looked about him.

Beyond the Haunted Woods, perched on a low sawgrass hill, loomed Horrible House, its jack-o'-lantern shutters hanging askew. And waving to him from one of the windows was no less than Monongahela Mouse himself, his lollipop ears alert.

"Ah," said Chiun. "The famous mouse will point the way, for he is always helpful and kind."

"Director, the tall one has entered the Tom Thumb Pavilion."

"Hah! Did you see that? I spooked the little gook. I made Lincoln say 'Fuck you' right in his face. Remind me to have a fart function installed in the Presidential Pavilion. Not just sound, but smell too. I want every Chief Executive, with his own distinctive and identifiable gas!"

"Director, shall I load the alternate program?"

"Huh? What? Oh, right. Switch over."

"Switching over."

> *"It's a life of wonder,*
> *"A life of gloom,*
> *"We live a life of storms,*
> *"And a life that's doomed.*
> *"It's a short, short life, don't you know?"*

"That's not how the song goes," Remo muttered as he entered the Tom Thumb Pavilion.

It was dark, but there was enough light to see by. Remo ignored the cake-frosting trolley cars and walked the track.

On either side of him stood tiny scenes. Ballerinas. Fairy woods. A tiny ice pond with skaters. Eskimo. Tahitians. Bavarians. All nationalities were portrayed. It was a celebration of the diversity of life on the planet Earth.

And it didn't go with the music being piped in from hidden loudspeakers. At all.

> *"We have just one life*
> *"And one atmosphere,*
> *"A few brief breaths*
> *"And you're in your bier.*
> *"Because the grave is deep*
> *"And long is our sleep."*

"That is definitely *not* how the song goes," Remo repeated.

And then, as the maddening music swelled, the miniature scenes sprang to life.

> *"It's a short, short life, don't you know?"*

The ballerinas exploded.

> *"It's a short, short life, don't you know?"*

The ice skaters burst into flames.

"It's a short, short life, don't you know?"

And the Eskimo family opened their happy mouths
and began to emit a poisonously yellow smoke Remo
knew wasn't exactly a cure for lung cancer.

He started running, dodging, ducking, as the maddening refrain repeated itself over and over again until
he was tempted to throw himself into one of the death
traps just to get it out of his brain.

"It's a short, short life, don't you know?
"It's a short, short life, don't you know?
"It's a short, short life, don't you know?"

"I know! I know!" Remo yelled back, as he wove
his way through the deadly missiles.

The foyer of Horrible House was dark. Electric can-
dles cast a sickly yellow-green light.

Hands tucked into the sleeves of his night-black
kimono, the Master of Sinanju studied the room. This
was plainly the entrance to the manor. The front doors
had been opened for him, as if by unseen fingers. Yet
there were no other doors, and the front portals had
locked themselves after he had passed through them.

He lifted his voice. "Mongo? Mongo Mouse? Are
you home?"

And the walls began to sink into the floor.

The Master of Sinanju looked upward.

A great crystal chandelier was coming closer. The
cracked and cobwebbed ceiling loomed larger and
larger.

His eyes warned him that the ceiling was coming
down to crush him, but his inner senses told another
story.

The floor was moving upward, carrying him with it.

Either way, the promised result would be the same.
A crushing, ignominious death.

Chiun waited, face calm. The Master of Sinanju,
Dispenser of Awesome Death, prepared to face death
itself.

At the last possible moment, the ceiling split along its longitudinal axis and flew upward in two sections, taking the fixed chandelier with it.

The floor lifted the Master of Sinanju level with the second story of Horrible House, and he stepped off the settling platform.

He found himself in a place of death.

There was a coffin at one end of a funeral parlor. Around it, silently weeping mourners huddled, dabbing eyes with black handkerchiefs. All were turned away from him in their noble grief.

The Master of Sinanju cleared his throat out of respect for the dead.

"I am looking for the Mouse of the house," he said solemnly, "and have no wish to disturb your grief."

At the sound of his voice, all heads turned—to show exposed bone and flaming eyes. Toothsome jaws dropped. Ghoulish laughter echoed off the crepe-hung walls.

And the coffin lid creaked slowly upward, impelled by a rotted purple hand.

"You are all dead," Chiun hissed.

The laughter returned, booming.

"And therefore you mock life," he snapped. "I will dispense with you all, shades of the living."

Sweeping in, the Master of Sinanju struck out with his deadly nails. They flashed and slashed through necks, impaled glaring eyeballs, and sliced at solar plexuses. All to no avail. The shades of the dead were insubstantial. They could not be harmed.

Eyes wide, the Master of Sinanju hurried from the room of the dead, slamming the heavy ironwood door behind him.

The next room was absolutely dark. Only the mocking laughter from beyond the door disturbed its vibrations.

But within a moment, a green witch was sporting along the black-painted ceiling.

She was a crone of rags and lank hair, her hat a black cone. She rode her ratty broom in furious circles that disturbed none of the quiet vibrations of the room.

The Master of Sinanju watched as, like a trapped bat, she swooped and climbed. This was beyond understanding. But even a creature of other realms could make a mistake.

The bottom of one long swoop brought her to within striking range. Chiun uncoiled like a striking viper.

His feet took him up, where he paused for a heart-beat. Then, with the witch about to veer away. he unsnapped his coiled limbs and struck out in all directions at once.

The witch passed through him without harm to either of them and he dropped to his feet, discouraged.

"Look at him," the Director chortled. "He looks like he doesn't know whether to shit or go blind!"

"Director, the other one is successfully negotiating the Tom Thumb Pavilion."

"He won't make it. He can't."

"Take a look for yourself."

The Director turned in his seat. His dead left eye, behind its patch, tried to focus by reflex. He cursed.

And when his one good eye had focused on the overhead screen, he cursed again and kept on cursing.

For there, moving like a figure in some nervous silent film, was the fruity man in black. Puppets exploded around him, or breathed thin lances of flam-ing oil, yet he managed to avoid every one of them.

"Where's the damned bear?" he growled.

"Cowering," Maus reported.

"Get him out there! Have him gun down that son of a bitch before he can get out the exit door!"

"Yes, Director."

"In my day, people did a day's work for a day's pay."

The Director returned to his screen. The tiny Asian man was looking around in the dark room, his figure as seen through the night-vision camera a greenish dappling of pixels.

"Agile little bugger, isn't he?" he muttered, reaching for a switch. He reset the control computer for Fatal Cycle, adding, "I've had enough fun with that little chink."

The entire floor dropped away under the Master of Sinanju's black-dyed sandals.

There was nothing for him to grasp and no time to think, so he did what his trained body told him to. He relaxed.

Limbs loose, he landed lightly twenty feet below in a chamber of rude stone. High in the ceiling the floor trap clapped shut, and in the sudden darkness yellow-orange cat's eyes blinked on at points high atop the walls.

These illuminated the grilled drains at ankle level, which began to gush cold water, quickly covering the floor in converging currents.

The Master of Sinanju watched the waterline creep upward. He was not concerned. It was only water. If it filled the entire chamber, he would simply float to the ceiling, where the trapdoor would surrender to his awesome skill.

And so he waited.

"Look at him! It's like he hasn't got a nerve in his entire scrawny body!" the Director complained.

"Perhaps he's paralyzed by fear, sir."

"Well, I'm going to *unparalyze* him. Here come the snakes."

They were water moccasins, and they eeled out of the lifting grates and twitched into the water angrily, wedge-shaped heads attempting to orient themselves to the unfamiliar environment.

When their eyes fell upon the Master of Sinanju's floating skirts and exposed legs, they arrowed toward them.

The water was now approaching the Master of
Sinanju's tiny waist.

He could float if he so wished. He did not wish this,
however. His hazel eyes watched the V-shaped wakes
of the approaching banded brown vipers with mild
interest.

And he began to stamp his feet in place, his hands
still concealed in his kimono sleeves. He would not
need his hands to discourage mere serpents.

The Director watched, aghast.

"The little runt is doing some kind of jig!"

Captain Maus came over.

"No, Director. Look at the blood in the water. He's
killing the snakes with his feet."

"By stepping on them? Just like that?"

"So it appears."

"Who does he think he is, Saint Patrick?"

"Unknown, sir."

"Well, let him try kicking bull gators around then!"

The alligators crawled and splashed from the grates
like khaki logs with stumpy legs. They yawned as they
came, disclosing unkempt toothy ripsaw mouths.

By this time, the Master of Sinanju was afloat. His
skirts hung low in the water, presenting, he knew, an
attractive enticement to the reptiles.

So he dived down into the water to meet them on
their own terms. One lacked a left eye. He came first.

There were three. They kicked and slashed about
with their muscular tails.

A corded tail came around, and the Master of
Sinanju blocked it with a pipe-stem wrist. The reptile,
his sluggish brain reacting to the pain of its encounter,
curled up in a ball and floated inert, one eye closed
and the other a black pit.

The other two circled, legs flippering.

One passed close enough for the Master of Sinanju
to seize its tail and arrest its progress. The grinning
head snapped around angrily. Chiun tugged. The jaws
snapped, and kept snapping. With the second gator in

a mood to bite anything it encountered, the Master of Sinanju gave it a gentle nudge in the direction of its third saurian brother.

Soon the two gators were chomping one another to shreds, and the water was turning a rusty red.

When the bodies had floated to the surface, the Master of Sinanju mounted them and stood resolute while the upward-creeping water brought him inexorably closer to the trapdoor and freedom.

"He killed my gators!" the Director raged, pounding the console with one gnarled fist. Plastic buttons cracked and popped up from their settings.

"Calhoun isn't dead, just stunned."

"Screw Calhoun! I want that slacker turned into shoes! I fed him a pitbull a day to develop his appetite, and he couldn't eat one bite-sized Chinaman when I needed it!"

"His nationality hasn't been definitely established, Director."

"I don't care if he's a pygmy. I want him dead. And the other one too!"

"The Bear is about to take him down, Director. You might want to watch."

"Now you're talking, Maus!" The fist came down again, cracking the console top.

"It's a short, short life, don't you know?
"It's a short, short life, don't you know?"
Remo ducked under a buzzing biplane no bigger than a robin. It was wire-guided. When it struck a light fixture, it chewed it to pieces and bored on into the wallboard like an angry mole.

Another came, and Remo was ready for it.

He grabbed the wire, snapped it free, and began spinning the biplane around his head in snarling circles.

"It's a short, short life, don't you know?
"It's a short, short life, don't you know?
"Shut up," Remo said, sending the biplane in the

direction of the incessant singing. It chewed into the speaker.

And to his surprise, the music stopped.

And another biplane dive-bombed him.

Remo snared it, and using the force of its flight, let it spin him around.

On the spin, he saw the hulking form of Mucky Moose step out from behind a replica of Big Ben and aim a pump-action shotgun in his direction.

Both barrels blew at once. They destroyed the ceiling, bringing cascades of plaster and lath down on his antlered head.

But Mucky Moose no longer cared.

He was already on his back, the biplane's stainless-steel propellor pureeing his heart muscle in the miocardial sac.

"Scratch one Moose," Remo said, pushing on the exit door bar.

When the water level had brought his bald yellow head to the ceiling trap, the Master of Sinanju, balanced atop two dead alligators, reached for the exposed hinge pins.

He used his right index fingernail to shear one and then the other clean off. They dropped into the water. The trap yawned, to hang down from its splintery lock. Slowly, like a rotting tooth, the weight began to tear the lock housing loose.

The Master of Sinanju couldn't wait. He took hold of the trap and whisked it into the brownish water.

Hands unseen in his sleeves again, he waited for the water to come level with the floor, then stepped off his saurian raft.

Each wall framed a door. He chose one, and passed through it.

The next room canted at a thirty-degree angle, and the one beyond also at a thirty-degree angle but on an opposite pitch.

There were no separating walls. The Master of Sinanju saw before him a long succession of twisted and canted rooms, like some drunken tunnel. Some

boasted furniture on the ceiling and light fixtures bolted
to the floor.

At the far end, he spied a familiar round-eared
shape. It waved at him, then beckoned with a white-
gloved finger.

"At last," murmured Chiun, starting along this gro-
tesque path.

The walls were decorated with ornate mirrors, he
saw.

Eyes alert, Chiun watched these as he walked at a
thirty-degree-cant through the first room. He knew
that mirrors sometimes concealed spying eyes—or foes
poised to strike.

In the first room his sharp eyes detected the reflection of a green ghost, dressed in chains and rags, following him.

He whirled, prepared to strike.

There was no green ghost. Yet the mirror had
shown one clearly.

He continued. And again, the green ghost appeared
in the mirror.

Again, he whirled. And again there was no ghost.

Frowning, the Master of Sinanju went to the mirror.
His reflection appeared undistorted. And behind him
was a ghost.

The Master of Sinanju broke the mirror with a tiny
fist, and when he resumed his progress he was not
molested.

Passing into the next room he found himself walking
at the opposite cant, but he shifted his inner balance
as easily as a fly walking on a sheer surface. A mirror
to his left showed clearly that a giant scarlet spider
was stalking him. Yet the opposite mirror reflected a
yellowish mummy, dragging his dusty wrappings.

This was an impossibility, he knew. He was being
stalked either by a spider or a mummy. Not both. The
mirrors each reflected one apparition, not two.

He stopped. The apparitions stopped. He continued. They followed. When the Master of Sinanju
leaped into the next room and stood poised to defend

himself, he saw that the room was empty of any
shapes, of this world or others.

"What sorcery is this?" he muttered darkly.

Thereafter, as he passed through the crazy procession of rooms, he simply ignored the obviously
bewitched mirrors and his progress was undisturbed.

In a room larger than the others, he encountered
the mouse.

Chiun lifted his voice.

"Mongo! Hail, entertainer of children. I bring you
greetings from the House of Sinanju."

Mongo spoke not a word. Laying a quieting finger
to his licorice lips, he beckoned the Master of Sinanju
to follow. Then he opened a secret panel in a wall.

"The Mouse has succeeded in drawing him into the
Slab Room, Director."

The Director looked away from the screen, which
framed Mucky Moose's quivering, defeated bulk.

"When he steps in, drop the ceiling on his head."

"The Mouse, too?"

"Mongo Mouse is immortal. He will never die."

"Yes, Director."

The Master of Sinanju stepped into the chamber
and smelled death. It hung in the close air. It was in
the walls, which appeared ordinary. The floors felt
like stone under his sandaled feet.

And when the Master of Sinanju looked up, he saw
that the ceiling too was stone, pitted and discolored
where scouring hadn't managed to remove all traces
of blood.

"You have lured me to this bitter place for a reason,
Mouse," he accused.

The black-and-white figure of Mongo Mouse grinned
starchily, and wriggled playful white-gloved fingers.

"Why do you not speak?" Chiun demanded.

The Mouse moved his head from side to side happily. But the Master of Sinanju could smell the sweat
he exuded.

Then, the ceiling began to grind downward.

And the mouse spoke.

"No, No, Uncle Sam! I'm your biggest fan!"

"You are not Monongahela Mouse," Chiun said suspiciously, hearing the unfamiliar voice.

"Damn straight, I'm not," said the Mouse, removing his head and throwing it at him. Chiun caught it easily, his eyes stricken with momentary surprise.

From an unseen loudspeaker an angry voice demanded, "Mongo, put your head back on. You are out of character."

In an ugly voice the mouse called back, "The ceiling is coming down, Captain. I'll be crushed!"

"Then die like Mongo would die. With his wooden shoes on."

"Screw you!" said the mouse with a human head, pounding on the walls like a trapped rat.

In its inexorable descent, the rumbling ceiling scraped wallpaper from the walls and knocked portraits off their nails.

The Master of Sinanju turned and attacked the only visible door. Thick and built of heavy panels, it was now fixed and immovable. Stripping the hinges did no good.

Chiun selected one panel and, using a fingernail that had been hardened by diet and exercise, outlined it swiftly. The wood screeched in protest. He repeated the action. Long shavings curled and fell to the floor. On the fourth circuit the panel fell out, leaving an aperture large enough for a child to use.

Tucking the prized mouse head under one arm, the Master of Sinanju passed through it easily. On the other side, he called to the frightened mouse impersonator. "Reveal to me the name of your master, and I will allow you to escape this way."

The mouse turned, said "Huh?" and clopped toward the hole.

The ceiling had swallowed half the cubic area of the room by this time, forcing the mouse to stoop, then crawl.

"Speak now!" Chiun urged.

"Out of my way, you old fart!"

The mouse-man reached the aperture, eyes wild, and attempted to struggle through. He got his head out. That was all.

As the ceiling inched toward the floor, the mouse's human eyes and tongue protruded. He gagged and made strangling noises deep in his throat. Then the blood began to run from eyes, ears, nose, and mouth, and something pinker than its tongue was forced from its mouth like an organic balloon.

Sternly, the Master of Sinanju watched the mouse in its death throes.

"So perish all imposters." Then he turned on his heel to go.

18

When Remo stepped out into the cool, orange blossom-scented sunlight, he spied the Master of Sinanju looking wet and bedraggled as he emerged from the rear of a cartoony-looking Louisiana Gothic mansion.

"Small world, isn't it?" he said dryly.

"Pah! I have been betrayed by a rodent."

"Not Mongo Mouse?" Remo asked in mock-horror.

"He attempted to lure me to what he thought would be my doom."

"I see you got his scalp," Remo said, nodding toward the black cap the Master of Sinanju now wore proudly atop his bald skull.

Chiun adjusted the round-eared skullcap.

"I now wear the crown of Beasley World, so that none will dare to harm me," he said.

"Don't count on it. This entire place is a death trap. Further proof that the Beasley Corporation is behind the whole thing."

"A base lie."

"I hate to burst your bubble, Little Father," Remo said, "but check out the flag."

Chiun followed Remo's pointing finger. It was directed toward the Sorcerer's Castle. Its pennant-like flag chattered in the morning breeze. Its was white. The design inside was black. A black circle, adorned by two smaller black circles.

"Remember the flags we found underground?" Remo asked.

"Mongo!" Chiun gasped in horror. "It is true!"

" 'Fraid so." Remo looked around. "The head cheese should clear this up. If we can only find him."

"I have seen nothing of Uncle Sam."

"And you won't. He's long in the ground. But *someone's* pulling the strings of this Punch and Judy horror show. My guess is it's the Beasley CEO, whoever that is. I can never remember his name."

The Master of Sinanju gazed about, his mouse ears like questing radar dishes.

"A chieftain might be expected to live in an edifice worthy of his domain," he said slowly.

"The Sorcerer's Castle," Remo said, eyeing its fluted spires. "Sounds farfetched, but at this late hour I wouldn't doubt anything."

The Master of Sinanju girded up his black skirts.

"Come, Remo. We will take the castle and wrest the throne from the wicked ruler."

"Come, Remo. We will take the castle and wrest the throne from the wicked ruler."

"Who *are* these buffoons?" roared the Director, pounding the console with his fist. It was becoming a wreck.

"No idea, sir. But Horrible House and the Tom Thumb Pavilion are no longer operational. We may not be able to open today."

"Of course we'll open! Sam Beasley World is open three hundred and sixty-five days a year, come rain, come shine."

"Not unless we can stop them cold in the next hour."

The Director stood up suddenly.

"Lure them into the Buccaneers of the Bahamas attraction."

"What good will that do, sir?"

"*Do!* It's the best damn ride in the park! And I'm going to be there to make sure those two walk the plank. Personally." He stood up, balancing on his silver-filagreed leg, and adjusted his eye patch.

"Yes, Director."

Captain Maus went to his microphone and began to issue terse instructions to the units in the field.

From every nook and crevice of Beasley World, they emerged. A kangaroo hopped out from behind a plastic toadstool and shoved his 9-mm Glock back into his pouch. A Transformed Tae Kwon Do Teen Terrapin popped a manhole cover and scampered down, leaving his scimitar behind.

Padded feet took flight all over the park. Every creature was headed in one direction.

"Look, Remo!" squeaked Chiun. "The forces of the treacherous mouse are in retreat before us!"

"Don't count on it."

"But they are fleeing."

"Looks to me like they're headed for the Buccaneers attraction."

"Then we will follow them."

"What if it's a trap?" asked Remo. "Not that's there's any doubt."

"Then they will die, and you and I will enjoy the sights of the Old West."

"Old West?"

"Yes. The Buccaneers of the Old West. Wyatt Burp. Buffalo Beef. Catastrophe Jane. And the other slowpokes."

"I think you mean 'cowpokes,' and you're confusing buckaroos with buccaneers. A buccaneer is a pirate."

"Let us not dawdle, for the sun climbs high. Soon it will be High Noon, a portentous time for buccaneers."

Remo rolled his eyes and followed.

They approached the Buccaneers attraction carefully. It was in the shape of a galleon that had run aground on an elkhorn coral reef. A Jolly Roger flapped and chattered in the wind.

The greeters were jumping into the open cannon ports all along the ship's hull, which clapped shut after them. They ignored the tiny boats that sat in the water surrounding the mock-shipwreck.

"What say, Little Father?" Remo asked, when they came to the water's edge. "Walk or ride?"

"We are the rightful lords of this domain. We shall ride."

"It's safer to walk."

"A ruler who cannot pass safely through his own kingdom does not truly rule."

"You're the one with the mouse ears," Remo said, drawing a boat to the shore for the Master of Sinanju to step aboard. Remo climbed in after him and shoved off.

"I don't see any paddles," Remo said, looking about the gunwhales.

The boat began to move. Remo went to the prow. He could see a submerged cable pulling them along. It dragged the boat around to the galleon's bow and passed waving mermaids on the shore. He returned to his seat.

A dark stove-in section of hull came into view and they were pulled into it.

As they passed into darkness, a mechanical jackdaw swiveled its beady eyes toward them and said, "Screw you jerks!" in a raucous voice.

The Master of Sinanju decapitated it with a piece of gingerbread ripped from the boat's stern.

Inside, they found themselves on a shakily illuminated underground stream. Fake rock walls reared up on either side of them. Indirect red lights shed a hellish, fitful illumination, bathing their frowning faces. Rusty, ill-smelling water lapped and sucked at the boat's knifing bow.

The the song began.

"Yo Ho Ho and a bucket of blood . . ."

"That is not how the song goes," murmured Chiun suspiciously.

"I don't give a hoot," Remo growled. "Anything to erase that other stupid song. I can't get it out of my mind."

"What other stupid song?" Chiun demanded.

" 'It's a short, short life, don't you know?' " Remo sang.

Chiun looked puzzled. "That is not how that song goes, either."

"Sue the management. I'm just here for the ride," Remo said sourly.

They passed under an overhang of rock, and a mechanical pirate lowered his stockinged head and brought an arm slowly toward them. The hand clutched an antique flintlock.

"Watch it, Little Father!" Remo warned.

A shot disturbed the air. The pistol blossomed in a flash of fire, and a hard round ball like a lead grape whistled past them, to punch a hole in a papier-maché outcropping.

As the boat slid by, Remo stood up and took hold of the pirate's head. He twisted. A spark flew out of the pirate's grinning mouth and when Remo sat down again, he was holding the corsair's glassy-eyed head.

The Master of Sinanju looked his question.

"Souvenir," Remo said nonchalantly.

"It is *my* pirate you have beheaded," Chiun said thinly.

"He might come in handy."

He did. They rounded a corner into a wider stretch of river and as the "Bucket of Blood" song swelled in their ears, they were surrounded by pirates.

They were stamping their feet to a mechanical fiddler crab sawing on a real fiddle, waving their muskets and flintlocks merrily. The weapons spat sparks and noise, but not balls.

"These creatures do not look like buccaneers," Chiun muttered. "Where are their half-pint hats?"

"I told you, you've got buccaneers mixed up with buckaroos. These are freaking buccaneers."

Suddenly the robots gathered themselves and, in synchronization, brought their weapons into line with the slow-moving boat and tracked it.

Remo brought the pirate head up in both hands and, from a sitting position, let it fly, like Wilt Chamberlain trying to sink a set shot.

The head struck the pirate captain in the face. Then there were two heads flying in two directions. Each struck another head, which in turn caromed off another. Within seconds the cavern was a chain reaction of mechanical heads rebounding in every direction.

Without their heads, the mechanical buccaneers and corsairs fired randomly, peppering the flimsy rocks and one another with grapeshot and lead ball.

A solitary head flew by their boat, forcing the Master of Sinanju to weave out of its path. It plopped into the brownish water.

"Not bad, huh?" Remo said with a grin, as they left the carnage behind them.

"One almost struck me," Chiun complained.

"It's been a while since I was on this ride," Remo said dryly.

Chiun made a wrinkled face. "This is terrible."

"You can fix them when we're done, okay?"

"That is not what I meant."

Remo lifted an eyebrow. "No?"

"This ride is a death trap. Therefore, impossible as it is to believe, what you have told me is true."

"Why is it so impossible that the Beasley Corporation is the culprit? They're Big Business. Anything's possible, when that much money's involved."

"It is not that."

"No?"

"It is that you were right," Chiun sniffed.

"Gee, when has that ever happened?"

"I do not recall," the Master of Sinanju said vaguely, as the tow cable pulled them from a stretch of darkness to another mechanical display.

This time, it was a depiction of a plank-walking. The plank jutted out in their path. Perched on the wavering tip was a fat merchant, his hands lashed behind his back. A freebooter in a red costume was prodding him with a cutlass. The merchant swiveled his head fearfully, his mouth agape.

As they came within hailing distance of the ship, every figure, including that of the terrified merchant, turned to regard them with unseeing glass eyes.

The freebooter took a step back and lifted his cutlass.

"Your turn," Remo prompted.

The Master of Sinanju came out of his seat like smoke from a hookah. His hands reached up to intercept the blade. It gleamed along its edge.

With both hands, Chiun reached around the wicked edge to grasp the pirate's cutlass arm by the wrist. He exerted little obvious effort, yet the arm, sword and all, came free, trailing multicolored wiring. It fell into the water and sank.

He returned to his seat and he and Remo ducked under the plank.

On the other side, they looked back to see the pirates hissing words at them.

"Fuck you! Fuck you!"

"Such language," Chiun sniffed.

"They're pirates."

"They swear like presidents."

"Huh?"

"Never mind. Look! Up ahead."

Remo's gaze followed Chiun's indicating finger. Ahead, bathed in a dancing red radiance, was a scene called FREEBOOTERS IN HELL, according to a crude sign.

Here, the pirates were getting the worst of it.

They were shoveling coal into mock fires, and being prodded by pitchforks wielded by plump green imps and a scarlet Lucifer figure.

"Looks like they got what they deserved," Remo said.

"I see no guns," Chiun pointed out.

"That's a good sign. They can't shoot us."

But they could throw pitchforks and hot coals—which they proceeded to do.

Standing up, Remo caught the pitchforks easily. He collected a handful with no more effort than if they had been stickball bats.

He sent them back the way they had come, impaling devils and the damned alike. Sparks snapped. Wires uncoiled, hissing.

The Master of Sinanju plucked the coals that fell into the thwarts of the boat with nimble fingers. A quick pinch with his fingernails and they sank hissing into the water.

"Nice try," Remo called back.

"Blow me," a pirate hurled back mechanically.

"Is it not 'Blow me down,' Remo?" Chiun wondered.

"Maybe they *are* buckaroos, after all," Remo said lightly.

"I will be glad when we come to the end of the trail," Chiun sniffed.

"No sweat. These guys aren't even in our class."

"The ride's not over yet," a raspy voice called out.

"Remo!" Chiun squeaked. "Who spoke?"

"One of the marionettes."

"That did not sound like a marionette."

"I don't hear a heartbeat."

The Master of Sinanju listened. Among the echoing sounds—the whine of hidden motors, and the buzz and click of relays—there was no gulping pump of a human heart.

But there was a raspy breathing.

"I hear lungs laboring," Chiun said thinly.

Remo listened. "Yeah. Me, too. But no heartbeat."

"How can there be lungs where there is no heart?"

"Maybe we nailed a real pirate, and he's on his way out."

"The voice that spoke did not sound dispirited in that way," Chiun pointed out.

"You're right," Remo said, looking worriedly about. "It is kinda spooky, at that. And the voice sounded familiar somehow."

Chiun narrowed his eyes to slits. "Beware, Remo. I sense great danger."

"I hear you," Remo said. He was standing up, his hands loose at his sides. His thick wrists rotated absently, an unconscious habit he had in situations like this.

Chiun pointed past the bow. "Look, Remo! There he is!"

Remo had been watching their wake. He turned, saying, "Who?"

"It is Uncle Sam. We have found him at last."

Remo narrowed his eyes.

Where the false rocks piled up, a lone figure stood balanced on a shiny peg leg. He wore a green felt sea captain's longcoat. His hat was a black tricorne, made rakish by a purple ostrich plume and a white skull-and-crossbones staring back from the upturned brim. He wore an eye patch.

Other than the costume and patch, he was the spitting image of Uncle Sam Beasley, right down to the frosted brush mustache and twinkling grandfatherly eye. He offered a folksy smile.

"It *is* him, Remo," Chiun said in a hushed voice.

"It's another marionette," Remo shot back. "Beasley's long dead. I told you that."

"I detect lungs."

Remo listened, interested. "Okay. Lungs. But where's the heart? It's a marionette. The lungs must be a bellows."

"The sound is coming from Uncle Sam."

"It's a bellows. Maybe he's getting ready to exhale poison gas."

"Why would he do that?" Chiun asked.

"Remember last year, when they had to close this ride? Stuff got in people's lungs. I'll bet this guy's the culprit."

"Very astute," said the pirate, in a cold voice.

Chiun's eye went round. "He answered, Remo!"

"Crap," said Remo. And as they watched, the pirate slowly lifted a hand to peel off his eye patch. It revealed a dark cavity like the orbit of a skull.

"What is this?" Chiun asked uncertainly.

"Offhand, I'd say a buccaneer who doesn't know his right from his left."

Without warning, the dark socket exploded in a flash of searing light.

Remo and Chiun were caught unawares. The light seared their eyeballs. It was no mere flashbulb. Their pupils irised down protectively, saving their sight. Still, the pain was excruciating. It sent synaptic needles into their brains.

"Damn!" Remo said, clapping his hand before his eyes.

The Master of Sinanju did the same. He expelled an angry breath past clenched teeth.

Through their pain, they caught the dry ratcheting back of a flintlock hammer.

Remo called, "Dive, Little Father!"

His shout was drowned in a splash of water. Chiun, moving first. Remo followed him into the cold, brackish brine.

A ball *whupped* into the water and knifed past them, sending rippling shock waves that made them separate like frightened dolphins.

Another shot struck the boat, knocking a hole in its bottom. It began to sink.

Remo, struggling to gain equilibrium, let his ears take him in the direction of the Master of Sinanju. His eyes were still closed. They stung terribly, as if heated pins had been driven through them.

When his bare arms felt the watery vibrations that told of Chiun's nearness, he reached out blindly. And got a wrist that was like a pair of long bones covered in loose chicken skin. It struggled.

He held on. Chiun calmed down. Like two groupers under a coral formation, they waited, not inhaling, and exhaling only slow beads of carbon dioxide that would not be visible in the darkness.

They waited. Through the water, the "Yo Ho Ho and a Bucket of Blood" song continued its rollicking cadence.

Remo began to wish the other song would come back. At least it was kind of catchy.

When the pain had lessened and he could trust his reflexes again, Remo let go of the Master of Sinanju and shot upward like a submarine-launched missile.

He emerged from the water a foot from the rocky river edge, hung a moment before gravity could reclaim him, and then, like a cartoon figure, simply stepped from his vertical position to the papier-mâché shelf.

Remo still couldn't see. But he could hear.

The marionette that strongly resembled Uncle Sam Beasley was still there, holding his smoking flintlock at the ready. The bellows sound and the smell of old-fashioned black powder told Remo that.

At the sight of Remo, it cracked a hideous grin and brought the long-barreled pistol in line with Remo's chest.

Remo stomped the papier-mâché under his feet and it split.

This stand of the outcropping collapsed, taking the peg leg pirate figure with it. He cursed like a cutthroat as he went down. Remo didn't hear a splash. But the bellows sound went away. He figured the mechanical thing was finally broken.

Remo returned to the water and, taking Chiun's wrist again, began to swim, the Master of Sinanju in tow. Chiun had lost his mouse ears.

They negotiated the underground river by feeling their way along the supporting shelf of slimy stone.

When daylight lightened the inner pink of their eyelids, they knew two things: that they were outside the attraction, and that their sight was gradually returning.

Remo was the first to the surface. The Master of Sinanju's bedraggled head surfaced a second later. His hazel eyes were like knife slits in his wrinkled visage as he released a squirt of brown water from his mouth.

"I think I got him," Remo said.

"That was not Uncle Sam," Chiun muttered.

"That's what I've been telling you," Remo said.

"Uncle Sam would never try to kill us."

"Have it your way," Remo said, looking around.

Sound from above them caused Remo to look up.

They were under the galleon's stern. Leaning over the rail of the poop deck was a menagerie of pop-eyed trademarks.

"The natives are about to revolt again," Remo said in a low warning voice.

Chiun looked up. His tiny mouth dropped open. He lifted a raging fist.

"Begone, vermin! Begone from my sight, or I will have all your heads on posts!"

A Terrapin brought a shotgun to his green shoulder, and aimed it downward. His movements were fluid, not jerky. A man in a suit.

The Master of Sinanju vanished beneath the waves.

The Terrapin redirected his weapon toward Remo's head.

"He wasn't kidding," Remo warned, as the creature adjusted his aim.

Before he could fire, the Terrapin tumbled over the rail, shell-over-flippers, into Remo's grasp. He pushed the bright green head down and kept it there, simultaneously bringing a knee upward.

The Terrapin mask cracked and leaked a cloud of blood. Remo released the floating flotsam.

Others began to fall. They were coming off the rail simply because the galleon itself was capsizing. They landed all around Remo.

Remo went to work, breaking necks and shattering spines. In a moment, the Master of Sinanju joined him. His technique was simpler. Remaining underwater, he began pulling the creatures down into the water, to hold them there like bunched grapes.

One by one they floated back to the surface, muzzles and snouts downward.

"I think that's all of them," Remo said when Chiun had resurfaced.

"I do not see the head buckaroo," Chiun complained.

"He wasn't real."

"Neither are these," said the Master of Sinanju coldly, indicating the dead. "Yet they bleed like persons."

"Point taken," said Remo. "What say we hit the castle?"

"No."

"No?"

"We will enter *my* castle as the conquerors we are."

19

The angry voice crackled over the loudspeaker.

"Damage report, damn it!"

"The galleon has been scuttled, Director."

"I know, you ninny! I was on it. I barely made it into the escape hatch in time."

"Three major attractions down, and they're headed for the Sorcerer's Castle. We have no greeters standing."

There was a pregnant pause over the connection.

"Order evacuation," said the Director, hoarsely.

"We're not opening, sir?"

"We're not staying! The lid is about to come off this entire base. We have to regroup. I'm moving B-Day up a day."

"I understand, sir. I'll blow retreat. What about Drake?"

"Tell him to play the goat."

"At once, Director."

Captain Maus punched the pound button on a telephone handset.

"Drake here. What the hell's going on?"

"No swearing in the ranks. You know the Director's feelings."

"Sorry."

"You've been watching?"

"With my Gumpy binoculars. This is a catastrophe. Half the attractions are in ruins."

"The Director has sounded retreat."

"Then it's over?"

"No. The operation continues. But we need time."

"What can I do?"

"Shield the Mouse."

"You can't be serious!"

"Shield the Mouse. Those are the Director's express wishes."

"He . . . he can't ask that of me! I've served him loyally!"

"Sorry. The Director's orders stand."

"But . . . but," sobbed Drake. "I . . . I was his biggest fan."

"And now he's asking you to make the ultimate sacrifice. You should be very proud."

"I . . . I am . . . !"

A sob broke over the loudspeaker before it cut out, leaving only silence.

20

Every avenue in Sam Beasley World led to the Sorcerer's Castle. It was like the fantastic hub of a great architectural wheel.

An iron portcullis barred the entrance. The drawbridge was in the half-raised position.

The moat held real alligators. They splashed their tails in sluggish warning.

Remo turned to the Master of Sinanju and said, "I think we can jump it."

"I will not be seen jumping into my own castle!" Chiun said stubbornly.

"We can't stay here."

"We will not. You will leap, and lower the drawbridge so that I may enter in a manner befitting my suzerainty."

"Oh, come on!"

"No. *You* go on."

Shrugging his shoulders, Remo stepped back and took a running jump. At the edge of the moat, he gave what looked like a weak double kick. But he seemed to take wing.

Remo landed on his feet on the precarious edge of the drawbridge. Without pausing, he snapped out with the edge of his right hand. It shattered one restraining chain. The drawbridge quivered, but held. Remo went to the other chain and took hold of a fistful of links. He gave it a hard twist and the drawbridge slammed down, throwing up dust.

Remo was left hanging onto the broken chain. He

released it and landed lightly on the still reverberating planks.

"How's that?" he asked, bowing and waving Chiun to enter.

Chiun frowned. "Was it necessary to break my chains?"

"You're welcome," Remo said sourly.

As they entered a stone-walled antechamber, they saw only suits of armor set in wall niches.

"I do not trust these guardians, Remo," Chiun said thinly. "Test their loyalty."

Remo went about, lifting visors. The suits proved to be empty.

"Satisfied?" he asked.

"No," said the Master of Sinanju.

"No?"

"They are ugly and will have to be replaced." He swept to the winding staircase and mounted it on sure, silent feet.

Frowning, Remo followed.

There was a honeycomb of chambers clustered at the highest point in the castle. One door lay open. Remo approached it cautiously. Cautiously, because he smelled the fresh, sour scent of human excrement.

A body slumped over a long conference table proved to be the source of the unpleasant odor.

Remo went to it, pulled it up in its chair.

"That's the guy!" he said.

"What guy?" Chiun asked, examining the dead face.

"The CEO of Beasley Corp. Whatever his name is."

The man's mouth hung slack. Stuck to his back teeth was a bright pink wad.

There was an open pack of Mongo Mouse chewing gum on the desk, next to a pocket dictaphone.

"Huh?" Remo said. "Smell."

Chiun sniffed the dead man's mouth delicately. "Almonds," he said.

"Cyanide. That's probably what killed Zorilla, too," said Remo, picking up the dictaphone. He fiddled with the rewind button until the device began to whir. When it had clicked to an automatic stop, Remo thumbed on the play-back.

The familiar but trembling voice of the Chairman of the Beasley Corporation began to vibrate from the tiny built-in speaker.

"This is the full confession of Eider Drake, Chairman and Chief Executive Officer of the Sam Beasley Corporation. It all began with our third quarter of fiscal 1991. . . ."

"A confession," Remo said, clicking the device off. "I'd better call Smith."

Harold W. Smith was changing in the Spartan privacy of his Folcroft office. He had not gone home. He had not slept, except in catnaps in his well-worn executive's chair.

Dawn was breaking over Long Island Sound as Smith replaced his gray trousers with an identical pair. His wrinkled white shirt came off his back and he struggled into a crisp white one. A fresh tie replaced the old. He examined his gray vest critically. It was still serviceable so he drew it on, patting the watch pocket to make certain his suicide pill was still there. It was.

Finally, he drew on his gray suit coat and returned to his still warm seat.

America slept. On the TV screen a test pattern sizzled. It was, unfortunately, a Spanish-language test pattern: the red-white-and-blue flag of Cuba and the words TELEREBELDE.

Havana had not yet relinquished its grip on South Florida airwaves, and the networks were perversely repeating the transmission in a desperate attempt to grab ratings.

Smith knew, because the President had informed him, that a surgical strike on a Cuban broadcast station was under active consideration in the War Room of the Pentagon. It would be justified not only in the name of the sanctity of U.S. airwaves, but as a tit for tat over the failed Turkey Point attacks.

At the moment there was a lull. But by afternoon—evening at the very latest—the next escalation was certain to take place. It was only a question of who would strike first.

And from Remo and Chiun, Smith had heard nothing.

A knock at the door and Eileen Mikulka, Smith's personal secretary, poked her head in. She saw an oblivious Harold Smith, looking as if he had just arrived refreshed by a full evening's sleep. Knowing how her boss detested any intrusion when he was concentrating, she quietly closed the door.

She saw he was working at his terminal again. It had always puzzled her. Sometimes it was there. Sometimes it wasn't.

She wondered if her starchy employer liked to play video games. Not a sheet of computer printout had ever crossed her desk. What could he be doing?

The blue contact phone rang and Harold Smith took it up.

"Remo. Report."

"Ultima Hora is history," Remo said.

"Good."

"Zorilla's dead"

"Yes?"

"So is Eider Drake."

"Who is Eider Drake?" Smith asked.

"Try punching him up on your computer," Remo suggested.

Smith obliged.

"Remo, the only Eider Drake I have is CEO of the Sam Beasley Corporation." And as it sunk in, Harold Smith's bleary eyes went wide.

"Remo! I promised Beasley World to Master Chiun!"

"No sweat, Smitty," Remo said cheerfully. "We've taken possession."

Smith's lemony mouth compressed into a bloodless pucker. His gray eyes took on an aghast look.

"Remo," he said tightly. "What about the mission?"

"Hey," Remo said. "After all the work we've done, don't we deserve a trip to Beasley World?"

"That is not funny!" Smith flared.

"Neither is what I'm about to tell you. Hold on to your truss, Smitty. It's been a long night."

"Proceed," Smith said, thin-lipped.

"We didn't kill Ultima Hora. Zorilla did. He musta got the word from his superior."

"Understood."

"We followed him. He led us to an underground military-style complex that seems to be headquarters of the whole operation."

Smith let out a pent-up breath. "Good," he said.

"Maybe. Maybe not. The underground complex is directly under Beasley World."

"Impossible."

"We fought our way out and ended on Pleasant Street, U.S.A. Then the mice and ducks tried to waste us."

"Come again?"

"The place was boobytrapped. Every freaking ride. And every swinging tail had a gun. And you have a *lot* of explaining to do to Chiun."

"Never mind that," Smith snapped testily. "What about Zorilla?"

"We found him dead. Might be suicide. Might not. But Drake definitely took his own life. He left a taped confession, and a new reason why Mongo Mouse chewing gum is bad for you."

"Remo, you are talking nonsense."

"Both Zorilla and Drake ate a stick and it killed them," Remo explained.

Harold Smith paused to digest the storm of information swirling through his confused brain.

"Remo, are you certain of your facts?" Smith asked, more calmly than he felt. "Certain that the Beasley people are behind this?"

"Remember the one thread that ran through this? Uncle Sam?"

"Yes?"

"Think about it." And Remo began humming the annoying tune still in his brain.

"Uncle Sam Beasley!" Smith exploded. "My God!"

"Drake left a taped confession. I'll Fedex it. But we still have the problem of the military complex under the park. Someone has to fumigate it. Chiun says he wants the vermin out by sundown. And he's not happy about the state of the park. A lot of it got trashed in the fighting."

Smith's voice became urgent. "Remo, hold the tape up to the phone and play it back, please."

"Okay. Here it comes."

Harold Smith pressed the receiver tight to his ear. He listened. And as he listened, his eyes grew wide enough that they threatened to drop out of their sockets.

The sound stopped abruptly. Remo's voice came back on the line.

"Crazy, huh?"

"That *was* Drake's voice," Smith said, tight-voiced. "It's incredible. But I have to accept it." Smith cleared his voice. "Remo, do not lose that tape. It's the proof we've needed to take before the U.N. Security Council."

A dull boom came across the miles of wire. Smith heard a faint jangle of glass.

"What was *that*?" he demanded.

"Dunno. Let me check."

Remo's voice came back on a moment later. "Hey! Future Realm just blew up! It's on fire!"

"My park!" Smith could hear Chiun wail in the background.

"Relax. You were going to tear it down anyway, right?" Remo reminded.

"But it is burning!" Chiun cried.

Remo's voice came back on. "Smitty, I think someone's hit the destruct button. What do we do?"

Another boom came. This time louder. The crash of glass was a short symphony, ending in a tinkling timpany.

"Remo! Take the tape and get out of there as fast as you can! Report from a secure location."

"Gotcha," said Remo. We'll—"

The line went dead, and Harold W. Smith went white as a sheet.

He composed himself and reached for the red phone. The President of the United States should have risen by now. This was going to be impossible to explain. . . .

Remo dropped the dead phone and turned to the Master of Sinanju.

"Smith says we're outta here. Now!"

"But my beautiful kingdom! It is under attack!"

"No help for it. Maybe Smith'll give you Beasleyland as a consolation prize."

"It is inferior," Chiun said distastefully.

"Tough," said Remo, snatching up the dictaphone. "Let's go!"

"Look! Remo, the villains are escaping!"

Remo returned to the window, now a jagged frame of glass.

At the back end of the park, trucks and cars were rumbling away. They were, he knew, escaping by means of the secret entrance through which they had penetrated the underground complex.

"We can't stop them by complaining about it," Remo said quickly. "Come on."

As they floated down the winding steps, the ground shook. A stone fell out of the wall, and mortar cracked everywhere. On the lower floors, the suits of armor were tumbling into inert piles of helmets and leggings and gauntlets.

They flashed across the drawbridge, above the panicky splashing of the gators. The ground under their feet felt strange.

Chiun looked around, his face dark with horror. "What is happening?" he squeaked.

"Feels like an earthquake," Remo said.

Then, in the exact center of the park, the ground cracked and began to settle.

"My park!" Chiun moaned. "The earth is swallowing my park!"

"It's a sinkhole! Let's get out of here!"

They ran for the entrance gate, as pavilions burst into flame or simply erupted skyward all about them. They dodged flying glass, uprooted trees, and once a sleek monorail car that rolled off its track and burst open like a loaf of bread.

As they ran, the spreading sinkhole edge followed them hungrily.

The entrance gates were already collapsing by the time they reached them, and they were forced to work around those.

The parking lots—there were acres of them—contained a few cars. Remo picked one whose color he liked and popped the ignition in jig time.

They roared out of the lot as the asphalt began to separate and sink, the victim of what the next day's *Furioso Guardian* would call "the largest sinkhole in Florida history."

"Anybody left in that underground complex is pressed ham by now," Remo said in a small voice.

21

By the time they'd gotten clear of the spreading sink-hole, it was too late to do anything about the escaping convoy of trucks.

"But they are responsible for this travesty!" Chiun raged, shaking a tiny fist in the air.

"Can't be helped. Smith says he needs this tape."

"And my magnificent kingdom is burning even as we speak!"

"It's insured," Remo said. "Count on it."

"So?"

"For millions of dollars," Remo added.

They were driving toward the outskirts of Furioso. The roar of sirens filled the air. Fire trucks and ambulances roared past them, filling the air with an ungodly cacophony. There were even some crash vehicles from nearby Furioso Airport racing back toward the park. Beasley World was the heart of Furioso's economy.

The stricken look faded from the Master of Sinan-ju's wrinkled countenance. "It is better to build these things from scratch," he sniffed, seemingly mollified.

"We gotta find a hotel to park for a while," Remo said.

"That is a good one," Chiun said, pointing east.

Remo looked east. He saw a tall white hotel. "What makes you say that?" he asked.

"It has a duck on its side. It is a good augury."

"Haven't we had enough of those? Ducks, I mean."

"One can never have enough duck. And I am in the mood for well-prepared duckling."

"Suit yourself," said Remo, taking the next exit.

The Podbury Hotel not only had a duck on its tower but a lobby filled with mallards, waddling about in an artificial pool. They shook water droplets off their down in the direction of a curious Master of Sinanju as Remo checked them in.

"Do not splash me," Chiun warned, stepping away from a spattering of water. "For I am in a foul mood. And hungry."

The mallards again shook their down in response, showering the Master of Sinanju's kimono.

Chiun quacked back at them, to no avail. He sounded like Dingbat Duck on an off day.

On the elevator ride to their room, Remo broke the bad news.

"No duckling on the menu."

"How can this be?"

"The desk clerk says that it would offend the guests who come to feed the lobby ducks."

"This is wrong," Chiun said huffily.

"Take it up with management. I gotta get this tape to Smith."

Abruptly, Chiun stabbed the sixth-floor button. The elevator instantly lurched to a stop and the doors slid apart.

"This isn't our floor," Remo pointed out.

"I must arrange for my trunks to be shipped from our last hotel to this one," Chiun said, stepping off the elevator. He turned and grazed the down button.

"What makes you think we're going to be here that long?" Remo asked, holding the door open with one hand.

"Why, I must supervise repairs to my Enchanted Village, soon to be renowned as Assassin's World."

"Give it up, Little Father. It's a crater now."

"Never," said the Master of Sinanju firmly.

"Suit yourself," said Remo, releasing the door. It closed, and the lift resumed its upward climb.

Remo entered his suite to find the phone ringing.

"Don't tell me Chiun maimed another member of the Hotel Workers Local," he grumbled as he reached for the receiver.

Before he could say hello, Harold Smith's lemony voice was saying, "Remo. Stay put. I am on my way."

"How'd you know we were here?" Remo blurted out.

"The hotel computer told my computer," said Smith, hanging up.

Harold W. Smith arrived at eleven-thirty sharp. He came into the suite carrying his ever-present well-worn briefcase. Not seeing the Master of Sinanju, he asked, "Where is Chiun?"

"Said something about going out for a bite to eat," said Remo. "The tape's over there," he added, indicating a coffee table.

Smith picked up the dictaphone and let it run.

The voice of Eider Drake came, dull with shock.

"This is the full confession of Eider Drake, Chairman and Chief Executive Officer of the Sam Beasley Corporation. It all began with our third quarter of fiscal 1991, when we realized that declining revenues, spiraling taxes, and unforeseen start-up costs for Euro-Beasley threatened the foundation of the company. I knew something would have to be done. My thoughts went to Cuba. There, I knew, was the perfect location for a new Beasley theme park, if only the current unpopular government could be toppled. I established contacts in the Cuban exile community toward this end. I realize now that I overreached my corporate authority, brought ruin down upon the company, and harmed the great memory of Sam Beasley. This, most of all, pains me. I am sorry. The idea was mine. The responsibility was mine. And I must pay the price. Everyone else was just following orders. Good-bye."

The tape ended.

"Not much of a confession," Remo remarked.

Wordlessly, Harold Smith placed the dictaphone in

a receptacle in his briefcase that also contained a portable terminal and cellular phone hookup.

"I have spoken with the President," he said, closing the case.

"Yeah?"

"He is incredulous, of course. But we have agreed that for the good of the country and to preserve the good name of Samuel Beasley, this . . . um . . . undertaking should never become public knowledge."

"Smitty, Sam Beasley World is now a sinkhole bigger than Rhode Island. How are you going to cover *that* up?"

"You have just explained it perfectly. It's a sinkhole. A natural phenomenon."

"Yeah? You heard the tape all the way through. It was disgusting. They were going to relocate Beasley World to *Cuba,* for crying out loud."

Smith rubbed his jaw. "Cuba was quite a resort island in its heyday. It is not so farfetched. Assuming they could seize control by force."

"Smitty, everyone who died, died for a *theme park*! Castro is trying to nuke us with one of our own power plants, because some suit didn't want to pay taxes!"

Smith frowned. "We will have to deal with the Beasley angle later. The crisis has not passed. A third MIG has been shot down. It's unlikely the Cuban Air Force will penetrate our coastal-defense net, but these continued provocations cannot go unanswered forever."

"This is crazy," Remo muttered, looking out the window.

"You seem troubled."

"I am. I grew up watching Sam Beasley on TV. A lot of kids were betrayed when Drake perverted the company. All I can think of is 'What would Uncle Sam say if he were alive to see this'?"

"Not important," Smith said flatly.

Remo turned, his eyes angry, "So that's it? You take the tape and tie it into a pretty ribbon?"

"Not quite," said Smith. "We must go through Utiliduck and destroy all evidence of the criminal conspiracy."

"Utiliduck?"

"That is the official designation of the underground command, control, and utility complex underlying Beasley World."

"Where'd you learn that? No, wait. Let me guess. Beasley's computers told yours."

"No. The complex is no secret, although off-limits to the general public. It is from there the attractions are controlled, largely by computer."

At that point the Master of Sinanju entered the suite, his hands concealed in his voluminous sleeves.

"Hail, Emperor Smith," he announced loudly, not stopping.

Smith nodded. "Master Chiun."

"Bestower of crumbling castles." And with that, Chiun swept into the other room. The door slammed.

Remo looked at Smith ironically. "Guess you're back in the doghouse."

"It will pass."

"Did you really intend to hand over Beasley World to him?"

"No," Smith admitted. "But I had to placate him. The situation was desperate, and Chiun can be exceedingly stubborn at times."

Remo raised an inquiring eyebrow. "At times? Next time you notice him *not* being stubborn, blow a whistle, will you? I'd like to take a photograph for posterity. But what are you going to do now? You're out from under the promise, but you know Chiun. He's going to want the moon if he's ever to work for you again."

Before Smith could answer, a mangled quack came from the other room.

"What was that?" Smith asked.

"Sounded like a duck," Remo said casually. Then it hit him. *"A duck!"*

Remo shot into the next room.

He discovered the Master of Sinanju in the act of squeezing the life out of a gasping, kicking mallard.

"Give me that!" Remo demanded.

Chiun clutched the wriggling duck's neck more tightly. "It is mine! It is dinner!"

"Did you steal that duck from the lobby pond?"

"What duck?"

"*That* duck."

Chiun looked injured. "It is a mallard. And it offered itself to me."

"It did not!"

"In return for a kernel of corn," Chiun admitted. The mallard was kicking its webbed feet violently now. Its eyes bulged.

"You lured that innocent duck up here? Children play with those ducks."

"I only took one," Chiun said in an injured tone. "There are many others for the children to play with. They will not miss this scrawny specimen, barely fit for eating."

Remo put out his hand. "The duck, Chiun. Now."

Grudgingly, the Master of Sinanju surrendered the now limp mallard. It began coughing quackily as soon as its slim neck had been freed.

Chiun turned his bleak hazel eyes in the direction of Harold Smith.

"This is what the head of the mightiest house of assassins in history has been reduced to," he said bitterly. "A vagabond existence, scrounging in low places for his next meal."

Smith adjusted the knot of his tie. "I am sure we can come to some accommodation, Master Chiun."

"I will not negotiate on an empty stomach. A caliph once locked himself into a stone chamber with Master Boo and won many concessions, because Boo could not stand the sound of his own growling stomach."

"I meant nothing of the kind," Smith said quickly.

"Did you bring my tape of the beauteous Cheeta?"

"Er, I forgot. Sorry."

"Another insult!"

"It was not meant that way," Smith protested.

"I could overlook it," Chiun said guardedly. "Perhaps."

"I would appreciate that, Master Chiun."

"In return for Beasleyland."

"Absolutely not!"

"Then a castle to be named later," Chiun said quickly.

Smith hesitated. Adjusting his glasses, his face grew reflective.

"Possibly," he said.

Before Remo could open his mouth to object, Harold Smith said, "Beasley World is thick with search teams and rescue trucks. We must move quickly, if we are to seize all evidence in this matter."

As they approached it, Sam Beasley World seemed more and more to resemble some fanciful lunar crater. Black smoke toiled upward, throwing the crumbled and drunken ramparts of Sorcerer's Castle into intermittent shadow.

The park was too big to rope off, but state police cars blocked the main entrance road.

Harold Smith offered a genuine-looking photo ID that said FEDERAL EMERGENCY MANAGEMENT AGENCY in intimidatingly large letters.

"How bad?" he asked.

"A lot of bodies down there, sir," a trooper said respectfully. "No survivors so far."

"Good," said Chiun.

"Hush," said Remo.

"We're going to look around," said Smith.

"The area isn't safe, sir."

"We'll chance it," Smith said.

They were waved through.

"My poor kingdom," Chiun said forlornly, his button nose pressed to the car window. "It is unsalvageable."

"Too bad," Remo said dryly. "The world really needed an Assassin's World. Right, Smitty?"

Smith said nothing. His pinched face was grim. The carnival desolation was appalling. The summit of Star Mountain had fallen in and was smoking like a volcano.

Remo fell silent.

They found a flat place in the outermost parking lot and picked their way over the jagged crevices and upflung shelves of asphalt. All around them lay ruins.

The ground had settled alarmingly. Phantom Lagoon had been drained of water, like a bizarre swimming pool. Monkey Domain was emitting a confusion of monkey chatterings and yeeps, evidently coming from tape machines all playing at different speeds—some too fast, some too slow.

Over by Horrible House—now a collapsed house of cards—rescue teams were extracting floppy bodies from a crack in the ground. None was human. A team of paramedics was trying to shock a seven-foot-tall rabbit back to life by applying electric paddles to his furry chest. They gave up when his long pink ears caught fire.

"Anybody trapped below when the ground fell in didn't have a prayer," Remo said quietly.

Smith asked, "Can you find the section where you emerged from underground?"

Remo led them to the disposal building that masqueraded as a fun house. It was in a quadrant of the park that was not as deeply sunken. They stepped in cautiously.

"We came up this tube," Remo said, indicating the pneumatic mechanism.

Smith peered down unhappily. "I am not sure I can negotiate this."

"No sweat. We'll give you a hand." And Remo cheerfully tucked a protesting Harold Smith under one arm. Paling, Smith closed his eyes.

Smith experienced a brief sensation of descent as Remo climbed downward. Then he found himself being set on his feet, as the Master of Sinanju stepped off the broken handholds in the side of the pipe.

Remo grinned. "How was that?" he asked, leading the way.

Smith straightened his coat and followed stiffly. He almost stepped on the body of Leopoldo Zorilla, but the Master of Sinanju assisted him around the tangled form.

At the broken end of the pipe, Smith endured the ignominy of being lowered by both hands to the polished white-tile floor, now shrouded in darkness.

He still clutched his briefcase, and from it he extracted a penlight. It whisked light about the long tunnel curiously.

"Remarkable," he said.

Remo and Chiun dropped lightly to his side. Remo said, "Follow me."

They walked.

Remo looked around. "Funny, this part isn't crushed flat like the rest."

"These walls are heavily reinforced," Smith said carefully. "It is my guess that this is not Utiliduck, but a secret wing."

"This is perfectly sensible," Chiun murmured.

"It is?" said Remo.

"All ducks have wings. Heh heh heh."

Remo rolled his eyes in silence.

They came to a sealed door. It resembled the guillotine-like entrance portal—a slab of steel plate, set in the grooves of a massive stainless-steel frame.

Smith's tiny ray found a magnetic keycard slot.

"Without a passcard, we cannot enter," he said.

"Wanna bet?" said Remo.

He placed his hands against the door, balanced himself on his feet, and pressed inward.

Nothing happened for some moments. Then Remo moved his flattened palms upward.

Smith clapped his hands over his ears to protect them from the interminable scream of tortured metal. The portal lifted, seemingly impelled by nothing more than the surface tension of Remo's flat palms.

When he had the door halfway up, Remo turned and said, "Slide under. I can't hold this thing forever."

Smith ducked under and in. The Master of Sinanju swept after him.

Remo gave the door a final lurch upward and rolled under the descending portal, which came roaring down behind him with a harsh, ringing clang.

The room was a nest of electronic equipment. Video monitors were lined up on overhead racks. Most were dead or filled with static. Tape spools gleamed. The console chairs were empty. There were no bodies to be seen, either.

Idly, Remo stabbed a button labeled TOM THUMB PAVILION.

To his surprise, a red light winked on and a set of reels began to turn.

Over the loudspeaker, a song warbled.

"It's a short, short life, don't you know?
"It's a short, short life, don't you know?"

"That is not right," Smith murmured.

Remo snapped the tape off, growling, "Tell me about it. Just when I got that thing out of my mind."

"What?"

"Never mind. It's been a long day."

Smith found another door. It was marked ANIMATION.

"Odd," he said. "I did not know the cartoonists worked underground."

They entered the door. It opened easily.

The room looked more like the War Room of a military base than an artist's studio.

In the center of a long table lay a topographically exact scale model of the island of Cuba.

"Here's your proof, Smitty," Remo said, indicating the walls with a wave of his hand.

Smith used his penlight. His brow furrowed at what he saw. Almost every square foot of wall space was covered with sheets of paper. Each sheet contained a drawing of some sort. They formed long rows of continuously depicted action.

"Odd," Smith said. "These appear to be storyboards."

"What?"

"Storyboards. Before they animate a cartoon, professional cartoonists work out the action in separate drawings, much like a comic strip," Smith explained.

"I say it's a War Room," Remo said firmly.

Chiun was examining the drawings critically.

"I do not understand this story," he said.

"That is because it is not a story," Smith said firmly. "These are the invasion plans for Cuba. Very clever. Instead of committing them to paper in text form, they worked them out as step-by-step cartoon illustrations."

"That is the goofiest thing I ever heard of," Remo said.

"It is not so farfetched," Smith suggested. "During World War Two, Sam Beasley loaned the government many of his artists for the war effort. They designed topographical models of Japanese-held Pacific Islands which were used in planning sessions, as well as so-called 'nose art' for bomber planes and camouflage details. He was quite a patriot."

Smith moved along one wall, following a line of drawings. They seemed to show a coastal area under invasion by waves of ocean-going military barges, while being defended by a large armed force.

"This calls for an amphibious landing at . . ." He went from the end of a row back to the beginning of the wall, to read the next tier of drawings.

Smith gasped. ". . . Zapata Swamp! At the Bay of Pigs!"

"Explains why Ultima Hora was training in a swamp," Remo said. "But why are these guys dressed like pirates?"

Smith came to Remo's side. His penlight followed the drawing sequence. In this sequence, the invading forces were standing up in their landing craft and returning fire. They wore costumes Remo had seen in the Buccaneers of the Bahamas attraction.

"This appears to be a secondary force," Smith ventured. "It is too small to be the spearhead for a full-scale invasion. But where is the main thrust?"

Chiun's voice piped up.

"Remo, if an animator is one who draws cartoons, what is a *re*animator?"

"Huh?"

"What is a reanimator?" repeated Chiun, indicating the sign on another door. It read: REANIMATION.

Remo and Smith joined him at the door. It looked like a submarine bulkhead door. It was locked, accessible only by passcard. Or as it turned out, by a fist that packed the power of a sledge-hammer. Remo casually punched the door off its hinges. It rang for a good half minute, even after they had stepped over it into the room beyond.

The Reanimation Room was lit up like a hospital. In fact, it looked a lot like an operating room. There was an operating table, an autoclave for sterilizing instruments, a defibrillator for restarting a stopped heart, and other medical paraphernalia.

"Must have an emergency generator," Smith mused, thumbing off his penlight. His face in the harsh white light appeared puzzled and sharp.

"Maybe it's an emergency hospital," Remo suggested. "Like a MASH unit."

"It does not appear to be portable," Smith said. He followed his inquisitive nose to a long stainless-steel capsule that sat in a corner. It might have been an old-fashioned iron lung, except that it was completely enclosed and stood upright. There was a face-sized porthole on one side near the top.

"Bomb?" Remo wondered.

Smith checked the support equipment. Tubes and coils ran from the long chamber to a framework of gleaming cylinders like oxygen tanks. They were labeled. One said OXYGEN. The others were labeled LIQUID NITROGEN. Various old-fashioned gauges were calibrated for pressure and temperature. The needles were dead.

Harold Smith stared at these a long time without speaking a word.

"You okay, Smitty?" Remo asked, noticing Smith's uncharacteristic stillness.

When Harold Smith turned around, his light-washed face was ghastly, his eyes sunken. "Remo," he croaked. "At any time during this operation, did you happen to encounter an individual who in any way resembled Sam Beasley?"

"Sure," Remo said brightly. "But I wouldn't call him an 'individual.' He was a marionette."

Smith asked in a dead voice, "A what?"

"A robot. You know, one of those animatronic things."

Smith let out a leaky sigh of relief, closing his eyes as if he had narrowly avoided walking off a cliff.

"It was no machine," Chiun inserted testily. "It was Uncle Sam himself."

At that, Harold W. Smith fainted dead away.

22

Dr. Osvaldo Revuelta was nervous. He did not understand what was happening. All he knew was that he was being whisked into the pages of history. To his destiny.

It had begun with a phone call. From the man known as "Maus," to whom he had reported his strange encounter with the thick-wristed Anglo and the elderly North Korean less than a day before.

"Be ready to move," Maus had said.

"Move?"

"Today is Beasley Day."

"I do not understand. What is this 'Beasley Day'?"

"You have loaned us your Ultima Hora."

"I loaned my *soldados* to Zorilla, the patriot."

"Zorilla is dead."

"It is sad. He was *muy Cubismo,* much Cuban."

"But you are *more* Cuban," the flattering voice had said. "You are *Cubissimo,* the most Cuban."

At that, Dr. Osvaldo Revuelta knew he was speaking to a comrade-in-arms.

The car whisked him to a pier, where a great cruise ship waited. The name on the stern was a well-known one. It read: BEASLEY ADVENTURE.

They took him up the gangplank, and two men in uniform escorted him to a stateroom. Their uniforms were white. Not army. Not navy. They bore simple insignia: three black circles in a white badge.

Somehow the men looked familiar.

"Do I not know jou?" he asked them.

"Sí," said one. And then Revuelta knew. They were Ultima Hora. *His* Ultima Hora. But they acted as if they no longer served him, but another.

"To whom are jou taking me?" he asked.

"To the Director."

"Director who?" he demanded, thinking that the CIA was run by a director. Perhaps they were secretly on his side, after all.

To that, they made no reply. Stone-faced, they escorted him to a cabin amidships and remained outside as he entered. It was incredibly hot in the cabin.

There was a figure seated behind a modest desk. He sat with his back to Revuelta, staring out a porthole at the blue sky. He wore some kind of a top hat. It looked black in silhouette.

"You are Osvaldo Revuelta?" the voice asked in a gravelly tone.

"Sí."

"Soon to be President of Cuba?"

"Who says this?" Revuelta snapped.

The figure turned in the creaky chair. His white-mustached face came into the light. The man was old, his face a fist of kindly wrinkles. Osvaldo Revuelta noticed that he wore a white eye patch. He also wore a tall hat of red and white vertical stripes.

It was not a face Revuelta immediately would have recognized. Except that in the center of the eye patch was a black insignia. Three joined circles. The same as on the crew's uniforms.

That was all that was needed. "Jou are *el Señor* Uncle Sam!" Revuelta exploded. "But, *Madre de Dios*—jou are *dead*!"

The man stood up and assumed a grandfatherly pose. He wore a long frock coat. The cut of the coat seemed ancient. It, too, partook of the style of the American flag, Revuelta saw.

"You know," he said, in a chuckling tone that was at once professorial and folksy, "some people laughed when I broke ground for Beasleyland. But I knew what I was doing. I saw the future clearly. I knew what people want. They want escape. They want fantasy. And I gave it to them." He chuckled inwardly. "Simple as that. No secret to it."

"I do not understand how jou cannot be dead," Revuelta said, dull-voiced.

The old man went on, as if unhearing. "Vision. That's what it's all about. Vision. Take my work on radio-animatronics. Robots. An old idea. But I made it come to life. People thought I was cracked. 'Why spend the money?' they asked. 'Stick with rides,' they said. 'That's where the money is.' "

The caricature of Uncle Sam paused, and fixed Osvaldo Revuelta with his single good eye.

"You know who Paul Winchell is?" he asked.

Dr. Osvaldo Revuelta shook his head no.

"Ventriloquist. Used to be on TV. Had a dummy named Jerry something-or-other. Not the point. Winchell perfected a valve that to this day is used in artificial hearts. Not many people know this. Not many would believe it. But it's true."

"*Si*, I have heard of this. But what does this mean?"

The weird old man smiled under his frosty mustache. "I'm a futurist. Always have been. The problem with being a futurist is that you never live to see all your works bear fruit. So when they told me I had a bum ticker back in '65, I thought it was the end. But I wasn't about to give up. Not me. So I went to my Concepteers—that's what I call the people who work up my ideas—and put the problem to them. They're good people. At first, they wouldn't touch it. Out of our depth, they said. But when I fired the first few, the others got hopping. That was when I first heard the word 'cryogenics.' That's from the Latin. Means 'the science of super-cold applications.' They explained that if I was willing to be frozen alive in a liquid nitrogen bath, some day a cure for heart disease might be found, and I could be defrosted like a mackerel and fixed up good as new."

The old man chuckled reflectively. "At first I told them they were crazy. I'd rather be dead. Then one of them happened to use the phrase 'suspended animation.' Well, that rang a bell with me, as you might expect. So I said, 'Tell me more.' The more I listened, the more it made sense. I liked the idea. It had vision. But I'm not a man to wait. I said, 'I'll go along, but you people have to pitch in. Do your part. I can't wait for science. I have plans.' Good thing, too, because I keeled over a year later. Massive coronary. I never knew what hit me."

"Jou have been frozen all these jears?" Revuelta gasped.

"You got it."

"But—but there has been no cure for heart disease that I have ever heard of," Revuelta pointed out.

The figure in the Uncle Sam outfit opened his coat and shirt with a single gesture, exposing a wrinkled, hairless chest and a long purple scar over his sternum. He clumped out from behind the desk and stood on an ornate silver peg leg that ended in a rubber cap.

"Transplant?" Revuelta croaked.

"Have a listen," said the old man. Revuelta made a face. "Come on, I don't bite!"

Reluctantly, Dr. Osvaldo Revuelta approached the odd figure. He placed one ear to the scarred chest.

"I hear no beating," he said in a strange voice.

"Animatronics," said the old man in a proud voice. "I own the world's first completely portable artificial ticker. They say it'll keep me going long past my hundredth birthday."

Dr. Revuelta straightened.

"Jou have an animatronic heart?" he gasped.

"When Winchell finds out, he's going to hemorrhage through that stupid dummy's mouth."

And Uncle Sam Beasley laughed his familiar grandfatherly laugh. But to Revuelta's ears, it sounded cracked.

23

Harold Smith's eyes snapped awake. They looked stark as they flicked from the open face of Remo Williams to Chiun's stern visage.

"You saw Sam Beasley?" he croaked.

Remo shook his head. "A pirate. It only looked like Beasley. He had a peg leg, for crying out loud!"

"No," Chiun insisted. "It was Beasley."

"Bulldookey," Remo said.

Smith said dully, "I fear Master Chiun is correct."

"What?"

"Help me to my feet," said Smith.

Remo obliged. Smith wobbled unsteadily on his feet. He leaned against the stainless-steel cryogenic capsule uncertainly.

"Are you okay, Smitty?" Remo asked worriedly.

"Do you recall a popular story about Sam Beasley?" Smith asked in a dry croak.

"That he drew all his own cartoons?"

"He did," Chiun inserted. "Everyone knows this."

"No. That upon his death the company had his body frozen in ice and preserved against the day a cure could be found for his failing heart."

"Boy, I haven't heard that in a long time. That was a myth, wasn't it? People said he was entombed under Star Mountain."

Smith looked upward. "Unless I miss my guess, we are under what remains of Star Mountain."

Remo folded his lean arms. "So?"

"Remo, I am leaning against a cryogenic chamber

designed to store a single human body in suspended animation," Smith said.

Remo's face acquired a strange expression. "Animation?"

Smith nodded. "The sign on the door says 'Reanimation,' " he pointed out.

Remo's eyes took on a look of deep horror. "You're not serious!"

"Remo, how many trucks did you see evacuating this installation?"

"For crying out loud!" Remo said plaintively. "This is *Uncle Sam Beasley* we're talking about!"

"How many?" Smith repeated.

"Six or seven."

"Hmmm. How many Ultima Hora soldiers were killed in Big Cypress?"

"Oh, twenty or so. Not a lot."

Smith frowned. He returned to the Animation Room, Remo and Chiun in tow, and splashed the drawings with his fading penlight.

"According to these," he said slowly, "a force of at least company strength is to be involved in the Zapata assault."

"That's what, a hundred men?"

"Exactly," said Smith, setting his briefcase on the tabletop model of Cuba. He flipped it open and lifted the receiver.

"Mr. President," he said after a brief pause. "This is Smith. I am afraid I have some bad news."

"Bad," groaned Remo in a sick voice. "This is terrible."

"I told you so," said the Master of Sinanju tartly.

But Remo Williams paid no heed. He was thinking that this wasn't over yet. He had wanted the guy who gave the orders to have Ultima Hora slaughtered. If Harold Smith was right, Remo was going to get his wish.

Smith completed his call and faced them stonily.

"The President agrees with my assessment of the situation."

Remo swallowed. "Which is?"

"You are to go to Guantánamo Naval Air Station. Immediately."

"Where's that?" Remo wanted to know.

"Cuba."

"You're sending us to a Cuban air base?"

"No, an American one."

"Since when do we have an air base on Cuba?" Remo demanded.

"Since 1903," Harold Smith said flatly.

Guantánamo Naval Air Station sprawled on the tail of the alligator shape that was the island of Cuba. It was surrounded by anti-submarine nets on the Guantánamo Bay side, and electrified fences, guard towers, and the largest mine field ever laid on the landward perimeters.

Hostile forces of the elite Cuban Frontier Brigade were picketed beyond the fence, always watching. Cuban aircraft buzzed this vast acreage daily. Other than by air or sea, the only way in or out was through a fenced-off corridor between the approximately fifty thousand antipersonnel mines.

On this, the second day of the Cuban crisis, no one was walking the narrow enclosure.

Navy Captain Bob Brown was explaining the crisis to his visitors as they stepped out of the C-130 cargo plane.

"Fidel's gone too far this time," he said bitterly. "I've skippered this place ten years now. It's never been this bad. Never!"

Remo looked past the airfield. "Gitmo"—as the captain had called it—was bigger than he'd imagined. It also looked pretty peaceful for a base that was, after all, in the middle of an enemy nation. He spotted a church steeple, nice homes—even the golden arches of a McDonald's.

"I don't see any trouble," said Remo, as they climbed into a waiting jeep. The captain drove.

"They blockaded our front gate!" he said savagely. "Nobody can go in or out. And we're on Water Condition Bravo."

"How bad is that?"

"How bad? I'll tell you how bad. The desalinization plant it on the fritz. There's been no water for the fairway for three weeks straight, and we're down to doing the wash on alternate days."

"Fairway?"

"We're blessed with an eighteen-holer. How do they expect us to defend democracy, if we can't break the monotony with a few rounds now and then?"

"Listen Captain—"

"Skipper. Call me Skipper. Everybody calls me Skipper."

"Let's get back to the security problem," Remo said.

"Problem? It's an unmitigated disaster! They've always allowed our Cuban help to pass through the front gate freely. The wash is not only backed up for lack of water, but we don't have anybody to do it." He plucked at his uniform. "Look at this. Wrinkled worse than my granny's face. And the fairway! The shade trees are dying. Ever try to play through eighteen holes without benefit of shade? It'll throw you off your game quicker than dysentery."

Remo was sitting beside the captain. He used his foot to press the captain's boot onto the brake. The jeep lurched to a halt. Remo grabbed the captain by the throat and squeezed.

"Listen," he bit out. "I'm only going to say this once. Never mind who we are. We represent the highest authorities. Got that? They sent us here to do a job. Out beyond the fence. Are you with me so far?"

Remo allowed the man a sip of air. It went whistling in past his larynx and came out a strangled grunt.

"I'll take that as a glimmer of understanding," said Remo. "Now, we don't have a lot of time. Take us to the entrance gate, and we'll leave you to your miserable existence."

Navy Captain Bob Brown went pale. His eyes seemed to retreat into his head. Remo encouraged him with a squeeze, then released him.

The captain got the jeep going. It went racing past

a crushed-coral golf course dotted with wilting mango trees, toward a line of guard towers manned by sharpshooters. Beyond were purple mountains and scooting fluffy clouds.

Moments later, the jeep pulled up at the inner-perimeter fence. There were triangular red signs that warned:

DANGER/PELIGRO
MINES/MINAS

"I take it this is the famous minefield," Remo said.

"Yes, sir."

"Don't 'sir' me. I'm a civilian." Remo spied a long thin dirt path through the field. Hurricane fences paralleled it.

"That the way out?" he asked.

"They've threatened to shoot anyone who sets foot on it," Captain Brown offered.

"They say anything about walking through the minefield?"

"No. But that's certain death."

"Only if you step on a mine," said Remo. He turned in his seat and said, "Coming, Little Father?"

The Master of Sinanju stepped from the vehicle. His face was tight.

"I do not like this assignment."

"You've been saying that all through the plane ride. Give it a rest."

Captain Brown looked interested. "You guys here to smoke Castro by any chance?"

"Hear hear," Chiun said.

"He wishes," Remo grumbled. "But orders are different this time out. We gotta protect him."

"From who?"

"Believe me, you'll sleep better if you don't know."

They started toward the minefield.

The captain called after them, "Hey, good luck! This base may have its down side, but there's no drugs, no guns, no juvenile delinquency, and no crime. I'd hate to be evaced to the States. It's not safe up there."

Chiun frowned. "I do not understand this lunacy."

"What lunacy?" asked Remo, as they approached the minefield fence. "The lunacy of being sent to protect Castro, or the lunacy of the skipper back there?"

"Both lunacies. If this bearded tyrant rules this island, why does he suffer the presence of his enemies? And if he is so weak as to allow this, why does Emperor Smith not simply have us dispatch him?"

"Politics are complicated."

"But death is the great toppler of dynasties."

They went to a gate in the minefield fence, and Remo sheared the padlock off with a sweep of his hand. He threw open the gate.

"Ready?" Remo asked.

Chiun nodded.

They walked into the minefield.

It was not as dangerous as it looked. For mines to be planted, soil has to be removed and repacked. No one who digs a hole and puts something in it ever gets all the soil back into the hole. That was certainly the case here. Rains had tamped down the loose soil around the mines. This wasn't noticeable to the naked eye, but as Remo and Chiun's feet inched through the minefield, their toes could feel the slight sponginess of the softer earth. Each time they encountered a spot of less resistance, they stepped around it.

By meandering through the hard-packed ground surrounding the mines, they reached the outer fence. It hummed. Electrified.

This presented a problem. Until Remo, using a spade-shaped hand, excavated a buried mine. He blew crumbs of moist soil off the top and placed it in a small depression the Master of Sinanju had cleared under the fence edge.

Then they retreated to a safe distance and threw a rock.

It struck the plunger. The mine made a surprisingly muffled boomlet . . . and there was a hole in the fence, like a torn sheet of paper.

They slipped through this hole easily.

Then the snipers of the Frontier Brigade, who had been watching in wide-eyed fascination, began to open fire.

It was lucky they did so. They first bullets missed Remo and Chiun completely. But they triggered mines placed on the other side of the perimeter fence.

"That idiot never said anything about another minefield!" Remo burst out.

"Perhaps these are *Cuban* mines," said Chiun.

A mine erupted a few yards in front of them, showering them with clods of dirt.

"Great," muttered Remo. "We're sitting ducks."

"Not if we keep our wits about us," said Chiun, bending down to scoop out a long-buried mine. It was gray, and shaped like a soup can with antennae.

He threw it. The mine, tumbling, sailed toward a royal palm tree, where a lone sniper was perched.

It landed, plungers down, in the swaying fronds. The top of the palm jumped apart. Palm fronds, rifle fragments, and assorted human limbs and organs showered down. The stone-gray bole now sported arty red stripes.

"Good thinking," said Remo.

Together, they excavated mines and tossed them at muzzle flashes. Before long, they had decapitated every palm in sight and cleared a lot of brush.

When the firing had stopped completely, they picked their way through the mines. It was easy, this time. The snipers had cleared most of the mines for them.

They found a jeeplike Russian-made Gazik vehicle, keys still in the ignition, and commandeered it. No one stopped them.

"Okay, on to Zapata Swamp," Remo said grimly.

"I am not looking forward to this," Chiun said thinly.

"I know what you mean."

"I have no desire to be the one to slay the illustrious Uncle Sam Beasley."

Remo said nothing, but he was thinking the same thing himself.

And he knew that before the day was done, he might have to kill his childhood hero in the name of his country. The thought made him sick to his stomach.

24

The President of Cuba puffed angrily as he stared out his office window. He had to be very angry, to puff in full view of the masses below. For he had sworn to them that he had given up his cherished cigars, as a token of the new Cuban smoking-prevention program he himself had inaugurated amid much fanfare.

He had said it was for the health and well-being of his beloved Cuba. It took him four hours of passionate speech-making to get his point across, appealing to the people's pride, their patriotism, their concern for their precious Socialist lungs.

In fact, the program was a blind to cover the sad fact that the tobacco crop had failed miserably, leaving only enough for the people to smoke their cigarettes— or Fidel his magnificent cigars.

That had been an easy choice. He would never give up his cigars. He would sooner shave his beloved beard.

An adjutant came in, gasping.

"Another MIG has been shot down!"

"Bah! Send another!"

"But El Lider, we have no more petrol to fuel them!"

El Lider turned angrily, puffing like a steam shovel.

"Then siphon some from my personal helicopter, dolt!"

The man saluted smartly. "At once, El Lider!"

An orderly came in a moment later. Fidel knew it was an orderly, because they were required to call him

El Presidente. Each rank of subordinates was restricted in the manner in which they could address him. His women invariably called him El Guapo Grosso.

"El Presidente!" gasped the orderly.

"What is it now?"

"A ship has been sighted bearing toward Havana Harbor."

The Maximum Leader turned from the window curiously. "What ship?"

"An American vessel."

"A warship?"

"No. A cruise ship. It bears the name *Beasley Adventure.*"

"Beasley! *El* Sam Beasley?"

"*Sí,* El Presidente."

The Maximum Leader of Cuba took his cigar from his bushy mouth and grinned fiercely. "He made *mucho gusto* cartoons in his day!"

"*Sí,* El Presidente. I personally am a fan of Dingbat Duck."

"Bah! He is nothing beside the pure flame that is Monongahela Mouse. A mouse after my own heart, that one! Now, as for this matter: The stupid *capitan* must be lost. Capture that ship! We will ransom it."

"*Sí,* El Presidente."

In the filthy waters off Havana Harbor, Cuban gunboats surrounded the *Beasley Adventure,* like minnows around a basking shark.

The captain of the flotilla lifted a megaphone to his mouth and shouted up.

"Prepare to be boarded, or jou will be blown out of the water!"

It was a colossal bluff. If a firing squad hadn't been the reward for disobedience, he would never have been so audacious as to risk it.

To his surprise, a white-uniformed captain leaned over the rail and shouted down through a megaphone of his own. It was quite powerful. It nearly blasted the Cuban captain's hat off his head with just two words.

"We surrender!"

"Jou will follow us to Habana Harbor!" the captain shouted back.

"Understood!"

And like a tamed and beaten Moby Dick, the leviathan cruise liner *Beasley Adventure* fell in behind the scooting gunboats.

All along the decks, Cuban naval guns fired into the air in joyous celebration.

The captain shared in none of it. He licked his lips in worriment, as the crumbling gray lines of Morro Castle loomed ahead.

"This is too easy," he muttered.

25

The sun was setting in the turquoise expanse of The Bay of Pigs when the first low shapes appeared on the horizon.

First there was but one.

Faustino Barranca, of the Cuban Territorial Troops Militia, saw it through the crimson haze of the setting sun, as if in a dream. He had been grilling alligator meat for his dinner. Since Option Zero, Faustino had personally thinned the alligator population of Zapata Swamp, overlooking the historic Bay of Pigs. It wasn't particularly tasty, but it was better than banana-rat stew.

He had been told of the failed U.S. incursion. All Cuba knew of it. It worried the people greatly, because El Loco Fidel had used it as an excuse to attack Florida. Unsuccessfully, it was true. But the rumors were that he would not give up until he had struck the Colossus of the North a mortal blow.

Everyone knew that the result of this insanity was beyond question: a small crater in Florida—and all of Cuba an inferno.

No one doubted the rationale for this. Socialism was failing. Cuba was crumbling. Castro would fall one day. He was not a man to fall gracefully. Not with his monumental ego.

The Maximum Leader would rather see armageddon, the utter destruction of Cuba, than accept the humiliation of political defeat.

So when the barges began to appear in the dancing

red reflections on the Caribbean, Faustino threw sand on his roasting fire to quench it and gathered up his Dragunov sniper's rifle.

If these were the Americans, it could only mean that Fidel had succeeded—and Cuba was as good as toast. He wept silently.

The barges grew in number, until they were strung out along the Bay like dark bars of soap.

From low superstructures, dishlike shapes revolved. Their designs were familiar, yet not. As he watched, Faustino came to recognize the odd configuration of three joined discs.

He blinked. *"Mongo?"*

Then the uniformed figures seated low in their seats stood up in unison. In perfect synchronization, they turned as one.

Rifles snapped to bulky shoulders. It was perfect. Not a man was out of order.

And as if a single button had been pressed, the murderous automatic weapons fire began to rake Zapata Swamp.

Faustino flung himself into the mangroves. He had no choice now but to return fire. He was a sharp-shooter. And he was good.

With his eye to the scope, he selected a soldier. The cross hairs lined up with the silhouette of his head, and Faustino squeezed the trigger.

The dark head exploded on its shoulders.

Faustino grinned through his sweat and fear. He had scored a direct hit with his first shot!

Then he laid his eyes against his scope again . . . and saw that the man he had shot, the headless man, was still firing. Firing without a head!

Faustino was so shocked by this sight that, unnerved, he jumped to his feet, the better to see this incredible thing.

A stitchery of bullets violently sewed his tunic to his chest and Faustino Barranca was flung into the mangrove tangle where the alligators would later find in him a tasty snack.

Mouse-eared radar dishes whirling, the amphibious

barges came on. Firing relentlessly. Without mercy. Without surcease.

Not even when the rumbling T-64 Cuban Revolutionary Armed Forces tanks came, and began to return the withering fire.

"What manner of *soldados* are these?!" the tank commander cried. For he saw through his binoculars men without arms, without heads, shattered and broken, yet still firing. Some wildly, others with unerring aim. "They are like machines, not *hombres*!"

26

The Maximum Leader of Cuba was beside himself.

The first reports from Zapata Swamp were incredible. A sea armada. Soldiers who continued to fire even as they were being blown to pieces.

He would have ordered the man who brought him the message shot for intoxication on duty, but the only alcohol on the entire island was safely housed in his private wine cellar.

"Our forces are being decimated, El Jefe!" The man was a major, so he was allowed to call him that. "Only your heroic presence will rally them!"

"Good thinking. Order my private helicopter to be readied. The one with the custom bar."

"But El Jefe, there is no petrol! It has been siphoned into a MIG, as per your instructions!"

Maximum Leader glowered. "Then summon the MIG back. We can bomb the nuclear plant later."

"It is too late, El Jefe! The MIG has been destroyed! Shot down!"

"Then we will *drive* to Zapata Swamp!" he bellowed. "Make it so!" he added, borrowing a line from his favorite American TV show.

"At once, El Jefe!"

Then another flunky came running in, with the news that the *Beasley Adventure* had been forcibly docked at the rusting oil terminal in the harbor.

"Has it been boarded yet?" he demanded.

"No, El Presidente."

Fidel struck a pose. "Good. Good. For I must be the one to board it personally."

"But El Jefe," the first man asked worriedly, "what of the Zapata incursion?"

"Order all forces mobilized to repel that cowardly assault. Hurl the *Yanquis* back into the bay. I have more important things to do."

"But . . . but—"

"*Go,* dolt!"

To the hovering orderly, he hissed, "Is Mongo on board?"

The orderly shrugged. "I did not see him, El Presidente."

"He will be aboard. For he is ever-present. I look forward to meeting him." The President drew on his campaign cap. "Let us go."

His personal customized Gazik whisked the Maximum Leader of Cuba from the Presidential Palace to the oil terminal. Traffic, normally light in these petroleum-starved times, was extraordinarily heavy. All of it consisted of military vehicles mobilized for the drive to Zapata Swamp. And all flowing in the opposite direction—out of Havana.

Cuba's leader was oblivious to the massive response to his all-powerful orders. A beaming grin struggled past his dark profusion of beard. He was looking forward to this rendezvous very much.

After all, he was Mongo Mouse's biggest fan.

27

Remo Williams had been supplied a detailed map of Cuba by Harold W. Smith. It showed all highways, significant roads and military installations, and mileage distance between. A big red circle indicated Guantánamo Naval Air Base and another highlighted Zapata Swamp, with a fat red line connecting the two.

Smith, after he had drawn the red parts, had pronounced the map foolproof.

Unfortunately, he had overlooked the fact that the map was a product of the nation's brief flirtation with the metric system. Mileage was given in kilometers.

"We're lost," grumbled Remo, who didn't know a kilometer from a kiloton. It was a balmy night in Cuba. The royal palms swayed in the breeze, like hula dancers with shaggy heads, as he tried to read the tiny mileage numbers by moonlight.

"How can we be lost?" Chiun said plaintively. "You have the Emperor's personal map."

"It's in kilometers. I only know miles."

"I have told you that you should be acquainted with all tongues," Chiun sniffed.

"Give me a break! The kilometer isn't a verb. It's a unit of measure. A stupid, useless unit of measure. I figure we've come thirty miles. What I want to know is, how many kilometers is that?" He looked toward a nearby city. "If that's Sancti Spíritus, we should take the left-hand road. But I don't see any signs saying it is."

"Even if you did," Chiun sniffed, "it would not help you, who cannot read elementary Spanish."

"I can read signs," Remo said defensively.

"If that is so, why can you not read a simple plan, on which circles and lines have been drawn for you in crayon? A child could follow that map."

Remo got the Gazik in gear, saying, "It's not crayon. It's Magic Marker."

Chiun sniffed. "An American crayon. There is no difference."

They received a lot of attention as they barreled along. Natives of amazingly varied skin colors waved to them as they passed.

It was crazy, but Remo took a chance and stopped.

"Sancti Spíritus?" he asked a roly-poly woman who looked amazingly like Aunt Jemima, pointing to the left-hand road. She was carrying her wet wash bundled on her head.

"*Sí, sí,*" she said pleasantly.

Remo threw her a *gracias* and took the left fork with confidence.

"The natives are unaccountably friendly," Chiun remarked.

"Or dumb as posts," Remo muttered. "We could be Schwarzkopf and Colin Powell, for all they know."

Behind them they heard a low roar, growing louder as it came closer. They looked back and saw a mechanized column approaching at a high rate of speed.

"Uh-oh," said Remo, pulling over to the side of the road. They got their vehicle into some brush and waited for the convoy to pass.

It was big. And long—consisting of T-64 tanks, BMP armored vehicles, and lurching Gaziks like their own. There was also a flock of military bicycles.

"They appear to be in a hurry," said Chiun, peering through rank foliage.

"I wonder," Remo muttered. "Could they be going where *we're* going?"

"If that is so, the attack has begun."

Remo got the stubborn engine going. "Let's follow them."

They shot out of the brush and fell in behind the column. Fortunately the roads were of hard-packed dirt, and the long tunnel of dust the convoy was generating was more than enough to conceal them.

At a major fork in the road the convoy encountered another and, after some argument over who would get to lead the march, formed one long olive-green line. A few miles along, the long convoy absorbed another.

Overhead, a lone observation helicopter sputtered along, heading north. It seemed to be running on empty.

"We may be too late," Remo said darkly.

By the time the swamp-stink had begun to tickle their sensitive noses, they could hear the sound of automatic weapons fire, punctuated by the relentless *boom-boom-boom* of artillery pieces and 125-mm tank cannon.

"We're too late!" Remo snapped. He was standing up in his seat, trying to make out the scene through the haze of gunsmoke and roiling oil smoke.

"What do you see?" asked Chiun, straining unsuccessfully on tippytoe.

"I see barges out in the water. They're taking a pounding."

"Is this good or is this bad?" Chiun wanted to know.

Remo had to think about that a minute.

"It's good for our mission, I think," he said slowly. "But it's bad for Cuba."

"Is it good for the bearded tyrant, the preempter of beauty and joy?" asked Chiun.

Remo's brow puckered. "Yeah. Dammit, it is."

Chiun's face darkened. "There is no justice."

"Let's see if we can't scare up our own," Remo said, dropping into the seat and sending the Gazik bumping and jouncing along the rough terrain.

As they drove, their tires popped the swarms of fleeing red crabs, with a sound like a symphony of flat tires.

When they had reached the edge of a vast swamp, they jumped out and climbed a hillock.

They had a panoramic view of the Bay of Pigs. The barges were as thick as ice cakes in an Arctic sea. As they watched, men in old-fashioned pirate costumes shouted in Spanish and swept the defenders strung along the swamp with concentrated fire. Remo recognized a few choice curses.

A number of barges had run aground and been blown up in the mangrove tangle. They were littered with heads and limbs and other body parts. There was no visible blood on the wrecked amphibious barges.

But they did notice the radar dishes shaped like Mongo Mouse heads.

"Why do they need radar?" Remo wondered.

"Because they are blind," said Chiun.

Remo looked down at the Master of Sinanju blankly. "Try me again, Little Father?"

Chiun beckoned for Remo to follow. Remo complied.

They came down the hillock, as the bullets and shells whistled all around them. They slipped down to the moonlit water and waded through the mangroves, which resembled multi-legged trees attempting to rise up out of the water.

They worked their way to one of the half-sunken barges.

"Behold!" cried Chiun, dragging a corsair off the rail where he had been slumped. His body ended at the waist, tapering into a male electronic connection the size of a fireplug.

Remo grunted. "Hey, this guy's animatronic!"

"All are," said Chiun. "This is why they need mouse heads to tell them where to point their boomsticks."

Remo looked out across the darkling Bay of Pigs. The pirates in the barges, some standing, some sitting, were firing in precise controlled bursts, stopping to reload with the same jerky economy of motion as a factory robot designed to fill empty cans with sliced peaches.

"I don't see any live guys," Remo said.

"There are none," Chiun said.

As they watched, a barge passed more or less unscathed through the murderous fire and coasted toward them. They slipped down until the rank water lapped at their lower eyelashes.

The barge nudged a mangrove clump, splintering it. The pirates, seated, continued to fire mechanically, while the mouse-head radar—with one ear blown off—continued its back-and-forth rotation.

"They're not getting out," Remo whispered, lifting his mouth free of the water to speak. He was not fired on.

"They are not created to perform that task," Chiun agreed. "For they have no legs."

"So what's the point? They can't take the beach—I mean, swamp. And the first rule of invasion is: grab a piece of land and hold it."

Chiun frowned.

"This is not the invasion," he said.

"Well, they're doing a bang-up imitation."

"This is a diversion," said Chiun.

"Maybe it's just to soften up the Cubans until the main force arrives," Remo suggested. "Remember Ultima Hora?"

"There is one way to find out. And that is to end this charade now."

With that, the Master of Sinanju porpoised into the water and swam toward the grounded barge.

Remo, ducking, followed.

Chiun floated under the barge and scored a circular hole in the flat-bottomed hull with one long fingernail. He tapped the circle with a knuckle. It popped in like a soup can lid.

The barge quickly filled, and they watched it as it sank. The pirates—and a ragtag crew they were—continued to fire as they sank. They gave off bluish-green sparks as water found their electronic components, and their guns sputtered into silence.

The last one vented a squawky *Tu Madre!* before it sank.

"Looks like a breeze," Remo said. "Let's do the job."

They swam out into the bay. The high-powered bullets were a nuisance, but they hit the water and immediately deflected at crazy shallow angles, to drop harmlessly to the ocean floor. The water was unnaturally warm.

Remo and Chiun split up and attacked the barges from below. Chiun scored holes with his nails. Remo, who had always resisted Chiun's insistence that he grow killing nails of proper length, used the blunt tip of his forefinger as a punch press instead. The stiff digit made thirsty drill-bit holes.

To the hunkered-down Cuban detachments along the beach at Playa Giron and stuck in the muck of Zapata Swamp, it looked as if their return fire was finally winning the day. One by one the barges had listed, capsized, or simply taken on water.

The order to cease firing came, and they watched in muted awe as the pirates continued to fire even as they went down with their ungainly ships. The water swallowed their muzzles and their still functioning mouths. Some of them were swearing in mechanical voices even afterward.

Silence settled over the Bay of Pigs.

And the crabs scuttled out of their places of concealment, and the long-necked buzzards floated over broken human carrion.

Remo and Chiun returned to a sheltered portion of the shore in the silence. They looked out over the bay. A huge full moon rose higher, seeming to shrink as it climbed.

"Guess there's no main task force," Remo muttered. "So where's the invasion?"

Then, from behind them, they heard excited cries in Spanish.

"What are they saying?" Remo asked Chiun. The Master of Sinanju listened with grim mien.

At length he said, "They are saying Habana does

not answer their radio calls. They fear it is under attack."

Remo dug out his map and looked at it.

"I don't see any 'Habana,' " he said.

"It is called 'Havana' on the map."

"Then why doesn't it *say* that?" Remo demanded, ripping the map to shreds and scattering it away.

The convoys started to back up. Between the damaged vehicles and the ones that had used their yearly allotment of gas to reach the combat zone, they managed only to create a logjam that trapped the rest. Spanish curses flew. Fights broke out over ownership of bicycles.

"So much for the Cuban cavalry," Remo grunted. "I'd say Fidel has been suckered good."

"So have we. For we must reach Havana immediately."

Remo looked around. He spotted the FAR helicopter, sitting like a droopy-winged dragonfly on a low hill.

"If there's any gas left in that bird, I think we have a chance," he said.

They flitted toward the waiting bird, avoiding the Cuban bodies—which the scarlet land crabs had already begun to attack hungrily.

28

The Maximum Leader of Cuba strode up the waiting gangplank to the gleaming white cruise ship, *Beasley Adventure*. It was magnificent! And so clean, it sparkled as if dusted by pixies.

Right then and there he decided not to ransom the opulent floating palace, but its crew and passengers only. He would keep it for his personal yacht. It was a prize worthy of the greatest soldier of the Americas, himself.

At the top of the gangplank two stewards in white waited for him, standing at attention. They were unarmed. In fact, they saluted crisply as he stepped onto the deck, trailed by a contingent of his loyal bodyguards.

"Why am I not met by the captain, as is fitting?" demanded the President of Cuba.

"The captain is expecting you in the main dining room, sir," one steward said politely.

El Lider blinked. He liked the treatment these men were according him. It was *muy* respectful.

"I will go to him!" he snapped. Motioning for his men to follow, he stormed along the deck, taking in the beauty of the prize that was now the flagship of the Cuban navy. Perhaps he would have it outfitted with surface-to-air missiles. No doubt the Beasley people would have fits, but in the historic struggle between ideologies the capitalists could expect no quarter.

They were two more stewards standing at attention

in front of the main dining salon, on B Deck. They
saluted with one hand, and with the other reached out
to open the doors.

El Lider nodded curtly as he swaggered into the
breathtaking crystalline sumptuousness of the salon.

He heard the muffled gunshots and turned, cigar
dropping from his mouth.

The stewards had each put a bullet into the brains
of his two closest bodyguards. They were crumpling
to the floor as, from places of concealment behind
gleaming white ventilators, others opened up on the
remnants of his protective contingent.

"*Mierda!*" he raged.

And the doors were clapped shut in his bearded
face.

"Welcome," a voice said.

The Cuban leader whirled, eyes stark.

Across the room, a captain in a starched white uniform sat quietly at the head table.

Making fists with his hands, El Lider stormed toward
the man. If necessary, he would break this dandy's
neck with his bare hands.

Out from under the tables, soldiers appeared. They
wore white jumpsuits and carried AR-15 automatic
rifles with ludicrously white stocks. There was an
insignia on each stock. The same insignia was on
patches stitched to their shoulders.

It was the world-famous silhouette of Monongahela
Mouse, he saw.

The rifles were all pointing toward him. He came
to a stop.

"I see, I see," he grumbled. "This is, how jou say,
a 'Troyan Horse'?"

"Not exactly," came a cool voice from behind him,
a voice with a kind of gravelly twinkle in it. "Although
this ship *is* just filled with young lads just waiting for
the signal to march into Havana. But you might say
what we have here is more of a kangaroo court."

The Maximum Leader of Cuba turned. And beheld
the last face in the world he had expected to see.

"*Uncle Sam?*"

*   *   *

The Cuban helicopter pilot was only too happy to give the Anglo and the old man from the East a ride to Habana. There was only one problem.

"There is no petrol, *señores!*"

"There enough to get us in the air?" asked the Anglo, holding him up as the waves of pain continued to converge on his poor heart.

"*Sí*. But how far, no one can say!"

"Let's take this one step at a time," said the Anglo.

And then, because the Anglo had been good enough to relocate his shoulders, the Cuban pilot happily lifted the helicopter into the air.

They had to stop twice for fuel. Petrol was a precious thing in the Cuban Revolutionary Army, and hoarded zealously. The Cuban pilot had told the pair of this, but they had seemed strangely unconcerned.

The pilot at last understood why, when they settled down next to a disabled T-64 tank and the two made the stranded tank crew perform the difficult act of siphoning the gas into the helicopter.

It was amazing, the things men could do even with their shoulders dislocated.

On the last leg of the trip the Anglo turned to the old man and, over the rattly clattering of the laboring helicopter, shouted, "Teach me some Spanish, Little Father."

"Why?"

"Because when I meet Castro, I want to give him a piece of my mind in his own tongue."

The President of Cuba wore the expression of a poleaxed zebu.

A figure stood up from behind a long banquet table. It was a ludicrous figure, dressed in the frock coat and top hat of the mythic symbol of American imperialism, Uncle Sam. Even his eye patch matched his costume. It was blue, and sprinkled with white stars.

But this Uncle Sam was not the graybeard of cartoons, but a cartoonist renowned throughout the world.

"But, jou . . . jou are *dead,* Uncle Sam Beasley!"

The man smiled under his frosty brush mustache. It was a reflective smile, if chilly.

"You know," he said thoughtfully, "when I first explained my ideas for Beasley Isle, a lot of my people thought I had been in the freezer too long."

" 'Beasley Isle'?"

" 'Cuba' sounds too ethnic. People don't want ethnicity in their leisure activities. That's why I had them call my French base EuroBeasley. Sounds more palatable. Anyway, I first got the idea after they pulled me out of that damn icebox."

"Icebox?"

"Everything had changed. Including our tax base. Revenue was down. Attendance off. But taxes were through the roof. I had bases all over the world, and the host countries were sucking every operation dry of operating capital through value-added taxes and every other kind of damn tax you could think of. So I asked myself, how can I be sure that the Beasley Corporation will survive into the next century, since it looks like I'm going to?"

"I do not know," El Lider said thickly, his mind still processing the impossibility of Uncle Sam Beasley standing before him, in the flesh.

"I'll tell you what came to me," said the star-spangled apparition. "I said, Beasley's too big now to be a corporation. It should be a nation. Think of it! An entire island that is also a theme park. It'll be bigger than all the other Beasley parks combined. Folks will flock from all over the world! And when they do, I'll just shut down the other parks. No more taxes. No more minimum-wage laws. No more government regulations. And maybe down the road when the fuss is over, after we're admitted into the U.N., I'll wrangle a seat on the Security Council and do really big things."

"Jou are going to turn my Cuba into a park!" El Lider roared.

The frost-tipped brush mustache quirked over snowy teeth. "I thought you'd be impressed."

"This will never happen! Never!"

"Thanks to Leo Zorilla, it will."

El Lider narrowed his eyes.

"That name sounds familiar," he mumbled, scratching his beard.

"Deputy Commandant, Cuban Air Force. Diabetic. He was picked up by this very vessel some months back. Unfortunately, the INS got to him before I could. But we got together. I offered him a job in return for whatever military secrets he cared to divulge."

"That traitor! I will have him shot!"

"Too late. He's history. Just as you, my friend, will be."

"Jou are *loco!*"

A twinkle came into the man's single visible eye. "You know what Leo told me? He told me that the weakest point in the Cuban coastal-defense net was the one everybody thought would be the strongest. Any idea where that is?"

The Maximum Leader suddenly turned green.

"Playa Giron?"

"Or Red Beach, as we say north of the border. It made sense to me. No one would want a repeat of the Bay of Pigs fiasco. You thought you could leave it unguarded, relatively speaking."

"Hah! The yoke is on jou. It is no longer unguarded. I have ordered the cream of the Revolution to that historic place!"

"That's right, you did. You've got practically all your regulars out there right now, shooting at animatronic soldiers."

"Animatronic?"

"You can't kill them, but they can kill you. Gives new meaning to the word 'expendable,' doesn't it?"

El Lider gaped. "A diversion?"

"I believe you said something about 'a Trojan Horse' earlier."

"And jou said something about a kangaroo court. I suppose you think jou can try me?"

"Intend to."

"Hah!" said the President of Cuba, pounding on his massive chest. "Do your worst! I am above your laws.

Above history. Jou cannot try me for war crimes. I have committed none. I am a revolutionary, a soldier of the Americas doing the work of the revolutionary. My interventions in other countries are no different than that of any great historical world power. The acts I have committed in my own country are the business of Cuba and Cuba alone. Jou cannot try me for these things."

"I don't expect to," said Uncle Sam Beasley in his dry-ice voice.

The President of Cuba plowed on as if unhearing. He was on a roll. He began ticking off points on his thick fingers.

"Jou cannot try me for crimes against the U.S.A., jou cannot try me for crimes against my people, jou cannot try me for—"

"Try copyright violations," said Uncle Sam.

El Lider's mouth dropped open in mid-word. "Copy—"

"You've been pirating my programs. I don't like that. I put a lot of sweat into those things." And with that, Uncle Sam Beasley took up a gavel and banged it twice on the banquet table.

From behind curtains came Mongo Mouse, Dingbat Duck, Screwball Squirrel, and a host of other fictitious characters. They took seats on either side of Uncle Sam, who then sat down.

"The Beasley Tribunal is in session," he snapped.

The President of Cuba blinked furiously. He had always understood the time might come when he would fall from power and be haled before a tribunal such as this. He looked at the jury again and thought, well, not exactly like *this*. . . .

He had practiced the speech he would give on this occasion. Every act of revolution he would defend fiercely, passionately, unassailably. He had dreamed of this moment. Looked forward to it almost, confident that his sharp wits and silver tongue would vindicate him before the world.

But he had certainly never taken the charge of copyright piracy into account. And here he was, forced to defend himself before the bizarre representatives of the most ferocious defenders of copyright on earth.

Feeling his bull-like shoulders sag, the Maximum Leader threw out his chest in defiance. "I insist upon being tried by my own countrymen. Only they can properly yudge me. Not these running dogs! No offense to jou, Gumpy."

Gumpy Dog cocked his floppy-eared head in an injured manner.

"Tell you what," said Beasley. "I'll throw in a Cuban." He lifted his voice. "Dr. Revuelta. Would you kindly join us?"

From behind the curtain came a Cuban the Cuban president knew only too well.

"*Jou! Jou terrorista!*" he raged.

"Dr. Revuelta will be installed as interim president," said Uncle Sam. "Having one of their own as head of the government will keep the population pacified."

The Cuban President shook a big fist. "Him? Never! He is a mediocrity."

"Actually, he's a gynecologist," Uncle Sam pointed out with a smile.

Dr. Revuelta took a seat beside Wacky Wolf.

"I understand you were a lawyer before you turned revolutionary," Uncle Sam said mildly. "I'll allow you to act as your own counsel."

"Challenge accepted."

Uncle Sam chuckled. "I thought you'd say that, you big blowhard. Seems I recall an old adage that goes, 'A man who acts as his own lawyer has a fool for a client.' "

"Bah!"

"So how do you plead?"

The Maximum Leader of Cuba gazed at the bizarre tribunal seated before him. His quick mind went back to his first trial, back in the old days. He had coined a phrase then. One which he still liked very much. It had resounded in the courtroom then, and he had shouted it to *las masas* ever since. It had gotten him through every political and strategic mistake he'd ever committed. He repeated it now.

"My guilt or innocence is not for such as jou to say!" he bellowed, shaking an agitated finger in their faces. "History will absolve me!"

And then he launched into a speech, which he intended to go down in history as the longest of his bombastic career.

For the more he kept talking, the more likely it was that his loyal soldiers would come to succor him.

29

The President of Cuba was appealing to Monongahela Mouse when his ears picked up the faint clattery rattle of helicopter blades. It was very near. He raised his bull voice to drown out the warning sounds. No doubt it was crack Cuban Marines of the Guevara Battalion, landing on the deck.

"Mongo, my brother," he said as he paced before the Beasley Tribunal. "I appeal to your renowned sense of fairness. Jou and I are *mucho hombres*. I am a man among men and jou, magnificent one, are a mouse among—how jou say?—mouses."

Mongo stared blankly, round-eared and round-eyed. It was impossible to tell if he was reaching the indefatigable rodent, so the Cuban kept talking.

"The children of Cuba love jou, as do I. How could I, their beloved Lider Maximo, deprive them of your adventures simply because our capitals do not have proper relations?"

The mouse cocked one ear to one side. The duck was nodding its orange beak imperceptibly. And best of all, Uncle Sam himself was growing sleepy of eye. It was working. They were becoming like silly putty in the grip of his oratorical might. Confident, he pressed on.

And the doors banged open.

Fidel turned, a broad grin splitting the bush that was his lower face.

"What took jou so—" He gulped, and swallowed his words.

A lone man stood framed in the salon entrance. He wore black. He was unarmed. Yet the expression on his face was one of utter confidence.

"What the fuck!" snarled Uncle Sam.

"Jou again!" gasped Dr. Revuelta.

"Que?" gulped Fidel Castro.

"Que sera, sera," said Remo, showing off his newly acquired knowledge of Spanish.

The Maximum Leader of Cuba looked at the dark-eyed Anglo with the high cheekbones and thick wrists, and spat out a harsh question in English.

"Who are jou, *Yanqui*?"

Remo smiled. *"Yo soy soldado de los Americas."*

And the Maximum Leader of Cuba did a slow burn that all but singed his curly beard. Who was this gringo, to claim the sacred mantle of the Latin American revolutionary?

Before he could voice the question, Uncle Sam Beasley thundered, "Somebody shoot that pain in the ass!"

It was an unfortunate order. Fully half the armed guards thought the pain in the ass was the Cuban leader. The others correctly took the command as directed toward the skinny guy in black.

"No! No! Not *that* pain in the ass! The other one!"

The soldiers who had been pointing their weapons at Remo redirected them at Fidel. Their opposite numbers executed the opposite maneuver.

Uncle Sam Beasley stood up, howling, *"No! No! No!* You're getting it all wrong! Listen to me, I'm the director here! Ten-*hup*! Right shoulder arms!"

Like marionettes, the soldiers clapped the AR-15s to their immaculate white shoulders. Their chins lifted at attention.

It was the perfect opportunity, so Remo swept in and grabbed the President of Cuba by his long gray beard. Without pausing, he gave a flick of one thick wrist, and suddenly the giant Cuban was whirling around Remo's head like a bull roarer. And emitting much the same howl.

"Don't shoot! Don't shoot!" Beasley yelled. "The trial isn't over yet!"

Remo released the beard. And the howling man flew, polished hobnailed combat boots first, toward one line of soldiers. They collapsed in a heap of bruises and broken bones.

Uncle Sam was screaming inarticulate orders now.

Remo was moving between the dining tables, casually flinging them about like oversized frisbees. They lopped off heads, broke rifles, and made short work of the white-uniformed soldiers with the corn-fed faces still on their feet.

Not a single shot was gotten off.

Remo stepped up and reached into a pile of tangled white arms and legs, to pull out a kicking olive-drab figure.

"I'm not done with you yet, Bushy," he growled.

He dragged the moaning President of Cuba back to the long banquet table, where assorted copyright and trademark characters sat very, very still.

"That was nice work," said Uncle Sam in a too-calm voice.

"Thanks," Remo said absently. He slammed the President of Cuba into one of the few still standing chairs.

Sam Beasley stood up. "No, I mean it."

Remo refused to look in the man's direction. "Okay, you mean it. I'll get to you in a minute."

"Seriously, I'd like to shake your hand, my boy."

Remo hesitated.

"Come on, come on. I won't bite. I know when I'm licked. I'm big enough to admit it."

Remo looked at the hand. It was empty. His ears picked up the bellows sounds of the man's ancient lungs. There was no heartbeat, but a steady humming from deep within his chest.

"What the heck," Remo said, reaching out his hand. "I used to be one of your biggest fans."

"And now you're the biggest chump on earth," snarled Uncle Sam, as he began to squeeze Remo's outstretched hand with the constrictive force of a trash-compacter.

Remo was so shocked by the unexpectedness of what was happening to him, that he did something he had not done in years. He screamed in pain.

The Master of Sinanju heard the scream while he was making the soldiers of Ultima Hora hors de combat. These were not evil men, so he had been going among them dislocating their shoulders. He did this by the deceptively simple action of grasping them by their shoulders and separating the arm bones from their rotator cuffs as he dodged their ineffectual blows. The motion was as simple as removing the lens cap from a Kodak.

Although the soldiers did scream louder than a camera would.

The sound of Remo's scream was unmistakable and unforgettable. Chiun had dragged such complaints out of Remo during the early difficult phases of Remo's training in Sinanju, when he had stubbornly persisted in eating meat and breathing incorrectly.

He flung himself up from the lower holds, where Ultima Hora awaited the signal to emerge and take unprotected Havana, and flashed toward the sound of Remo's agony.

Remo Williams was unaccustomed to pain. On the one hand, his nerves had been trained to sublimate ordinary pain. On the other, his entire body had been raised to enormous levels of sensitivity to external stimuli. And he had been caught by surprise.

Excruciating agony made his highly refined nervous system explode into white noise. His senses shut down. Red sparks danced before his eyes. He could feel his finger bones and metacarpals grinding together under a handshake that he realized too late was composed not of ordinary flesh and bone but of some powerful hydraulic mechanism sheathed in a realistic-looking fleshlike covering.

Worst of all, he couldn't pull loose.

"Left my right hand in the freezer, as it were," a familiar voice chuckled. "But the animators gave me a new one. Like it?"

Waves of pain rolled through Remo's stunned brain. His training told him to lash out at the source of the agony, but his mind warned him that he would be killing Sam Beasley. Uncle Sam. The kindly old Uncle Sam who had told him stories way way back in another life, spent around an old staticky black-and-white TV set, watching cartoons with his fellow orphans.

And as he hesitated the pain redoubled, and Remo had lost his chance to strike. No longer in control of his body, he went down on one knee, his teeth clamping tight and a black cloud passing over his thoughts.

Then another voice came. High and commanding. "Hold!" it said. Chiun!

Uncle Sam's voice turned icy with anger. "I'd like to know who the hell you two are."

"I am the Master of Sinanju," Chiun said in his most dramatic voice. "And that is my son you are harming. Release him at once!"

"My pink ass!"

And through the roaring in his ears, Remo heard the tiny gasp that came from Chiun's offended mouth.

"You are not Uncle Sam!"

"The hell I'm not!"

"Uncle Sam would never use such language."

"A lot you know. And who are you two clowns, CIA?"

The question was ignored. Chiun pitched his voice to Remo's roaring ears. "Remo. This man is an imposter. Smite him at once."

"I—I can't!" Remo gasped.

"Banish the pain," Chiun urged.

"It's not the freaking pain. This is Uncle Sam! The real one! I can't hurt him!"

"Nonsense."

"He's got an animatronic freaking heart!"

"*Radio*-animatronic," Uncle Sam corrected in his

famous professorial tone. "Use the correct terminology, please."

"Radio?" It was the dazed voice of the President of Cuba.

The hand slackened its excruciating grip. Remo forced his eyes open. He looked up. Uncle Sam, dressed in the Stars and Stripes, loomed over him, grinning wickedly.

"Controlled and kept beating indefinitely by an outside signal. No need to change batteries, or replace defective parts. They say I've got another ninety years in me, at least."

"You are a machine," Chiun accused.

"I'm just as human as the next guy. I've only been augmented."

"Chiun," Remo gasped. "Don't just stand there debating. Do something!"

The Master of Sinanju's eyes became slits. Coldly, he intoned, "Remo, stand up. Do not shame me before this bearded ruffian of a tyrant. Show that you are worthy of the training bestowed upon you."

"I can't kill him! You know who he is!"

"You must!"

"Look, *you* do it!"

"Remo! I cannot have the children of Sinanju believing that I dispatched their favorite white in all the universe. You must do this yourself."

Remo started to rise. The hydraulic hand clamped down hard.

"Another move like that," Beasley warned, "and I'll squeeze his hand to bloody pulp."

"Another word like that, and my pupil will grind you into powdered bone meal," Chiun countered.

"I can't do it, Chiun!"

Across the room the Master of Sinanju stood his ground, his hands having retreated to their concealing sleeves. He looked to his pupil, humbled before the very eyes of Mongo Mouse and the others. It was unseemly.

He noticed the bearded tyrant. Castro struggled to his feet.

"Jou," he groaned, addressing Chiun. "I will give jou anything jou name if jou save me from this *loco gringo.*"

"Have you gold?" asked Chiun, interest flavoring his voice.

"*Sí. Sí.* As much as jou wish."

"Five billion," Chiun said quickly.

"*Que?*"

"Five billion in gold. Will you pay?"

"No! It is a preposterous amount. Who do jou think jou are?"

"I am the Master of Sinanju," Chiun said haughtily, eyeing the tyrant to see what his reaction was.

"By the beard of Ché! I have heard of you!"

Chiun smiled thinly. "I thought you would."

"Jou are a North Korean."

"Correct."

"The last of my trustworthy allies," the Cuban President said hollowly. "Have *they* strayed from the Socialist path, as well?"

"I am no tool of Pyongyang," Chiun spat.

"Then who do jou work for?"

"Your mortal enemy."

Castro groaned. "Then I am a dead man."

"Only if this is my wish," Chiun said dryly.

Dr. Osvaldo Revuelta had had enough of this charade. Every moment delayed his assuming the presidency of Cuba, his beloved island.

He stood up, saying, "Enough. It is time to yudge the tyrant. I say, 'Death to Castro!' " He turned his thumb downward. "What say jou, members of the yury?"

One by one, the others followed suit. Mongo turned his white-gloved thumb downward. Dingbat dropped a webbed hand. Wacky Wolf lowered his shortest claw.

The verdict was unanimous. Except for Uncle Sam Beasley. His thumb was occupied at the moment, as he continued to squeeze the white man's fist into submission.

"*I* say when we vote!" he snarled.

"We are wasting time," Revuelta complained. "We must launch our attack. My Ultima Hora jearn to liberate Cuba!"

"No," said Chiun. "They writhe and groan in the holds below. I have accepted their surrender."

"Bullshit!" said Beasley hotly. He squeezed his unfeeling hand in anger, producing a yelp from Remo.

"Look," Revuelta protested. "I am to be the new El Presidente!"

"Think again," snapped Beasley. "You're just a puppet. I'll pull the strings and you'll dance."

Revuelta looked horrified. "What are jou saying to me?"

"And if you get out of line," Beasley added, "I'll just have my Concepteers make an animatronic copy of you. One that *won't* get out of line."

"Jou are a fraud!" cried Revuelta, reaching for Beasley's throat. "Jou—"

Beasley was too quick. With his free hand, he whipped off his eye patch. Dr. Osvaldo Revuelta's face was less than a foot in front of the exposed electronic eye. When it exploded like the biggest flashbulb in the universe, he was looking directly at it.

Revuelta reeled back, howling and covering his eyes.

"Blind! I am blinded!"

He stumbled in the direction of the Master of Sinanju, who calmly tripped him and stepped on his writhing neck. A dull crunching came, and Revuelta wa. still after a moment's busy quivering.

Remo Williams drained the pain coming down his right wrist into the rest of his body, diffusing it, absorbing it. His teeth ground together. Sweat was coming off his brow. He was regaining control. With his free hand, he clutched the tablecloth. It slipped off the table.

And he happened to see a black box under the long

banquet table. It looked like a boom box, except there was no speaker or tape deck. But there were lights and digital displays.

One continued to count off numbers sequentially until it got to 26. Then the indicator reset to zero, and started over.

A spectrographic indicator coursed up and down a calibrated scale. It matched exactly the humming vibration coming from the chest of Uncle Sam.

Through the receding pain, Remo Williams made a connection. Between the bar and the heart hum. Between the number twenty-six and the human heart.

He steeled himself for more agony. And reached under the table for the black box.

"What the hell are you doing down there?" Sam Beasley roared suddenly.

Remo's fingers touched something. Then the pain came slamming back, and he was being hoisted off his knees.

But not before he turned a dial.

Remo was lifted face-to-face with Sam Beasley. The man's stale breath was in his face, filling him with revulsion. But Remo had already made up his mind. He knew what he had to do.

This was not Uncle Sam. Not the Uncle Sam of his childhood. Maybe that Uncle Sam had never really existed. Maybe he was just as much a fantasy as Mongo Mouse. Whatever he was, he had to die. Even if the act would haunt Remo Williams for the rest of his life.

Remo's free hand formed the tip of a spear. He willed his fingers into absolute rigidity. There was no telling what they would have to penetrate—soft loose flesh or armor plate. He brought the hand up with deliberate control. He would have only one shot. It had to be good.

Uncle Sam Beasley snarled at him. Then, his face went pale. His mouth opened and closed spasmodically. His good eye rolled up into his head. The other, a machined steel orb with a pulsing red light in the center, began to dim.

"You bastard!" he hissed, and the red pinpoint pupil exploded in a laser burst designed to destroy the sight of anyone looking into it.

Remo, hearing a cybernetic relay click, shut his eyes a split-second ahead of the red-hot flash.

The light seared through his eyelids, and his vision became a very shocking pink color riddled with delicate red veinwork.

Sam Beasley emitted a strangled sound and began to wheeze like an accordion. His vise-like hand stopped squeezing Remo's hand, and he began to gasp and flail with his free hand. It reached up for his own throat.

And while he was doing that, Remo reached out blindly and pried the hydraulic fingers free of his own hand. One snapped off.

He stepped back, clutching his mangled fingers in a fist.

The Master of Sinanju rushed up to meet him. He grasped Remo's hand, turned it over and back, examining it critically.

"I do not think it is broken," he muttered.

"I can't tell," Remo gasped.

"There is one way to find out," said Chiun, suddenly unbending Remo's clenched fist.

Remo screamed louder than ever.

Chiun beamed back. "The bones work. It is fine."

Which was more than could be said for Uncle Sam Beasley. He lay on the ground, thrashing and gasping like a beached fish. His teeth chattered as if from cold. He was turning blue.

His assorted creations hovered around him, crying plaintively.

"Uncle Sam! Uncle Sam! Don't leave us! Not again! We need you, Uncle Sam!"

The Master of Sinanju swept into the middle of the creatures, scattering them and crying, "Begone, vermin!"

He looked down upon the face of Uncle Sam Beasley and, with an extended fingernail, imploded the electronic laser eye.

Uncle Sam paid the maiming no heed. He continued to writhe in his slow death-throes. His peg leg pounded the floor like a slow drumstick. His voice was a croak. "Maus . . . Maus . . . shield . . . mouse."

"What's he saying?" Remo asked.

"He is calling for someone," Chiun said slowly.

Remo listened. "Sounds like 'mouse.' Must mean Mongo. Where is he, anyway?"

The Master of Sinanju raked the demoralized jury with cold eyes. He pointed an accusing finger at Mongo Mouse.

"You! Remain where you are, if you value your scalp. I know how treacherous is your kind."

Mongo Mouse proffered open hands, in a clear gesture of compliance.

The President of Cuba cautiously approached. He pointed to the box. "That is what is keeping him alive. We must destroy it." And he lifted a combat boot.

The Master of Sinanju swept a hand out and found the sensitive back of the Cuban leader's knee. He used his fingernails to inflict maximum pain on the Maximum Leader.

And the Maximum Leader of Cuba hopped away, holding his leg and howling Spanish invective through his beard.

Remo looked down. "We can't let him die, can we?"

"No," said Chiun.

Remo knelt and examined the box. The digital readout was counting only up to 7 before resetting itself. Remo touched the dial he had hit before. He turned it one way. The number reset to 0, and Sam Beasley began to quiver and gasp for air.

"Oops!" Remo turned it the other way. The man began to breathe, jerkily but more regularly. The number cycle climbed to 15.

Remo experimented with the heart cycle until he had found a setting—19—that kept Beasley on his back and breathing, but still helpless.

He stood up. "I think that does it."

The President of Cuba limped up. His face was pale and incredulous.

"Jou have saved my Revolution," he whispered hoarsely. "This lunatic was going to try me for imaginary crimes."

Chiun eyed him coldly. "Speak to me not of your crimes, preempter of beauty."

"*Que?*"

"He means," Remo said dryly, "you knocked his favorite TV show off the air."

The Maximum Leader of Cuba blinked. "Are jou all mad? First this one complains that I am stealing his cartoons. Now jou are angry because I have interrupted a mere television program."

"Wrong thing to say, bushy," Remo warned.

The Master of Sinanju drew himself up haughtily. "Cheeta Ching is no mere television personality. She is all that is good and beautiful and pure in the universe."

"You are *loco*. I responded to aggression. No more."

The Master of Sinanju puffed out his cheeks.

"You admit your guilt, then!"

"I am proud of it." The President of Cuba lifted an authoritarian finger. "I will rub the *Yanquis'* noses in their folly at every opportunity."

"Then you must die a thousand deaths!" proclaimed Chiun, starting after the man.

"Hold it, Chiun." Remo warned. "You know what Smith said."

Chiun stopped. His eyes narrowed. "Since I am forbidden to send you to the fate you so richly deserve," he fumed, "I must visit a less suitable punishment than I would like."

And with grim purpose the Master of Sinanju backed the fear-struck President of Cuba up against a wall.

Remo Williams, clutching his wounded hand, was powerless to prevent what happened next.

The screams of the Maximum Leader came in bursts, like those of a misfiring machine gun.

It was such a horrific sight, Remo was forced to turn away.

Off in one corner Dingbat Duck, Gumpy Dog, and the others covered their faces and cowered in fear.

No one noticed that Mongo Mouse had slipped away.

Below deck, Captain Ernest Maus went to an emergency locker and armed himself with a Glock pistol and a big box of Ricky Rabbit fruit drops. He broke open the inner plastic wrapping, and the unleashed scent of almonds floated upward.

He found the main Ultima Hora force trapped in the hold, milling about, their arms hanging numb at their sides. That made it easy to feed them the drops, although some did fight. He shot those ones.

When he had left, all were dead.

In other areas of the ship, such as the staterooms and the gym, many were already unconscious or dead. The Beasley employees willingly accepted their allotment—although with sobs and hot tears in their eyes—and succumbed, after first whispering the praises of Uncle Sam.

It was all accomplished in a surprisingly short period of time. When Maus finally doffed his mouse head in exchange for a scuba mask and air tanks, only he remained alive.

He leaned against the gleaming brass rail of the stern and let the heavy tanks carry him over into the polluted water of Havana Harbor.

No one heard the splash. No one saw him make for a puttering ramshackle fishing boat and climb aboard. There was only an old man at the wheel, piloting his craft out into open water.

Maus stopped his heart by thrusting into his back a marlin spike left lying on the deck. He took the wheel and returned the aging craft to its course.

In his brain there lingered a deep distaste for what he had done. But he had executed his orders. He had shielded the mouse. The future would take care of itself.

He was the Beasley Corporation now.

30

Two days later, Harold W. Smith was escorting the Master of Sinanju and Remo Williams to the security wing of Folcroft Sanitarium. Smith's footsteps echoed off the well-scrubbed walls. As usual, Remo and Chiun made no sounds as they walked.

"I could see no other viable option," Smith was saying.

"This is a correct attitude," Chiun said with approval.

"It would have been better had the man expired in action. Still, the world need never know he returned from the dead."

"No way was I going to waste him," said Remo.

"Nor I," said Chiun.

"And turning him over to the Cuban authorities wasn't exactly on the menu," Remo added.

They turned a corner.

"Understood," Smith said grimly. He stopped before a heavy door, and they took turns peering through a thick pane of plate glass reinforced by wire mesh.

Inside, a man sat on the edge of a simple cot in his Dingbat Duck pajamas, with a writing tablet balanced on the padded knee of his silver left leg. He wore an ordinary black eye patch over one eye. His right hand ended in a stump. He was using his left to draw on the tablet.

"Cartoons?" Remo asked.

"No. He is storyboarding his escape," Smith said thinly.

"Uh-oh."

"It will not happen," Smith said. "Not with his hydraulic hand removed and his laser eye destroyed."

"Any other tricks?"

"None that the X-rays could find. The pegleg is solid silver. The laser, by the way, is similar to one under Pentagon development. It's designed to immobilize enemy forces by permanently shocking the optic nerve."

"The fiend!" said Chiun indignantly.

"Yeah. I read about it." Remo went to the next room and looked through the screened window panel. This was a rubber-walled room. In one corner a young man with long blond hair sat, rocking in a straightjacket.

"I see you put him next to Purcell," Remo said.

"Pah!" Chiun said in distaste. "Another foulness in human form."

"Getting to be a regular rogue's gallery in here," Remo said, thinking back on what a grave threat Jeremiah Purcell, the Dutchman—the only living person other than Remo and Chiun to have mastered Sinanju—had posed before he had lost his mind.

"Neither the Dutchman nor Beasley will bother us again," said Smith. They moved away from the doors and retraced their steps.

"What's the latest out of Havana?" asked Remo.

"Utter silence," Smith said. "The President is very pleased. The *Beasley Adventure* has been returned to the corporation without comment. Inasmuch as there seem to have been few survivors among Ultima Hora and the Beasley operatives, the suppression of the truth will be comparatively easy."

"Do not forget that Mongo got away," Chiun sniffed. "After completing his wicked work."

"One anonymous operative should pose no future threat," Smith said. "This chapter would appear to be closed. There has been no further broadcast-jamming from Cuba, and satellite reconnaissance indicates that the Cubans are dismantling their signal-transmission nest, as promised."

"We made that a condition of our leaving Havana harbor peacefully," Remo pointed out.

"A wise move. It is interesting that Castro has not appeared on television or in public since the event."

Chiun beamed. "Interesting, yes. But not without cause."

Smith looked down. "Master Chiun?"

From one sleeve, the Master of Sinanju pulled a rolled-up olive-drab campaign cap. He unrolled it and offered it to Harold Smith by the bill.

Smith accepted the offering and looked into the shallow cloth bowl of the cap itself. It was filled with what appeared to be the makings of a rat's nest.

"What is this?" Smith asked.

"A gift to you," beamed Chiun. "I would have preferred the ears in a box, but this was not possible."

Smith looked blank. "I do not understand."

"What Chiun's trying to say," said Remo, "is that it'll be a long time before Fidel shows his face in public again. Chiun plucked his face bare as a baby's behind. And twice as ugly."

Harold Smith's eyes went wide with horror. Then, on reflection, a dry lemony humor seemed to suffuse them.

"Master Chiun, I will treasure this gift always," he said without perceptible warmth.

Chiun waved a dismissive hand. "A mere token of my esteem. Now that we have saved your realm once again, it is time to get down to the business of the upcoming contract."

Smith looked disturbed. "Er, what did you have in mind?"

"I believe something was said about a castle."

"You are no longer interested in Beasleyland?"

Chiun made a face. "It is for children. And I no longer look upon mice with the same innocent eyes."

"I can make no promises, but it may be that something can be worked out."

"I am *not* living in a frigging castle," Remo said tightly.

"With an outhouse for Remo," Chiun added.

"You mean *guest* house," Remo corrected.

"That too," said Chiun. "For guests. Such as my beloved Cheeta, soon to be fulfilled due to my beneficence. And this reminds me that it is nearly the appointed hour for her nightly poem to America."

And as the Master of Sinanju hurried along the corridors of Folcroft Sanitarium, humming contentedly to himself, Remo Williams and Harold Smith exchanged horrified glances as they realized they faced a potential security problem that threatened to make the one they had just resolved seem like a passing stormcloud.

"He *is* the father," Smith said in a shocked tone.

"No way I'm living under the same roof as that Korean barracuda," Remo said fiercely. "No way, Smitty."

Harold Smith swallowed hard and said nothing, his gray face slowly turning bruise-green.